Georg Manville Fenn

Begumbagh, a story of the Indian Mutiny, and other stories

Georg Manville Fenn

Begumbagh, a story of the Indian Mutiny, and other stories

ISBN/EAN: 9783337304669

Printed in Europe, USA, Canada, Australia, Japan

Cover: Foto ©Andreas Hilbeck / pixelio.de

More available books at **www.hansebooks.com**

A

TALE OF THE INDIAN MUTINY

AND OTHER STORIES

BY

GEORGE MANVILLE FENN

AUTHOR OF
'THE DINGO BOYS;' 'RAJAH OF DAH;' 'IN THE KING'S NAME;'
'DICK O' THE FENS;' 'THE GOLDEN MAGNET;' ETC.

W. & R. CHAMBERS, LIMITED
LONDON AND EDINBURGH

CONTENTS.

PAGE

BEGUMBAGH: A TALE OF THE INDIAN MUTINY............ 5

THE GOLDEN INCUBUS..124

IN A GOWT..171

A FIGHT WITH A STORM 183

'I had crept close, and was in the act of leaping on him.'

BEGUMBAGH,

A TALE OF THE INDIAN MUTINY.

INTRODUCTION.

’VE waited all these years, expecting some one or another would give a full and true account of it all; but little thinking it would ever come to be my task. For it's not in my way; but seeing how much has been said about other parts and other people's sufferings, while ours never so much as came in for a line of newspaper, I can't think it's fair; and as fairness is what I always did like, I set to, very much against my will; while, on account of my empty sleeve, the paper keeps slipping and sliding about, so that I can only hold it quiet by putting the lead inkstand on one corner, and my tobacco-jar on the other. You see, I'm not much at home at this sort of thing; and though, if you put a pipe and a glass of something before me, I could tell you all about it, taking my time, like, it seems that won't do. I said: 'Why don't you write it down as I tell it, so as other people could read all about it?' But 'No,' he says; 'I could do it in my fashion, but I want it to be in your simple unadorned style; so set to and do it.'

I daresay a good many of you know me—seen me often in
Bond Street, at Facet's door—Facet's, you know, the great
jeweller, where I stand and open carriages, or take messages,
or small parcels with no end of valuables in them, for I'm
trusted.   Smith, my name is, Isaac Smith; and I'm that
tallish, grisly fellow with the seam down one side of my face,
my left sleeve looped up to my button, and not a speck to be
seen on that 'commissionaire's' uniform, upon whose breast
I've got three medals.

I was standing one day, waiting patiently for something
to do, when a tallish gentleman came up, nodded as if he
knew me well, and I saluted.

'Lose that limb in the Crimea, my man?'

'No, sir. Mutiny,' I said, standing as stiff as use had
made nature with me.

And then he asked me a lot more questions, and I
answered him; and the end of it was that one evening I
went to his house, and he had me in, and did what was
wanted to set me off. I'd had a little bit of an itching to
try something of the kind, I must own, for long enough, but
his words started me; and in consequence I got a quire of
the best foolscap paper, and a pen'orth of pens, and here's
my story.

CHAPTER I.

Dub-dub-dub-dub-dub-dub.   Just one light beat given by
the boys in front—the light sharp tap upon their drums,
to give the time for the march; and in heavy order there
we were, her Majesty's 156th Regiment of Light Infantry,
making our way over the dusty roads with the hot morning
sun beating down upon our heads.   We were marching very
loosely, though, for the men were tired, and we were longing
for the halt to be called, so that we might rest during the

heat of the day, and then go on again. Tents, baggage-wagons, women, children, elephants, all were there ; and we were getting over the ground at the rate of about fifteen miles a day, on our way up to the station, where we were to relieve a regiment going home.

I don't know what we should have done if it hadn't been for Harry Lant, the weather being very trying, almost as trying as our hot red coats and heavy knapsacks, and flower-pot busbies, with a round white ball like a child's plaything on the top ; but no matter how tired he was, Harry Lant had always something to say or do, and even if the colonel was close by, he'd say or do it. Now, there happened to be an elephant walking along by our side, with the captain of our company, one of the lieutenants, and a couple of women in the howdah ; while a black nigger fellow, in clean white calico clothes, and not much of 'em, and a muslin turban, and a good deal of it, was striddling on the creature's neck, rolling his eyes about, and flourishing an iron toasting-fork sort of thing, with which he drove the great flap-eared patient beast. The men were beginning to grumble gently, and shifting their guns from side to side, and sneezing, and coughing, and choking in the kicked-up dust, like a flock of sheep, when Captain Dyer scrambles down off the elephant, and takes his place alongside us, crying out cheerily : 'Only another mile, my lads, and then breakfast.'

We gave him a cheer, and another half-mile was got over, when once more the boys began to flag terribly, and even Harry Lant was silent, which, seeing what Harry Lant was, means a wonderful deal more respecting the weather than any number of degrees on a thermometer, I can tell you ; but I looked round at him, and he knew what it meant, and, slipping out, he goes up to the elephant. 'Carry your trunk, sir,' he says ; and taking gently hold of the great beast's soft nose, he laid it upon his shoulder, and marched on like that, with the men roaring with laughter.

'Pulla-wulla.   Ma-pa-na,' shouted the nigger who was driving, or something that sounded like it, for of all the rum lingoes ever spoke, theirs is about the rummest, and always put me in mind of the fal-lal-la or tol-de-rol chorus of a song.

'All right. I'll take care!' sings out Harry; and on he marched, with the great soft-footed beast lifting its round pats and putting them down gently so as not to hurt Harry; and, trifling as that act was, it meant a great deal, as you'll see if you read on, while just then it got our poor fellows over the last half-mile without one falling out; and then the halt was called; men wheeled into line; we were dismissed; and soon after we were lounging about, under such shade as we could manage to get in the thin tope of trees.

CHAPTER II.

THAT'S a pretty busy time, that first half-hour after a halt: what with the niggers setting up a few tents, and getting a fire lighted, and fetching water; but in spite of our being tired, we soon had things right. There was the colonel's tent, Colonel Maine's—a little stout man, that we all used to laugh at, because he was such a little, round, good-tempered chap, who never troubled about anything, for we hadn't learned then what was lying asleep in his brave little body, waiting to be brought out. Then there was the mess tent for the officers, and the hospital tent for those on the sick-list, beside our bell tents, that we shouldn't have set up at all, only to act as sun-shades. But, of course, the principal tent was the colonel's.

Well, there they were, the colonel and his lady, Mrs Maine—a nice, kindly-spoken, youngish woman: twenty years younger than he, she was; but, for all that, a happier couple never breathed; and they two used to seem as if the regiment, and India, and all the natives were made on purpose to fall down and worship the two little golden idols they'd set up—a little girl and a little boy, you know. Cock Robin and Jenny Wren, we chaps used to call them, though Jenny Wren was about a year and a half the oldest. And I believe it was from living in France a bit, that the colonel's wife had got the notion of dressing them so; but it would have done your heart good to see those two children—the boy with his little red tunic and his sword, and the girl with her red jacket and belt, and a little canteen of wine and water, and a tiny tin mug; and them little things driving the old black ayah half-wild with the way they used to dodge away from her to get amongst the men, who took no end of delight in bamboozling the fat old woman when she was hunting for them; sending them here, and there, and everywhere, till she'd turn round and make signs with her hands, and spit on the ground, which was her way of cursing us. For I must say that we English were very, very careless about what we did or said to the natives. Officers and men, all alike, seemed to look upon them as something very little better than beasts, and talked to them as if they had no feelings at all, little thinking what fierce masters the trampled slaves could turn out, if ever they had their day—the day that the old proverb says is sure to come for every dog; and there was not a soul among us then that had the least bit of suspicion that the dog—by which, you know, I mean the Indian generally—was going mad, and sharpening those teeth of his ready to bite.

Well, as a matter of course, there were other people in our regiment that I ought to mention: Captain Dyer I did name; but there was a lieutenant, a very good-looking young fellow, who was a great favourite with Mrs Colonel Maine; and he dined a deal with them at all times, besides being a great chum of Captain Dyer's—they two shooting together, and being like brothers, though there was a something in Lieutenant Leigh that I never seemed to take to. Then there was the doctor—a Welshman he was, and he used to make it his boast that our regiment was about the healthiest anywhere; and I tell you what it is, if you were ill once, and in hospital, as we call it—though, you know, with a marching regiment that only means anywhere till you get well—I say, if you were ill once, and under his hands, you'd think twice before you made up your mind to be ill again, and be very bad too before you went to him. Pestle, we used to call him, though his name was Hughes; and how we men did hate him, mortally, till we found out his real character, when we were lying cut to pieces almost, and him ready to cry over us at times as he tried to bring us round. 'Hold up, my lads,' he'd say, 'only another hour, and you'll be round the corner!' when what there was left of us did him justice. Then, of course, there were other officers, and some away with the major and another battalion of our regiment at Wallahbad; but they've nothing to do with my story.

I do not think I can do better than introduce you to our mess on the very morning of this halt, when, after cooling myself with a pipe, just the same as I should have warmed myself with a pipe if it had been in Canady or Nova Scotia, I walked up to find all ready for breakfast, and Mrs Bantem making the tea.

Some of the men didn't fail to laugh at us who took our tea for breakfast; but all the same I liked it, for it always took me home, tea did—and to the days when my poor old mother used to say that there never was such a boy for bread and butter as I was; not as there was ever so much butter that she need have grumbled, whatever I cost for bread; and though Mrs Bantem wasn't a bit like my mother, she brought up the homely thoughts. Mrs Bantem was, I should say, about the biggest and ugliest woman I ever saw in my life. She stood five feet eleven and a half in her stockings, for Joe Bantem got Sergeant Buller to take her under the standard one day. She'd got a face nearly as dark as a black's; she'd got a moustache, and a good one too; and a great coarse look about her altogether. Measles —I'll tell you who he was directly—Measles used to say she was a horse god-mother; and they didn't seem to like one another; but Joe Bantem was as proud of that woman as she was of him; and if any one hinted about her looks, he used to laugh, and say that was only the outside rind, and talk about the juice. But all the same, though, no one couldn't be long with that woman without knowing her flavour. It was a sight to see her and Joe together, for he was just a nice middle size—five feet seven and a half—and as pretty a pink and white, brown-whiskered, open-faced man as ever you saw. We all got tanned and coppered over and over again, but Joe kept as nice and fresh and fair as on the day we embarked from Gosport years before; and the standing joke was that Mrs Bantem had a preparation for keeping his complexion all square.

Joe Bantem knew what he was about, though, for one day when a nasty remark had been made by the men of another regiment, he got talking to me in confidence over our pipes, and he swore that there wasn't a better woman living; and he was right, for I'm ready now at this present moment to take the Book in my hand, and swear the same thing before all the judges in Old England. For you see we're such duffers, we men: shew us a pretty bit of pink and white, and we run mad after it; while all the time we're running away from no end of what's solid and good, and true, and such as'll wear well, and shew fast colours, long after your pink and white's got faded and grimy. Not as I've much room to talk. But present company, you know, and setra. What, though, as a rule, does your pretty pink and white know about buttons, or darning, or cooking?

Why, we had the very best of cooking; not boiled tag and rag, but nice stews and roasts and hashes, when other men were growling over a dog's-meat dinner. We had the sweetest of clean shirts, and never a button off; our stockings were darned; and only let one of us—Measles, for instance—take a drop more than he ought, just see how she'd drop on to him, that's all. If his head didn't ache before, it would ache then; and I can see as plain now as if it was only this minute, instead of years ago, her boxing Measles' ears, and threatening to turn him out to another mess if he didn't keep sober. And she would have turned him over too, only, as she said to Joe, and Joe told me, it might have been the poor fellow's ruin, seeing how weak he was, and easily led away. The long and short of it is, Mrs Bantem was a good motherly woman of forty; and those who had anything to say against her, said it out of jealousy, and all I have to say now is what I've said before : she only had one fault, and that is, she never had any little Bantems to make wives for honest soldiers to come; and wherever she is, my wish is that she may live happy and venerable to a hundred.

That brings me to Measles. Bigley his name was; but he'd had the small-pox very bad when a child, through not being vaccinated; and his face was all picked out in holes, so round and smooth that you might have stood peas in them all over his cheeks and forehead, and they wouldn't have fallen off; so we called him Measles. If any of you say 'Why?' I don't know no more than I have said.

He was a sour-tempered sort of fellow was Measles, who listed because his sweetheart laughed at him; not that he cared for her, but he didn't like to be laughed at, so he listed out of spite, as he said, and that made him spiteful. He was always grumbling about not getting his promotion, and sneering at everything and everybody, and quarrelling with Harry Lant, him, you know, as carried the elephant's trunk; while Harry was never happy without he was teasing him, so that sometimes there was a deal of hot water spilled in our mess.

And now I think I've only got to name three of the drum-boys, that Mrs Bantem ruled like a rod of iron, though all for their good, and then I've done.

Well, we had our breakfast, and thoroughly enjoyed it, sitting out there in the shade. Measles grumbled about the water, just because it happened to be better than usual; for sometimes we soldiers out there in India used to drink water that was terrible lively before it had been cooked in the kettle; for though water-insects out there can stand a deal of heat, they couldn't stand a fire. Mrs Bantem was washing up the things afterwards, and talking about dinner; Harry Lant was picking up all the odds and ends, to carry off to the great elephant, standing just then in the best bit of shade he could find, flapping his great ears about, blinking his little pig's eyes, and turning his trunk and his tail into two pendulums, swinging them backwards and forwards as regular as clockwork, and all the time watching Harry, when Measles says all at once : ' Here come some lunatics !'

CHAPTER III.

Now, after what I've told you about Measles' listing for spite, you will easily understand that the fact of his calling any one a lunatic did not prove a want of common reason in the person spoken about; but what he meant was, that the people coming up were half-mad for travelling when the sun was so high, and had got so much power.

I looked up and saw, about a mile off, coming over the long straight level plain, what seemed to be an elephant, and a man or two on horseback; and before I had been looking above a minute, I saw Captain Dyer cross over to the colonel's tent, and then point in the direction of the coming elephant. The next minute, he crossed over to where we were. 'Seen Lieutenant Leigh?' he says in his quick way.

'No, sir; not since breakfast.'

'Send him after me, if he comes in sight. Tell him Miss Ross and party are yonder, and I've ridden on to meet them.'

The next minute he had gone, taken a horse from a sycee, and in spite of the heat, cantered off to meet the party with the elephant, the air being that clear that I could see him go right up, turn his horse round, and ride gently back by the side.

I did not see anything of the lieutenant, and, to tell the truth, I forgot all about him, for I was thinking about the party coming, for I had somehow heard a little about Mrs Maine's sister coming out from the old country to stay with her. If I recollect right, the black nurse told Mrs Bantem, and she mentioned it. This party, then, I supposed contained the lady herself; and it was as I thought. We had had to leave Patna unexpectedly to relieve the regiment ordered home; and the lady, according to orders, had followed us, for this was only our second day's march.

I suppose it was my pipe made me settle down to watch the coming party, and wonder what sort of a body Miss Ross would be, and whether anything like her sister. Then I wondered who would marry her, for, as you know, ladies are not very long out in India without picking up a husband. 'Perhaps,' I said to myself, 'it will be the lieutenant;' but ten minutes after, as the elephant shambled up, I altered my mind, for Captain Dyer was ambling along beside the great beast, and his was the hand that helped the lady down —a tall, handsome, self-possessed girl, who seemed quite to take the lead, and kiss and soothe the sister, when she ran out of the tent to throw her arms round the new-comer's neck.

'At last, then, Elsie,' Mrs Colonel said out aloud.   'You've had a long dreary ride.'

'Not during the last ten minutes,' Miss Ross said, laughing in a bright, merry, free-hearted way.   'Lieutenant Leigh has been welcoming me most cordially.'

'Who?' exclaimed Mrs Colonel, staring from one to the other.

'Lieutenant Leigh,' said Miss Ross.

'I'm afraid I am to blame for not announcing myself,' said Captain Dyer, lifting his muslin-covered cap.   'Your sister, Miss Ross, asked me to ride to meet you, in Lieutenant Leigh's absence.'

'You, then'——

'I am only Lawrence Dyer, his friend,' said the captain smiling.

It's a singular thing that just then, as I saw the young lady blush deeply, and Mrs Colonel look annoyed, I muttered to myself, 'Something will come of this,' because, if there's anything I hate, it's for a man to set himself up for a prophet.   But it looked to me as if the captain had been taking Lieutenant Leigh's place, and that Miss Ross, as was really the case, though she had never seen him, had heard him so much talked of by her sister, that she had welcomed him, as she thought, quite as an old friend, when all the time she had been talking to Captain Dyer.

And I was not the only one who thought about it; else why did Mrs Colonel look annoyed, and the colonel, who came paddling out, exclaim loudly: 'Why, Leigh, look alive, man! here's Dyer been stealing a march upon you. Why, where have you been?'

I did not hear what the lieutenant said, for my attention was just then taken up by something else, but I saw him go up to Miss Ross, holding out his hand, while the meeting was very formal; but, as I told you, my attention was taken up by something else, and that something was a little, dark,

bright, eager, earnest face, with a pair of sharp eyes, and a
little mocking-looking mouth; and as Captain Dyer had
helped Miss Ross down with the steps from the howdah, so
did I help down Lizzy Green, her maid; to get, by way of
thanks, a half-saucy look, a nod of the head, and the sight
of a pretty little tripping pair of ankles going over the hot
sandy dust towards the tent.

But the next minute she was back, to ask about some
luggage—a bullock-trunk or two—and she was coming up
to me, as I eagerly stepped forward to meet her, when she
seemed, as it were, to take it into her head to shy at me,
going instead to Harry Lant, who had just come up, and
who, on hearing what she wanted, placed his hands, with a
grave swoop, upon his head, and made her a regular eastern
salaam, ending by telling her that her slave would obey her
commands.   All of which seemed to grit upon me terribly;
I didn't know why, then, but I found out afterwards, though
not for many days to come.

We had the route given us for Begumbagh, a town that,
in the old days, had been rather famous for its grandeur;
but, from what I had heard, it was likely to turn out a very
hot, dry, dusty, miserable spot; and I used to get reckoning
up how long we should be frizzling out there in India before
we got the orders for home; and put it at the lowest calcu-
lation, I could not make less of it than five years.   But
there, we who were soldiers had made our own beds, and
had to lie upon them, whether it was at home or abroad;
and, as Mrs Bantem used to say to us, 'Where was the use
of grumbling?'   There were troubles in every life, even if
it was a civilian's—as we soldiers always called those who
didn't wear the Queen's uniform—and it was very doubtful
whether we should have been a bit happier, if we had been
in any other line.   But all the same, government might
have made things a little better for us in the way of suitable
clothes, and things proper for the climate.

And so on we went : marching mornings and nights ; camping all through the hot day ; and it was not long before we found that, in Miss Ross, we men had got something else beside the children to worship.

But I may as well say now, and have it off my mind, that it has always struck me, that during those peaceful days, when our greatest worry was a hot march, we didn't know when we were well off, and that it wanted the troubles to come before we could see what good qualities there were in other people. Little trifling things used to make us sore— things such as we didn't notice afterwards, when great sorrows came. I know I was queer, and spiteful, and jealous, and no great wonder that, for I always was a man with a nastyish temper, and soon put out ; but even Mrs Bantem used to shew that she wasn't quite perfect, for she quite upset me, one day, when Measles got talking at dinner about Lizzy Green, Miss Ross's maid, and, what was a wonderful thing for him, not finding fault. He got saying that she was a nice girl, and would make a soldier as wanted one a good wife ; when Mrs Bantem fires up as spiteful as could be—I think, mind you, there'd been something wrong with the cooking that day, which had turned her a little— and she says that Lizzy was very well, but looks weren't everything, and that she was raw as raw, and would want no end of dressing before she would be good for anything ; while, as to making a soldier's wife, soldiers had no busi- ness to have wives till they could buy themselves off, and turn civilians. Then, again, she seemed to have taken a sudden spite against Mrs Maine, saying that she was a poor, little, stuck-up, fine lady, and she could never have forgiven her if it had not been for those two beautiful children ; though what Mrs Bantem had got to forgive the colonel's wife, I don't believe she even knew herself.

The old black ayah, too, got very much put out about this time, and all on account of the two new-comers ; for when

Miss Ross hadn't got the children with her, they were along
with Lizzy, who, like her mistress, was new to the climate,
and hadn't got into that dull listless way that comes to
people who have been some time up the country. They were
all life, and fun, and energy, and the children were never
happy when they were away ; and of a morning, more to
please Lizzy, I used to think, than the children, Harry Lant
used to pick out a shady place, and then drive Chunder
Chow, who was the mahout of *Nabob*, the principal elephant,
half wild, by calling out his beast, and playing with him all
sorts of antics. Chunder tried all he could to stop it, but it
was of no use, for Harry had got such influence over that
animal that when one day he was coaxing him out to lead
him under some trees, and the mahout tried to stop him,
Nabob makes no more ado, but lifts his great soft trunk, and
rolls Mr Chunder Chow over into the grass, where he lay
screeching like a parrot, and chattering like a monkey, rolling
his opal eyeballs, and shewing his white teeth with fear, for
he expected that *Nabob* was going to put his foot on him,
and crush him to death, as is the nature of those great
beasts. But not he : he only lays his trunk gently on Harry's
shoulder, and follows him across the open like a great flesh-
mountain, winking his little pig's eyes, whisking his tiny
tail, and flapping his great ears ; while the children clapped
their hands as they stood in the shade with Miss Ross and
Lizzy, and Captain Dyer and Lieutenant Leigh close
behind.

'There's no call to be afraid, miss,' says Harry, saluting
as he saw Miss Ross shrink back ; and seeing how, when he
said a few words in Hindustani, the great animal minded
him, they stopped being scared, and gave Harry fruit and
cakes to feed the great beast with.

You see, out there in that great dull place, people are very
glad to have any little trifle to amuse them, so you mustn't
be surprised to hear that there used to be quite a crowd to

see Harry Lant's performances, as he called them. But all the same, I didn't like his upsetting old Chunder Chow; and it seemed to me even then, that we'd managed to make another black enemy—the black ayah being the first.

However, Harry used to go on making old *Nabob* kneel down, or shake hands, or curl up his trunk, or lift him up, finishing off by going up to his head, lifting one great ear, saying they understood one another, whispering a few words, and then shutting the ear up again, so as the words shouldn't be lost before they got into the elephant's brain, as Harry explained, because they'd got a long way to go. Then Harry would lie down, and let the great beast walk backwards and forwards all over him, lifting his great feet so carefully, and setting them down close to Harry, but never touching him, except one day when, just as the great beast was passing his foot over Harry's breast, a voice called out something in Hindustani—and I knew who it was, though I didn't see—when *Nabob* puts his feet down on Harry's chest, and Lizzy gave a great scream, and we all thought the poor chap would be crushed; but not he: the great beast was took by surprise, but only for an instant, and, in his slow quiet way, he steps aside, and then touches Harry all over with his trunk; and there was no more performance that day.

'I've got my knife into Master Chunder for that,' says Harry to me, 'for I'll swear that was his voice.' And I started to find he had known it.

'I wouldn't quarrel with him,' I says quietly, 'for it strikes me he's got his knife into you.'

'You've no idea,' says Harry, 'what a nip it was. I thought it was all over; but all the same, the poor brute didn't mean it, I'd swear.'

CHAPTER IV.

WHO could have thought just then that all that nonsense of Harry Lant's with the elephant was shaping itself for our good, but so it was, as you shall by-and-by hear. The march continued, matters seeming to go on very smoothly—but only seeming, mind you, for let alone that we were all walking upon a volcano, there was a good deal of unpleasantry brewing. Let alone my feeling that, somehow or another, Harry Lant was not so true a mate to me as he used to be, there was a good deal wrong between Captain Dyer and Lieutenant Leigh, and it soon seemed plain that there was much more peace and comfort in our camp a week earlier than there was at the time of which I am now writing.

I used to have my turns as sentry here and there; and it was when standing stock-still with my piece, that I used to see and hear so much—for in a camp it seems to be a custom for people to look upon a sentry as a something that can neither see nor hear anything but what might come in the shape of an enemy. They know he must not move from his post, which is to say that he's tied hand and foot, and perhaps from that they think that he's tied as to his senses. At all events, I got to see that when Miss Ross was seated in the colonel's tent, and Captain Dyer was near her, she seemed to grow gentle and quiet, and her eyes would light up, and her rich red lips part, as she listened to what he was saying; while, when it came to Lieutenant Leigh's turn, and he was beside her talking, she would be merry and chatty, and would laugh and talk as lively as could be. Harry Lant said it was because they were making up matters, and that some day she would be Mrs Leigh; but I didn't look at it in that light, though I said nothing.

I used to like to be sentry at the colonel's tent, on our halting for the night, when the canvas would be looped up, to let in the air, and they'd got their great globe-lamps lit, with the tops to them, to keep out the flies, and the draughts made by the punkahs swinging backwards and forwards. I used to think it quite a pretty sight, with the ladies and the three or four officers, perhaps chatting, perhaps having a little music, for Miss Ross could sing like—like a nightingale, I was going to say; but no nightingale that I ever heard could seem to lay hold of your heart and almost bring tears into your eyes, as she did. Then she used to sing duets with Captain Dyer, because the colonel wished it, though it was plain to see Mrs Maine didn't like it, any more than did Lieutenant Leigh, who, more than once, as I've seen, walked out, looking fierce and angry, to strike off right away from the camp, perhaps not to come back for a couple of hours.

It was one night when we'd been about a fortnight on the way, for during the past week the colonel had been letting us go on very easily, I was sentry at the tent. There had been some singing, and Lieutenant Leigh had gone off in the middle of a duet. Then the doctor, the colonel, and a couple of subs were busy over a game at whist, and the black nurse had beckoned Mrs Maine out, I suppose to see something about the two children; when Captain Dyer and Miss Ross walked together just outside the tent, she holding by one of the cords, and he standing close beside her.

They did not say much, but stood looking up at the bright silver moon and the glittering stars; while he said a word now and then about the beauty of the scene, the white tents, the twinkling lights here and there, and the soft peaceful aspect of all around; and then his voice seemed to grow lower and deeper as he spoke from time to time, though I could hardly hear a word, as I stood there like a statue watching her beautiful face, with the great clusters of hair knotted back from her broad white forehead, the moon shining full on it, and seeming to make her eyes flash as they were turned to him.

They must have stood there full half an hour, when she turned as if to go back, but he laid his hand upon hers as it held the tent cord, and said something very earnestly, when she turned to him again to look him full in the face, and I saw that her hand was not moved.

Then they were silent for a few seconds before he spoke again, loud enough for me to hear.

'I must ask you,' he said huskily; 'my peace depends upon it. I know that it has always been understood that you were to be introduced to Lieutenant Leigh. I can see now plainly enough what are your sister's wishes; but hearts are ungovernable, Miss Ross, and I tell you earnestly, as a simple, truth-speaking man, that you have roused feelings that until now slept quietly in my breast. If I am presumptuous, forgive me—love is bold as well as timid—but at least set me at rest: tell me, is there any engagement between you and Lieutenant Leigh?'

She did not speak for a few moments, but met his gaze—so it seemed to me—without shrinking, before saying one word, so softly, that it was like one of the whispers of the breeze crossing the plain—and that word was 'No!'

'God bless you for that answer, Miss Ross—Elsie,' he said deeply; and then his head was bent down for an instant over the hand that rested on the cord, before Miss Ross glided away from him into the tent, and went and stood resting with her hand upon the colonel's shoulder, when he, evidently in high glee, began to shew her his cards, laughing and pointing to first one, and then another, for he seemed to be having luck on his side.

But I had no more eyes then for the inside of the tent, for Captain Dyer just seemed to awaken to the fact that I was standing close by him as sentry, and he gave quite a start as he looked at me for a few moments without speaking. Then he took a step forward.

'Who is this? Oh, thank goodness!' (he said those few words in an undertone, but I happened to hear them). 'Smith,' he said, 'I forgot there was a sentry there. You saw me talking to that lady?'

'Yes, sir,' I said.

'You saw everything?'

'Yes, sir.'

'And you heard all?'

'No, sir, not all; only what you said last.'

Then he was silent again for a few moments, but only to lay his hand directly after on my chest.

'Smith,' he said, 'I would rather you had not seen this; and if it had been any other man in my company, I should perhaps have offered him money, to insure that there was no idle chattering at the mess-tables; but you I ask, as a man I can trust, to give me your word of honour as a soldier to let what you have seen and heard be sacred.'

'Thank you, captain,' I said, speaking thick, for somehow his words seemed to touch me. 'You shan't repent trusting me.'

'I have no fear, Smith,' he said, speaking lightly, and as if he felt joyful, and proud, and happy.—'What a glorious night for a cigar;' and he took one out of his case, when we both started, for, as if he had that moment risen out of the ground, Lieutenant Leigh stood there close to us; and even to this day I can't make out how he managed it, but all the same he must have seen and heard as much as I had.

'And pray, is my word of honour as a soldier to be taken, Captain Dyer? or is my silence to be bought with money? —Confound you! come this way, will you!' he hissed; for Captain Dyer had half turned, as if to avoid him, but he stepped back directly, and I saw them walk off together amongst the trees, till they were quite out of sight; and if ever I felt what it was to be tied down to one spot, I felt it then, as I walked sentry up and down by that tent watching for those two to return.

CHAPTER V.

Now, after giving my word of honour to hold all that sacred, some people may think I'm breaking faith in telling what I saw; but I made that right by asking the colonel's leave—he is a colonel now—and he smiled, and said that I ought to change the names, and then it would not matter.

I left off my last chapter saying how I felt being tied down to one spot, as I kept guard there; and perhaps everybody don't know that a sentry's duty is to stay in the spot where he has been posted, and that leaving it lightly might, in time of war, mean death.

I should think I watched quite an hour, wondering whether I ought to give any alarm; but I was afraid it would appear foolish, for perhaps after all it might only mean a bit of a quarrel, and I could not call to mind any quarrel between officers ending in a duel.

I was glad, too, that I did not say anything, for at last I saw them coming back in the clear moonlight—clear-like as day; and then in the distance they stopped, and in a moment one figure seemed to strike the other a sharp blow, which sent him staggering back, and I could not then see who it was that was hit, till they came nearer, and I made out that it was Captain Dyer; while, if I had any doubts at first, I could have none as they came nearer and nearer, with Lieutenant Leigh talking in a big insolent way at Captain Dyer, who was very quiet, holding his handkerchief to his cheek.

So as to be as near as possible to where they were going

to pass, I walked to the end of my tether, and, as they came up, Lieutenant Leigh says, in a nasty spiteful whisper : ' I should have thought you would have come into the tent to display the wound received in the lady's cause.'

' Leigh,' said Captain Dyer, taking down his white handkerchief—and in the bright moonlight I could see that his cheek was cut, and the handkerchief all bloody—' Leigh, that was an unmanly blow. You called me a coward ; you struck me ; and now you try to poison the wound with your words. I never lift hand against the man who has taken that hand in his as my friend, but the day may come when I can prove to you that you are a liar.'

Lieutenant Leigh turned upon him fiercely, as though he would have struck him again ; but Captain Dyer paid no heed to him, only walked quietly off to his quarters ; while, with a sneering, scornful sort of laugh, the lieutenant went into the colonel's tent ; though, if he expected to see Miss Ross, he was disappointed, for so long as I was on guard, she did not shew any more that night.

Off again the next morning, and over a hotter and dustier road than ever ; and I must say that I began to wish we were settled down in barracks again, for everything seemed to grow more and more crooked, and people more and more unpleasant. Why, even Mrs Bantem that morning before starting must shew her teeth, and snub Bantem, and then begin going on about the colonel's wife, and the fine madam, her sister, having all sorts of luxuries, while poor hardworking soldiers' wives had to bear all the burden and heat of the day ; while, by way of winding up, she goes up to Harry Lant and Measles, who were, as usual, squabbling about something, and boxes both their ears, as if they had been bad boys. I saw them both colour up fierce ; but the next minute Harry Lant bursts out laughing, and Measles does the same, and then they two did what I should think they never did before—they shook hands ; but Mrs Bantem had no sooner turned away with tears in her eyes, because she felt so cross, than the two chaps fell out again about some stupid thing or another, and kept on snarling and snapping at each other all along the march.

But there, bless you! that wasn't all: I saw Mrs Maine talking to her sister in a quick earnest sort of way, and they both seemed out of sorts; and the colonel swore at the tent-men, and bullied the adjutant, and he came round and dropped on to us, finding fault with the men's belts, and that upset the sergeants. Then some of the baggage didn't start right, and Lieutenant Leigh had to be taken to task by Captain Dyer, as in duty bound; while, when at last we were starting, if there wasn't a tremendous outcry, and the young colonel—little Cock Robin, you know—kicking, and screaming, and fighting the old black nurse, because he mightn't draw his little sword, and march alongside of Harry Lant!

Now, I'm very particular about putting all this down, because I want you to see how we all were one with the other, and how right through the battalion little things made us out of sorts with one another, and hardly friendly enough to speak, so that the difference may strike you, and you may see in a stronger light the alteration and the behaviour of people when trouble came.

All the same, though, I don't think it's possible for any-body to make a long march in India without getting out of temper. It's my belief that the grit does it, for you do have that terribly; and what with the heat, the dust, the thirst, the government boots, that always seem as if made not to fit anybody, and the grit, I believe even a regiment all chaplains would forget their trade.

Tramp, tramp, tramp, day after day, and nearly always over wide, dreary, dusty plains. Now we'd pass a few muddy paddy-fields, or come upon a river, but not often; and I many a time used to laugh grimly to myself, as I thought what a very different place hot, dusty, dreary India was, to the glorious country I used to picture, all beautiful trees and flowers, and birds with dazzling plumage. There are bright places there, no doubt, but I never came across one, and my recollections of India are none of the most cheery.

But at last came the day when we were crossing a great wide-spread plain, in the middle of which seemed to be a few houses, with something bright here and there shining in the sun; and as we marched on, the cluster of houses appeared to grow and grow, till we halted at last in a market square of a good-sized town; and that night we were once more in barracks. But, for my part, I was more gritty than ever; for now we did not see the colonel's lady or her sister, though I may as well own that there was some one with them that I wanted to see more than either.

They were all, of course, at the colonel's quarters, a fine old palace of a place, with a court-yard, and a tank in the centre, and trees, and a flat roof, by the side of the great square; while on one side was another great rambling place, separated by a narrowish sort of alley, used for stores and hospital purposes; and on the other side, still going along by the side of the great market square, was another building, the very fellow to the colonel's quarters, but separated by a narrow footway, some ten feet wide, and this place was occupied by the officers.

Our barracks took up another side of the square; and on the others were mosques and flat-roofed buildings, and a sort of bazaar; while all round stretched away, in narrow streets, the houses of what we men used to call the niggers. Though, speaking for myself, I used to find them, when well treated, a nice, clean, gentle sort of people. I used to look upon them as a big sort of children, in their white muslin and calico, and their simple ways of playing-like at living; and even now I haven't altered my opinion of them in

general, for the great burst of frenzied passion that ran
through so many of them was just like a child's uncon-
trolled rage.

Things were not long in settling down to the regular life:
there was a little drill of a morning, and then, the rest of
the day, the heat to fight with, which seemed to take all
the moisture out of our bodies, and make us long for
night.

I did not get put on as sentry once at the colonel's
quarters, but I heard a little now and then from Mrs
Bantem, who used to wash some of Mrs Maine's fine things,
the black women doing everything else; and she'd often
have a good grumble about 'her fine ladyship,' as she called
her, and she'd pity her children. She used to pick up a
good deal of information, though, and, taking a deal of
interest as I did in Miss Ross, I got to know that it seemed
to be quite a settled thing between her and Captain Dyer;
and Bantem, who got took on now as Lieutenant Leigh's
servant, used to tell his wife about how black those two
were one towards the other.

And so the time went on in a quiet sleepy way, the men
getting lazier every day. There was nothing to stir us, only
now and then we'd have a good laugh at Measles, who'd
get one of his nasty fits on, and swear at all the officers
round, saying he was as good as any of them, and that if
he had his rights he would have been made an officer before
then. Harry Lant, too, used to do his bit to make time
pass away a little less dull, singing, telling stories, or getting
up to some of his pranks with old *Nabob*, the elephant,
making Chunder, the mahout, more mad than ever, for, no
matter what he did or said, only let Harry make a sort of
queer noise of his, and just like a great flesh-mountain,
that elephant would come. It didn't matter who was in
the way: regiment at drill, officer, rajah, anybody, old *Nabob*
would come straight away to Harry, holding out his trunk

for fruit, or putting it in Harry's breast, where he'd find some bread or biscuit; and then the great brute would smooth him all over with his trunk, in a way that used to make Mrs Bantem say, that perhaps, after all, the natives weren't such fools as they looked, and that what they said about dead people going into animals' bodies might be true after all, for, if that great overgrown beast hadn't a soul of its own, and couldn't think, she didn't know nothing, so now then!

CHAPTER VI.

BUT it was always the same; and though time was when I could have laughed as merrily as did that little Jenny Wren of the colonel's at Harry's antics, I couldn't laugh now, because, it always seemed as if they were made an excuse to get Miss Ross and her maid out with the children.

A party of jugglers, or dancing-girls, or a man or two with pipes and snakes, were all very well; but I've known clever parties come round, and those I've named would hardly step out to look; and my heart, I suppose it was, if it wasn't my mind, got very sore about that time, and I used to get looking as evil at Harry Lant as Lieutenant Leigh did at the captain.

But it was a dreary time that, after all, one from which we were awakened in a sudden way, that startled us to a man.

First of all, there came a sort of shadowy rumour that something was wrong with the men of a native regiment, something to do with their caste; and before we had well realised that it was likely to be anything serious, sharp and swift came one bit of news after another, that the British officers in the native regiments had been shot down—here, there, in all directions; and then we understood that what we had taken for the flash of a solitary fire, was the firing of a big train, and that there was a great mutiny in the land. And not, mind, the mutiny or riot of a mob of roughs, but of men drilled and disciplined by British officers, with leaders of their own caste, all well armed and provided with ammunition; and the talk round our mess when we heard all this was, How will it end?

I don't think there were many who did not realise the fact that something awful was coming to pass. Measles grinned, he did, and said that there was going to be an end of British tyranny in India, and that the natives were only going to seize their own again; but the next minute, although it was quite clean, he takes his piece out of the rack, cleans it thoroughly all over again, fixes the bayonet, feels the point, and then stands at the ' present!'

'I think we can let 'em know what's what, though, my lads, if they come here,' he says, with a grim smile; when Mrs Bantem, whose breath seemed quite taken away before by the way he talked, jumped up quite happy-like, laid her great hand upon his left side, and then, turning to us, she says: 'It's beating strong.'

'What is?' says Bantem, looking puzzled.

'Measles' heart,' says Mrs Bantem: 'and I always knew it was in the right place.'

The next minute she gave Measles a slap on the back as echoed through the place, sending him staggering forward; but he only laughed and said: 'Praise the saints, I ain't Bantem.'

There was a fine deal of excitement, though, now. The colonel seemed to wake up, and with him every officer, for we expected not only news but orders every moment. Discipline, if I may say so, was buckled up tight with the tongue in the last hole; provisions and water were got in; sentries doubled, and a strange feeling of distrust and fear came upon all, for we soon saw that the people of the place hung away from us, and though, from such an inoffensive-looking lot as we had about us, there didn't seem much to fear, yet there was no knowing what treachery we might have to encounter, and as he had to think and act for others beside himself, Colonel Maine—God bless him—took every possible precaution against danger, then hidden, but which was likely to spring into sight at any moment.

There were not many English residents at Begumbagh, but what there were came into quarters directly; and the very next morning we learned plainly enough that there was danger threatening our place by the behaviour of the natives, who packed up their few things and filed out of the town as fast as they could, so that at noonday the market-place was deserted, and, save the few we had in quarters, there was not a black face to be seen.

The next morning came without news; and I was orderly, and standing waiting in the outer court close behind the colonel, who was holding a sort of council of war with the officers, when a sentry up in the broiling sun, on the roof, calls out that a horseman was coming; and before very long, covered with sweat and dust, an orderly dragoon dashes up, his horse all panting and blown, and then coming jingling and clanking in with those spurs and that sabre of his, he hands despatches to the colonel.

I hope I may be forgiven for what I thought then, but, as I watched his ruddy face, while he read those despatches, and saw it turn all of a sickly, greeny white, I gave him the credit of being a coward; and I was not the only one who did so. We all knew that, like us, he had never seen a shot fired in anger; and something like an angry feeling of vexation came over me, I know, as I thought of what a fellow he would be to handle and risk the lives of the four hundred men under his charge there at Begumbagh.

'D'yer think I'd look like that?' says a voice close

to my ear just then. 'D'yer think if I'd been made an officer, I'd ha' shewed the white-feather like that?' And turning round sharp, I saw it was Measles, who was standing sentry by the gateway; and he was so disgusted, that he spat about in all directions, for he was a man who didn't smoke, like any other Christian, but chewed his tobacco like a sailor.

'Dyer,' says the colonel, the next moment, and they closed up together, but close to where we two stood—'Dyer,' he says, 'I never felt before that it would be hard to do my duty as a soldier; but, God help me, I shall have to leave Annie and the children.' There were a couple of tears rolling down the poor fellow's cheeks as he spoke, and he took Captain Dyer's hand.

'Look at him! Look there!' whispers Measles again; and I kicked out sharp behind, and hit him on the shin. 'He's a pretty sort of a'——

He didn't say any more just then, for, like me, he was staggered by the change that took place.

I think I've said Colonel Maine was a little, easy-going, pudgy man, with a red face; but just then, as he stood holding Captain Dyer's hand, a change seemed to come over him; he dropped the hand he had held, tightened his sword-belt, and then took a step forward, to stand thoughtful, with despatches in his left hand. It was then that I saw in a moment that I had wronged him, and I felt as if I could have gone down on the ground for him to have walked over me, for whatever he might have been in peace, easy-going, careless, and fond of idleness and good-living—come time for action, there he was with the true British officer flashing out of his face, his lips pinched, his eyes flashing, and a stern look upon his countenance that I had never seen before.

'Now then!' I says in a whisper to Measles. I didn't say anything else, for he knew what I meant. 'Now then—now then!'

'Well,' says Measles then, in a whisper, 'I s'pose women and children will bring the soft out of a man at a time like this; but, why! what did he mean by humbugging us like that!'

I should think Colonel Maine stood alone thoughtful and still in that court-yard, with the sun beating down upon his muslin-covered forage-cap, while you could slowly, and like a pendulum-beat, count thirty. It was a tremendously hot morning, with the sky a bright clear blue, and the shadows of a deep purply black cast down and cut as sharp as sharp. It was so still, too, that you could hear the whirring, whizzy noise of the cricket things, and now and then the champ, champ of the horse rattling his bit as he stood outside the gateway. It was a strange silence, that seemed to make itself felt; and then the colonel woke into life, stuck those despatches into his sword-belt, gave an order here, an order there, and the next minute—Tantaran-tantaran, *Tantaran-tantaran*, TANTARAN-TANTARAN, *Tantaran-tay*—the bugle was ringing out the assemblée, men were hurrying here and there, there was the trampling of feet, the court-yard was full of busy figures, shadows were passing backwards and forwards, and the news was abroad that our regiment was to form a flying column with another, and that we were off directly.

Ay, but it was exciting, that getting ready, and the time went like magic before we formed a hollow square, and the colonel said a few words to us, mounted as he was now, his voice firm as firm, except once, when I saw him glance at an upper window, and then it trembled, but only for an instant. His words were not many; and to this day, when I think of the scene under that hot blue sky, they come ringing back; for it did not seem to us that our old colonel was speaking, but a new man of a different mettle, though it was only that the right stuff had been sleeping in his breast, ready to be wakened by the bugle.

'My lads,' he said, and to a man we all burst out into a

C

ringing cheer, when he took off his cap, and waved it round
—‘My lads, this is a sharp call, but I've been expecting it,
and it has not found us asleep. I thank you for the smart
way in which you have answered it; for it shews me that a
little easy-going on my part in the piping times of peace has
not been taken advantage of. My lads, these are stern times;
and this despatch tells me of what will bring the honest
British blood into every face, and make every strong man
take a firm gripe of his piece as he longs for the order to
charge the mutinous traitors to their Queen, who, taking her
pay, sworn to serve her, have turned, and in cold blood
butchered their officers, slain women, and hacked to pieces
innocent babes. My lads, we are going against a horde of
monsters; but I have bad news—you cannot all go’——

There was a murmur here.

‘That murmur is not meant,’ he continued; ‘and I know
it will be regretted when I explain myself. We have women
here and children : mine—yours—and they must be protected’
(it was here that his voice shook). ‘Captain Dyer's company
will garrison the place till our return, and to those men
many of us leave all that is dear to us on earth. I have
spoken. God save the Queen !’

How that place echoed with the hearty ‘Hurray !’ that
rung out ; and then it was, ‘Fours right. March !’ and only
our company held firm, while I don't know whether I felt
disappointed or pleased, till I happened to look up at one of
the windows, to see Mrs Maine and Miss Ross, with those
two poor little innocent children clapping their hands with
delight at seeing the soldiers march away ; one of them, the
little girl, with her white muslin and scarlet sash over her
shoulder, being held up by Lizzy Green ; and then I did
know that I was not disappointed, but glad I was to
stay.

But to shew you how a man's heart changes about when
it is blown by the hot breath of what you may call love, let

me tell you that only half a minute later, I was disappointed again at not going; and dared I have left the ranks, I'd have run after the departing column, for I caught Harry Lant looking up at that window, and I thought a handkerchief was waved to him.

Next minute, Captain Dyer calls out, 'Form four—deep. Right face. March!' and he led us to the gateway, but only to halt us there, for Measles, who was sentry, calls out something to him in a wild excited way.

'What do you want, man?' says Captain Dyer.

'O sir, if you'll only let me exchange. 'Taint too late. Let me go, captain.'

'How dare you, sir!' says Captain Dyer sternly, though I could see plainly enough it was only for discipline, for he was, I thought, pleased at Measles wanting to be in the thick of it. Then he shouts again to Measles: ''Tention—present arms!' and Measles falls into his right position for a sentry when troops are marching past. 'March!' says the captain again; and we marched into the market-place, and—all but those told off for sentries—we were dismissed; and Captain Dyer then stood talking earnestly to Lieutenant Leigh, for it had fallen out that they two, with a short company of eight-and-thirty rank and file, were to have the guarding of the women and children left in quarters at Begumbagh.

CHAPTER VII.

It seemed to me that, for the time being, Lieutenant Leigh was too much of a soldier to let private matters and personal feelings of enmity interfere with duty; and those two stood talking together for a good half-hour, when, having apparently made their plans, fatigue-parties were ordered out; and what I remember then thinking was a wise move, the

soldiers' wives and children in quarters were brought into
the old palace, since it was the only likely spot for putting
into something like a state of defence.

I have called it a palace, and I suppose that a rajah did
once live in it, but, mind you, it was neither a very large nor
a very grand place, being only a square of buildings, facing
inward to a little court-yard, entered by a gateway, after the
fashion of no end of buildings in the east.

Water we had in the tank, but provisions were brought
in, and what sheep there were. Fortunately, there was a
good supply of hay, and that we got in ; but one thing we
did not bargain for, and that was the company of the great
elephant, *Nabob*, he having been left behind. And what
does he do but come slowly up on those india-rubber cushion
feet of his, and walk through the gateway, his back actually
brushing against the top ; and then, once in, he goes quietly
over to where the hay was stacked, and coolly enough begins
eating !

The men laughed, and some jokes were made about his
taking up a deal of room, and I suppose, really, it was
through Harry Lant that the great beast came in ; but no
more was said then, we all being so busy, and not one of
us had the sense to see what a fearful strait that great
inoffensive animal might bring us to.

I believe we all forgot about the heat that day as we
worked on, slaving away at things that, in an ordinary way,
we should have expected to be done by the niggers. Food,
ammunition, wood, particularly planks, everything Captain
Dyer thought likely to be of use ; and soon a breastwork
was made inside the gateway ; such lower windows as looked
outwards carefully nailed up, and loopholed for a shot at the
enemy, should any appear ; and when night did come at last,
peaceful and still, the old palace was turned into a regular
little fort.

We all knew that all this might be labour in vain, but all

the same it seemed to be our duty to get the place into as good a state of defence as we could, and under orders we did it. But, after all, we knew well enough that if the mutineers should bring up a small field-piece, they could knock the place about our ears in no time. Our hope, though, was that, at all events while our regiment was away, we might be unmolested, for, if the enemy came in any number, what could eight-and-thirty men do, hampered as they were with half-a-dozen children, and twice as many women? Not that all the women were likely to hamper us, for there was Mrs Bantem, busy as a bee, working here, comforting there, helping women to make themselves snug in different rooms; and once, as she came near me, she gave me one of her tremendous slaps on the back, her eyes twinkling with pleasure, and the perspiration streaming down her face the while. 'Ike Smith,' she says, 'this is something like, isn't it? But ask Captain Dyer to have that breastwork strengthened—there isn't half enough of it. Glad Bantem hasn't gone. But, I say, only think of that poor woman! I saw her just now crying, fit to break her poor heart.'

'What poor woman?' I said, staring hard.

'Why, the colonel's wife. Poor soul, it's pitiful to see her! it went through me like a knife.—What! are you there, my pretties?' she cried, flumping down on the stones as the colonel's two little ones came running out. 'Bless your pretty hearts, you'll come and say a word to old Mother Bantem, won't you?'

'What's everybody tying about?' says the little girl, in her prattling way. 'I don't like people to ty. Has my ma been whipped, and Aunt Elsie been naughty?'

'Look, look!' cries the boy excitedly; 'dere's old *Nabob!*' And toddling off, the next minute he was close to the great beast, his little sister running after him, to catch hold of his hand; and there the little mites stood close to, and staring up at the great elephant, as he kept on amusing himself by twisting up a little hay in his trunk, and then lightly scattering it over his back, to get rid of the flies—for what nature could have been about to give him such a scrap of a tail, I can't understand. He'd work it, and flip it about hard enough; but as to getting rid of a fly, it's my belief that if insects can laugh, they laughed at it, as they watched him from where they were buzzing about the stone walls and windows in the hot sunshine.

The next minute, like a chorus, there came a scream from one of the upper windows, one from another, and a sort of howl from Mrs Bantem, and we all stood startled and staring, for what does Jenny Wren do, but, in a staggering way, lift up her little brother for him to touch the elephant's trunk, and then she stood laughing and clapping her hands with delight, seeing no fear, bless her! as that long, soft trunk was gently curled round the boy's waist, he was drawn out of his sister's arms; and then the great beast stood swinging the child to and fro, now up a little way, now down between his legs, and him crowing and laughing away all the while, as if it was the best fun that could be.

I believe we were all struck motionless; and it was like taking a hand away from my throat to let me breathe once more, when I saw the elephant gently drop the little fellow down on a heap of hay, but only for him to scramble up, and run forward shouting: 'Now 'gain, now 'gain;' and, as if *Nabob* understood his little prattling, half-tied tongue, he takes him up again, and swings him, just as there was a regular rush made, and Mrs Colonel, Miss Ross, Lizzy, and the captain and lieutenant came up.

'For Heaven's sake, save the child!' cries Mrs Maine.— 'Mr Leigh, pray, do something.'

Miss Ross did not speak, but she looked at Captain Dyer; and those two young men both went at the elephant directly, to get the child away; but, in an instant, *Nabob* wheeled round, just the same as a stubborn donkey would at home with a lot of boys teasing it; and then, as they dodged round his great carcass, he trumpeted fiercely, and began to shuffle off round the court.

I went up too, and so did Mrs Bantem, brave as a lion; but the great beast only kept on making his loud snorting noise, and shuffled along, with the boy in his trunk, swinging him backwards and forwards; and it was impossible to help thinking of what would be the consequence if the elephant should drop the little fellow, and then set on him one of his great feet.

It seemed as if nothing could be done, and once the idea —wild enough too—rushed into my head that it would be advisable to get a rifle put to the great beast's ear, and fire, when Measles shouted out from where he was on guard: 'Here's Chunder coming!' and, directly after, with his opal eye-balls rolling, and his dark, treacherous-looking face seeming to me all wicked and pleased at what was going on, came the mahout, and said a few words to the elephant, which stopped directly, and went down upon its knees. Chunder then tried to take hold of the child, but somehow that seemed to make the great beast furious, and getting up again, he began to grunt and make a noise after the fashion of a great pig, going on now faster round the court, and sending those who had come to look, and who stood in his way, fleeing in all directions.

Mrs Maine was half fainting, and, catching the little girl to her breast, I saw her go down upon her knees and hide her face, expecting, no doubt, every moment, that the next one would be her boy's last; and, indeed, we were all alarmed now, for the more we tried to get the little chap away, the fiercer the elephant grew; the only one who did not seem to mind being the boy himself, though his sister now began to cry, and in her little artless way I heard her ask her mother if the naughty elephant would eat Clivey.

I've often thought since that if we'd been quiet, and left

the beast alone, he would soon have set the child down; and I've often thought, too, that Mr Chunder could have got the boy away if he had liked, only he did nothing but tease and irritate the elephant, which was not the best of friends with him. But you will easily understand that there was not much time for thought then.

I had been doing my best along with the others, and then stood thinking what I could be at next, when I caught Lizzy Green's eye turned to me in an appealing, reproachful sort of way, that seemed to say as plainly as could be : 'Can't you do anything?' when all at once Measles shouts out : ''Arry, 'Arry!' and Harry Lant came up at the double, having been busy carrying arms out of the guard-room rack.

It was at one and the same moment that Harry Lant saw what was wrong, and that a cold dull chill ran through me, for I saw Lizzy clasp her hands together in a sort of thankful way, and it seemed to me then, as Harry ran up to the elephant, that he was always to be put before me, and that I was nobody, and the sooner I was out of the way the better.

All the same, though, I couldn't help admiring the way Harry ran up to the great brute, and did what none of us could manage. I quite hated him, I know, but yet I was proud of my mate, as he went up and says something to *Nabob*, and the elephant stands still. 'Put him down,' says Harry, pointing to the ground; and the great flesh-mountain puts the little fellow down. 'Now then,' says Harry, to the horror of the ladies, 'pick him up again;' and in a twinkling the great thing whips the boy up once more. 'Now, bring him up to the colonel's lady.' Well, if you'll believe me, if the great thing didn't follow Harry like a lamb, and carry the child up to where, half fainting, knelt poor Mrs Maine. 'Now, put him down,' says Harry; and the next moment little Clive Maine—Cock Robin, as we called him—was being hugged to his mother's breast. 'Now go down on your knees, and beg the ladies' pardon,' says Harry laughing. Down goes the elephant, and stops there, making a queer chuntering noise the while. 'Says he's very sorry, ma'am, and won't do so no more,' says Harry, serious as a judge; and in a moment, half laughing, half crying, Mrs Maine caught hold of Harry's hand, and kissed it, and then held it for a moment to her breast, sobbing hysterically as she did so.

'God bless you! You're a good man,' she cried; and then she broke down altogether; and Miss Ross, and Mrs Bantem, and Lizzy got round her, and helped her in.

I could see that Harry was touched, for one of his lips shook; but he tried to keep up the fun of the thing; and turning to the elephant, he says out loud : 'Now, get up, and go back to the hay; and don't you come no more of those games, that's all.'

The elephant got up directly, making a grunting noise as he did so.

'Why not?' says Harry, making-believe that that was what the great beast said. 'Because, if you do, I'll smash you. There!'

Officers and men, they all burst out laughing, to see little Harry Lant—a chap so little that he wouldn't have been in the regiment only that men were scarce, and the standard was very low when he listed—to see him standing shaking his fist at the great monster, one of whose legs was bigger than Harry altogether—stand shaking his fist in its face, and then take hold of the soft trunk and lead him away.

Perhaps I did, perhaps I didn't, but I thought I caught sight of a glance passing between Lizzy Green, now at one window, and Harry, leading off the elephant; but all the same I felt that jealous of him, and to hate him so that I could have quarrelled with him about nothing. It seemed as if he was always to come before me.

And I wasn't the only one jealous of Harry, for no

sooner was the court pretty well empty, than he came
slowly up towards me, in spite of my sour black looks,
which he wouldn't notice ; but before he could get to me,
Chunder Chow, the mahout, goes up to the elephant,
muttering and spiteful-like, with his hook-spear thing, that
mahouts use to drive with ; and being, I suppose, put out,
and jealous, and annoyed at his authority being taken away,
and another man doing what he couldn't, he gives the
elephant a kick in the leg, and then hits him viciously with
his iron hook thing.

Well ! Bless you ! it didn't take an instant, and it seemed
to me that the elephant only gave that trunk of his a gentle
swing against Chunder's side, and he was a couple of
yards off, rolling over and over in the hay scattered
about.

Up he jumps, wild as wild ; and the first thing he
catches sight of is Harry laughing fit to crack his sides,
when Chunder rushes at him like a mad bull.

I suppose he expected to see Harry turn tail and run ;
but that being one of those things not included in drill, and
a British soldier having a good deal of the machine about
him, Harry stands fast, and Chunder pulls up short, grinning,
rolling his eyes, and twisting his hands about, just for all
the world like as if he was robbing a hen-roost, and wringing
all the chickens' necks.

'Didn't hurt much, did it, blacky ?' says Harry coolly.
But the mahout couldn't speak for rage ; and he kept
spitting on the ground, and making signs, till really his face
was anything but pretty to look at. And there he kept on,
till, from laughing, Harry turned a bit nasty, for there was
some one looking out of a window ; and from being half-
amused at what was going on, I once more felt all cold and
bitter. But Harry fires up now, and makes towards Mr
Chunder, who begins to retreat ; and says Harry : 'Now I
tell you what it is, young man ; I never did you any ill

turn ; and if I choose to have a bit of fun with the elephant, it's government property, and as much mine as yours. But look ye here—if you come cussing, and spitting, and swearing at me again in your nasty heathen dialect, why, if I don't—— No,' he says, stopping short, and half-turning to me, 'I can't black his eyes, Isaac, for they're black enough already ; but let him come any more of it, and, jiggermaree, if I don't bung 'em !'

CHAPTER VIII.

CHUNDER didn't like the looks of Harry, I suppose, so he walked off, turning once to spit and curse, like that turn-coat chap, Shimei, that you read of in the Bible ; and we two walked off together towards our quarters.

'I ain't going to stand any of his nonsense,' says Harry.

'It's bad making enemies now, Harry,' I said gruffly. And just then up comes Measles, who had been relieved, for his spell was up now; and another party were on, else he would have had to be in the guard-room.

'There never was such an unlucky beggar as me,' says Measles. 'If a chance does turn up for earning a bit of promotion, it's always some one else gets it. Come on, lads, and let's see what Mother Bantem's got in the pot.'

'You'll perhaps have a chance before long of earning your bit of promotion without going out,' I says.

'Ike Smith's turned prophet and croaker in ornary,' says Harry, laughing. 'I believe he expects we're going to have a new siege of Seringapatam here, only back'ards way on.'

'Only wish some of 'em would come this way, says

Measles grimly ; and he made a sort of offer, and a hit out
at some imaginary enemy.

'Here they are,' says Joe Bantem, as we walked in.
'Curry for dinner, lads—look alive.'

'What, my little hero !' says Mrs Bantem, fetching
Harry one of her slaps on the back. 'My word, you're in
fine plume with the colonel's lady.'

Slap came her hand down again on Harry's back ; and as
soon as he could get wind : 'Oh, I say, don't,' says Harry.
'Thank goodness, I ain't a married man.—Is she often as
affectionate as this with you, Joe ?'

Joe Bantem laughed ; and soon after we were all making,
in spite of threatened trouble and disappointment, an
uncommonly hearty dinner, for, if there ever was a woman
who could make a good curry, it was Mrs Bantem ; and
many 's the cold winter's day I've stood in Facet's door
there in Bond Street, and longed for a plateful. Pearls
stewed in sunshine, Harry Lant used to call it ; and really
to see the beautiful, glistening, white rice, every grain tender
as tender, and yet dry and ready to roll away from the
others—none of your mosh-posh rice, if Mrs Bantem boiled
it—and then the rich golden curry itself : there, I've known
that woman turn one of the toughest old native cocks into
what you'd have sworn was a delicate young Dorking chick
—that is, so long as you didn't get hold of a drumstick,
which perhaps would be a bit ropy. That woman was a
regular blessing to our mess, and we fellows said so, many
a time.

One, two, three days passed without any news, and we in
our quarters were quiet as if thousands of miles from the
rest of the world. The town kept as deserted as ever, and
it seemed almost startling to me when I was posted sentry
on the roof, after looking out over the wide, sandy, dusty
plain, over which the sunshine was quivering and dancing,
to peer down amongst the little ramshackle native huts

without a sign of life amongst them, and it took but little thought for me to come to the conclusion that the natives knew of something terrible about to happen, and had made that their reason for going away. Though, all the same, it might have been from dread lest we should seek to visit upon them and theirs the horrors that had elsewhere befallen the British.

I used often to think, too, that Captain Dyer had some such feelings as mine, for he looked very, very serious and anxious, and he'd spend hours on the roof with his glass, Miss Ross often being by his side, while Lieutenant Leigh used to watch them in a strange way, when he thought no one was observing him.

I've often thought that when people are touched with that queer complaint folks call love, they get into a curious half-delirious way, that makes them fancy that people are nearly blind, and have their eyes shut to what they do or say. I fancy there was something of this kind with Miss Ross, and I'm sure there was with me when I used to go hanging about, trying to get a word with Lizzy ; and, of course, shut up as we all were then, often having the chance, but getting seldom anything but a few cold answers, and a sort of show of fear of me whenever I was near to her.

But what troubled me as much as anything was the behaviour of the four Indians we had shut up with us— Chunder Chow, the old black nurse, and two more—for they grew more uppish and bounceable every day, refusing to work, until Captain Dyer had one of the men tied up to the triangles and flogged, down in a great cellar or vault place that there was under the north end of the palace, so that the ladies and women shouldn't hear his cries. He deserved all he got, as I can answer for, and that made the rest a little more civil, but not for long ; and, just the day before something happened, I took the liberty of saluting

Captain Dyer, after he had been giving me some orders, and took that chance of speaking my mind.

'Captain,' I says, 'I don't think those black folks are to be trusted.'

'Neither do I, Smith,' he says. 'But what have you to tell me?'

'Nothing at all, captain, only that I have my eye on them; and I've been thinking that they must somehow or another have held communication outside; and I don't like it, for those people don't get what we call cheeky without cause.'

'Keep both eyes on them then, Smith,' says Captain Dyer, smiling; 'and, no matter what it is—if it is the most trivial thing in any way connected with them, report it.'

'I will, sir,' I says; and the very next day, much against the grain, I did have something to report.

CHAPTER IX.

THE next morning was hotter, I think, than ever, with no prospect either of rain or change; and, after doing what little work I had to get over, it struck me that I might as well attend to what Captain Dyer advised—give two eyes to Chunder and his friends; so I left Mrs Bantem busy over her cooking, and went down into the court.

All below was as still as death—sunshine here, shadow there, but, through one of the windows, open to catch the least breeze that might be on the way, and taking in instead the hot, sultry air, came now and then the silvery laughter of the children—that pleasant cheery sound that makes the most rugged old face grow a trifle smoother.

I looked here, and I looked there, but could only see old *Nabob* amusing himself with the hay, a sentry on the roof to the east, and another on the roof to the west, and one in the gateway, broiling almost, all of them, with the heat.

The ladies and the children were seldom seen now, for they were in trouble; and Mrs Maine was worn almost to skin and bone with anxiety, as she sat waiting for tidings of the expedition.

Not knowing what to do with myself, I sauntered along by where there was a slip of shade, and entered the south side of the palace—an old half-ruinous part; and after going first into one, and then into another of the bare empty rooms, I picked out what seemed to be the coolest corner I could find, sat down with my back propped against the wall, filled and lit my pipe, and then putting things together in my mind, thoroughly enjoyed a good smoke.

There was something wonderfully soothing in that bit of tobacco, and it appeared to me cooling, comforting, and to make my bit of a love-affair seem not so bad as it was. So, on the strength of that, I refilled, and was about half-way through another pipe, when things began to grow very dim round about me, and I was wandering about in my dreams, and nodding that head of mine in the most curious and wild way you can think of. What I dreamed about most was about getting married to Lizzy Green; and in what must have been a very short space, that event was coming off at least half-a-dozen times over, only *Nabob*, the elephant, would come in at an awkward time and put a stop to it. But at last, in my dreamy fashion, it seemed to me that matters were smoothed over, and he consented to put down the child, and, flapping his ears, promised he'd say yes. But in my stupid, confused muddle, I thought that he'd no sooner put down the child with his trunk than he wheeled round and took him up with his tail; and so on, backwards and forwards, when, getting quite out of patience,

I caught Lizzy's hand in mine, saying: 'Never mind the elephant—let's have it over;' and she gave a sharp scream.

I jumped to my feet, biting off, half swallowing a bit of pipe-shank as I did so, and then stood drenched with perspiration, listening to a scuffling noise in the next room; when, shaking off the stupid confused feeling, I ran towards the door just as another scream—not a loud, but a faint excited scream—rang in my ears, and the next moment Lizzy Green was sobbing and crying in my arms, and that black thief Chunder was crawling on his hands and knees to the door, where he got up, holding his fist to his mouth, and then he turned upon me such a look as I have never forgotten.

I don't wonder at the people of old painting devils with black faces, for I don't know anything more devilish-looking than a black's phiz when it is drawn with rage, and the eyes are rolling about, now all black flash, now all white, while the grinning ivories below seem to be grinding and ready to tear you in pieces.

It was after that fashion that Chunder looked at me as he turned at the door; but I was then only thinking of the trembling, frightened girl I held in my arms, trying at the same time to whisper a few gentle words, while I had hard work to keep from pressing my lips to her white forehead.

But the next minute she disengaged herself from my grasp, and held out her little white hand to me, thanking me as sweetly as thanks could be given.

'Perhaps you had better not say a word about it,' she whispered. 'He's come under pretence of seeing the nurse, and been rude to me once or twice before. I came here to sit at that window with my work, and did not see him come behind me.'

I started as she spoke about that open window, for it looked out upon the spot where I sometimes stood sentry;

but then, Harry Lant sometimes stood just in the same place, and I don't know whether it was a strange impression caused by his coming, that made me think of him, but just then there were footsteps, and, with his pipe in his mouth, and fatigue-jacket all unbuttoned, Harry entered the room.

'Beg pardon; didn't know it was engaged,' he says lightly, as he stepped back; and then he stopped, for Lizzy called to him by his name.

'Please walk back with me to Mrs Maine's quarters,' she said softly; and once more holding her hand out to me, with her eyes cast down, she thanked me; and the question I had been asking myself—Did she love Harry Lant better than me?—was to my mind answered, and I gave a groan as I saw them walk off together, for it struck me then that they had engaged to meet in that room, only Harry Lant was late.

'Never mind,' I says to myself; 'I've done a comrade a good turn.' And then I thought more and more of there being a feeling in the blacks' minds that their hour was coming, or that ill-looking scoundrel would never have dared to insult a white woman in open day.

Ten minutes after, I was on my way to Captain Dyer, for, in spite of what Lizzy had said, I felt that, being under orders, it was my duty to report all that occurred with the blacks; for we might at any time have been under siege, and to have had unknown and treacherous enemies in the camp would have been ruin indeed.

'Well, Smith,' he said, smiling as I entered and saluted, 'what news of the enemy?'

'Not much, sir,' I said; what I had to tell, going, as I have before said, very much against the grain. 'I was in one of the empty rooms on the south side, when I heard a scream, and running up, I found it was Miss Ross'——

'What!' he roared, in a voice that would have startled a stronger man than I.

'Miss Ross's maid, sir, with that black fellow Chunder, the mahout, trying to kiss her.'

'Well?' he said, with a black angry look overspreading his face.

'Well, sir,' I said, feeling quite red as I spoke, 'he kissed my fist instead—that's all.'

Captain Dyer began to walk up and down, playing with one of the buttons on his breast, as was his way when eager and excited.

'Now, Smith,' he said at last, stopping short before me, 'what does that mean?'

'Mean, sir?' I said, feeling quite as excited as himself. 'Well, sir, if you ask me, I say that if it was in time of peace and quiet, it would only mean that it was a bit of his black—— I beg your pardon, captain,' I says, stopping short, for, you see, it was quite time.

'Go on, Smith,' he said quietly.

'His black impudence, sir.'

'But, as it is not in time of peace and quiet, Smith?' he said, looking me through and through.

'Well, sir,' I said, 'I don't want to croak, nor for other people to believe what I say; but it seems to me that that black fellow's kicking out of the ranks means a good deal; and I take it that he is excited with the news that he has somehow got hold of—news that is getting into his head like so much green 'rack. I've thought of it some little time now, sir; and it strikes me that if, instead of our short company being Englishmen, they were all Chunder Chows, before to-morrow morning, begging your pardon, Captain Dyer and Lieutenant Leigh would have said "Right wheel" for the last time.'

'And the women and children!' he muttered softly: but I heard him.

He did not speak then for quite half a minute, when he turned to me with a pleasant smile.

'But you see, though, Smith,' he said, 'our short company is made up of different stuff; and therefore there's some hope for us yet; but—— Ah, Leigh, did you hear what he said?'

'Yes,' said the lieutenant, who had been standing at the door for a few moments, scowling at us both.

'Well, what do you think?' said Captain Dyer.

'Think?' said Lieutenant Leigh contemptuously, as he turned away—'nothing!'

'But,' said Captain Dyer quietly, 'really I think there is much truth in what he, an observant man, says.'

There was a challenge from the roof just then; and we all went out to find that a mounted man was in sight; and on the captain making use of his glass, I heard him tell Lieutenant Leigh that it was an orderly dragoon.

A few minutes after, it was plain enough to everybody; and soon, man and horse dead beat, the orderly with a despatch trotted into the court.

It was a sight worth seeing, to look upon Mrs Maine clutching at the letter enclosed for her in Captain Dyer's despatch. Poor woman! it was a treasure to her—one that made her pant as she hurriedly snatched it from the captain's hand, for all formality was forgotten in those days; and then she hurried away to where her sister was waiting to hear the news.

CHAPTER X.

THE orderly took back a despatch from Captain Dyer, starting at daybreak the next morning; but before then, we all knew that matters were getting to wear a terrible aspect. At first, I had been disposed to think that the orderly was romancing, and giving us a few travellers' tales; but I soon found out that he was in earnest; and more than once I felt a shiver as he sat with our mess, telling us of how regiment after regiment had mutinied and murdered their officers; how station after station had been plundered, collectors butchered, and their wives and daughters sometimes cut down, sometimes carried off by the wretches, who had made a sport of throwing infants from one to the other on their bayonets.

'I never had any children,' sobbed Mrs Bantem then; 'and I never wished to have any; for they're not right for soldiers' wives; but only to think—the poor sweet, suffering little things. Oh, if I'd only been a man, and been there!'

We none of us said anything; but I believe all thought as I did, that if Mrs Bantem had been there, she'd have done as much—ah, perhaps more—than some men would have done. Often, since then, as I think of it, and recall it from the bygone, there I can see Mother Bantem—though why we called her mother, I don't know, unless it was because she was like a mother to us—with her great strapping form; and think of the way in which she'——

Halt! Retire by fours from the left.

Just in time; for I find handling my pen's like handling a commander-in-chief's staff, and that I've got letters which make words, which make phrases, which make sentences, which make paragraphs, which make chapters, which make up the whole story: and that is for all the world like the army with its privates made into companies, and battalions. and regiments, and brigades. Well, there you are: if you don't have discipline, and every private in his right place, where are you? Just so with me; my words were coming out in the wrong places, and in another minute I should have spoiled my story, by letting you know what was coming at the wrong time.

Well, we all felt very deeply the news brought in by that orderly, for soldiers are not such harum-scarum roughs as some people seem to imagine. For the most part, they're

men with the same feelings as civilians ; and I don't think
many of us slept very sound that night, feeling as we did
what a charge we had, and that we might be attacked at any
time ; and a good deal of my anxiety was on account of Lizzy
Green ; for even if she wouldn't be my wife, but Harry Lant's,
I could not help taking a wonderful deal of interest in her.

But all the same it was a terribly awkward time, as you
must own, for falling in love ; and I don't know hardly
whom I pitied most, Captain Dyer or myself ; but think I
had more leanings towards number one, because Captain
Dyer was happy ; though, perhaps, I might have been ; only
like lots more hot sighing noodles, I never once thought of
asking the girl if she'd have me. As for Lieutenant Leigh,
I never once thought of giving him a bit of pity, for I did
not think he deserved it.

Well, the trooper started off at daybreak, so as to get well
on his journey in the early morning ; and about an hour
after he was gone, I had a fancy to go into the old ruined
room again, where there was the bit of a scene I've told you
of. My orders from Captain Dyer were, to watch Chunder
strictly, both as to seeing that he did not again insult any of
the women, and also to see if he had any little game of his
own that he was playing on the sly ; for though Lieutenant
Leigh, on being told, pooh-poohed it all, and advised a
flogging, Captain Dyer had his suspicions—stronger ones, it
seemed, than mine ; and hence my orders and my being
excused from mounting guard.

It was all very still, and cool, and quiet as I walked from
room to room, slowly and thoughtfully, stopping to pick up
my broken pipe, which lay where I had dropped it ; and
then going on into the next room, where, under the window,
lay the bit of cotton cobweb and cat's-cradle work Lizzy had
been doing, and had left behind. I gave a bit of a gulp as
I picked that up, and I was tucking it inside my jacket
when I stopped short, for I thought I heard a whisper.

I listened, and there it was again—a low, earnest whispering of first one and then another voice in the next room,
whose wide broken doorway stood open, for there wasn't a
bit of woodwork left.

I have heard about people saying, that in some great
surprise or fright, their hearts stood still; but I don't believe
it, because it always strikes me that, when a person's heart
does stand still, it never goes on again. All the same,
though, my heart felt then as if it did stand still with the
dead, dull, miserable feeling that came upon me. Only to
think that on this, the second time I had come through
these ruined rooms, and they were here again! It was
plain enough Harry Lant and Lizzy made this their
meeting-place, and only they knew how many times they'd
met before.

Time back, I could have laughed at the idea of me, a
great strapping fellow, feeling as I did; but now I felt very
wretched; and as I thought of Harry Lant kissing those
bright red lips, and looking into those deep dark eyes, and
being let pass his hand over the glossy hair, with the
prospect of some day calling it all his own, I did not burn
all over with a mad rage and passion, but it was like a
great grief coming upon me, so that, if it hadn't been for
being a man, I could have sat down and cried.

I should think ten minutes passed, and the whispering
still went on, when I said to myself: 'Be a man, Isaac; if
she likes him better, hasn't she a right to her pick?' But
still I felt very miserable as I turned to go away, when a
something, said a little louder than the rest, stopped me.

'That ain't English,' I says to myself. 'What! surely
she's not listening to that black scoundrel?'

I was red-hot then in a moment; and as to thinking
whether this or that was straightforward, or whether I was
playing the spy, or anything of that sort, such an idea never
came into my head. Chunder was evidently talking to

Lizzy Green in that room; and for a few seconds I felt blind with a sort of jealous savage rage—against her, mind, now; and going on tip-toe, I looked round the doorway, so as to see as well as hear.

I was back in an instant, with a fresh set of sensations busy in my breast. It was Chunder, but he was alone; there was no Lizzy there; and I don't know whether my heart beat then for joy at knowing it, or for shame at myself for having thought such a thing of her.

What did it mean, then?

I did not have to ask myself the question twice, for the answer came—Treachery! And stealing to the slit of window in the room I was in, I peeped cautiously out in time to see Chunder throwing out what looked like a white packet. I could see his arm move as he threw it down to a man in a turban—a dark wiry-looking rascal; and in those few seconds I seemed to read that packet word for word, though no doubt the writing was in one of the native dialects, and my reading of it was, that it was a correct list of the defenders of the place, the women and children, and what arms and ammunition there were stored up.

It was all plain enough, and the villain was sending it by a man who must have brought him tidings of some kind.

What was I to do? That man ought to be stopped at all hazards; and what I ought to have done was to steal back, give the alarm, and let a party go round to try and cut him off.

That's what I ought to have done; but I never did have much judgment.

Now for what I did do.

Slipping back from the window, I went cautiously to the doorway, and entered the old room where Chunder was standing at the window; and I went in so quietly, and he was so intent, that I had crept close, and was in the act of leaping on to him before he turned round and tried to avoid me.

He was too late, though, for with a bound I was on him, pinioning his hands, and holding him down on the window-sill, with his head half out, as bearing down upon him, I leaned out as far as I could, yelling out: 'Sentry in the next roof, mark man below. Stop him, or fire.'

The black fellow below drew a long, awkward-looking pistol, and aimed at me, but only for a moment. Perhaps he was afraid of killing Chunder, for the next instant he had stuck the pistol back in his calico belt, and, with head stooped, was running as hard as he could run, when I could hardly contain myself for rage, knowing as I did how important it was for him to have been stopped.

'Bang!'

A sharp report from the roof, and the fellow made a bound.

Was he hit?

No : he only seemed to run the faster.

'Bang!'

Another report as the runner came in sight of the second sentry.

But I saw no more, for all my time was taken up with Chunder ; for as the second shot rang out, he gave a heave, and nearly sent me through the open window.

It was by a miracle almost that I saved myself from breaking my neck, for it was a good height from the ground ; but I held on to him tightly with a clutch such as he never had on his arms and neck before ; and then, with a strength for which I shouldn't have given him credit, he tussled with me, now tugging to get away, now to throw me from the window, his hot breath beating all the time upon my cheeks, and his teeth grinning, and eyes rolling savagely.

It was only a spurt, though, and I soon got the better of him.

I don't want to boast, but I suppose our cold northern bone and muscle are tougher and stronger than theirs; and at the end of five minutes, puffing and blown, I was sitting on his chest, taking a paper from inside his calico.

That laid me open; for, like a flash, I saw then that he had a knife in one hand, while before another thought could pass through my mind, it was sticking through my jacket and the skin of my ribs, and my fist was driven down against his mouth for him to kiss for the second time in his life.

Next minute, Captain Dyer and a dozen men were in the room, Chunder was handcuffed and marched off, and the captain was eagerly questioning me.

'But is that fellow shot down or taken—the one outside?' I asked.

'Neither,' said Captain Dyer; 'and it is too late now: he has got far enough away.'

Then I told him what I had seen, and he looked at the packet, his brow knitting as he tried to make it out.

'I ought to have come round, and given the alarm, captain,' I said bitterly.

'Yes, my good fellow, you ought,' he said; 'and I ought to have had that black scoundrel under lock and key days ago. But it is too late now to talk of what ought to have been done; we must talk of what there is to do.—But are you hurt?'

'He sent his knife through my jacket, sir,' I said, 'but it's only a scratch on the skin;' and fortunately that's what it proved to be, for we had no room for wounded men.

CHAPTER XI.

AN hour of council, and then another—our two leaders not seeming to agree as to the extent of the coming danger. Challenge from the west roof : 'Orderly in sight.'

Sure enough, a man on horseback riding very slowly, and as if his horse was dead beat.

'Surely it isn't that poor fellow come back, because his horse has failed ? He ought to have walked on,' said Captain Dyer.

'Same man,' said Lieutenant Leigh, looking through his glass ; and before very long, the poor fellow who had gone away at daybreak rode slowly up to the gate, was admitted, and then had to be helped from his horse, giving a great sobbing groan as it was done.

'In here, quick !' I said, for I thought I heard the ladies' voices ; and we carried him in to where Mrs Bantem was, as usual, getting ready for dinner, and there we laid him on a mattress.

'Despatches, captain,' he says, holding up the captain's letter to Colonel Maine. 'They didn't get that. They were too many for me. I dropped one, though, with my pistol, and cut my way through the others.'

As he spoke, I untwisted his leather sword-knot, which was cutting into his wrist, for his hacked and blood-stained sabre was hanging from his hand.

'Wouldn't go back into the scabbard,' he said faintly ; and then with a harsh gasp : ' Water—water !'

He revived then a bit ; and as Captain Dyer and Mrs Bantem between them were attending to, and binding up his wounds, he told us how he had been set upon ten miles off, and been obliged to fight his way back ; and, poor chap, he had fought ; for there were no less than ten lance-wounds in his arms, thighs, and chest, from a slight prick up to a horrible gash, deep and long enough, it seemed to me, to let out half-a-dozen poor fellows' souls.

Just in the middle of it, I saw Captain Dyer start and look strange, for there was a shadow came across where we were kneeling; and the next instant he was standing between Miss Ross and the wounded man.

'Pray, go, dear Elsie; this is no place for you,' I heard him whisper to her.

'Indeed, Lawrence,' she whispered, 'am I not a soldier's daughter? I ought to say this is no place for you. Go, and make your arrangements for our defence.'

I don't think any one but me saw the look of love she gave him as she took sponge and lint from his hand, pressing it as she did so, and then her pale face lit up with a smile as she met his eyes; the next moment she was kneeling by the wounded trooper, and in a quiet firm way helping Mrs Bantem, in a manner that made her, poor woman, stare with astonishment.

'God bless you, my darling,' she whispered to her, as soon as they had done, and the poor fellow was lying still— a toss-up with him whether it should be death or life; and I saw Mrs Bantem take Miss Ross's soft white hand between her two great rough hard palms, and kiss it just once.

'And I'd always been abusing and running her down for a fine madam, good for nothing but to squeak songs, and be looked at,' Mrs Bantem said to me, a little while after. 'Why, Isaac Smith, we shall be having that little maid shewing next that there's something in her.'

'And why not?' I said gruffly.

'Ah, to be sure,' says she, with a comical look out of one eye; 'why not? But, Isaac, my lad,' she said sadly, and looking at me very earnestly, 'I'm afraid there's sore times coming; and if so, God in heaven help those poor bairns!

Oh, if I'd been a man, and been there!' she cried, as she
recollected what the trooper had told us; and she shook her
fist fiercely in the air. 'It's what I always did say:
soldiers' wives have no business to have children; and it's
rank cruelty to the poor little things to bring them into the
world.'

Mrs Bantem then went off to see to her patient, while
I walked into the court, wondering what would come next,
and whether, in spite of all the little bitternesses and
grumbling, everybody, now some of the stern realities of life
were coming upon us, would shew up the bright side of his
or her nature; and somehow I got very hopeful that they
would.

I felt just then that I should have much liked to have a
few words with Lizzy Green, but I had no chance, for it was
a busy time with us. Captain Dyer felt strongly enough his
responsibility, and not a minute did he lose in doing all he
could for our defence; so that after an anxious day, with
nothing more occurring, when I looked round at what had
been done in barricading and so on, it seemed to me,
speaking as a soldier, that, as far as I could judge, there was
nothing more to be done, though still the feeling would come
home to me that it was a great place for forty men to defend,
if attacked by any number. Captain Dyer must have seen
that, for he had arranged to have a sort of citadel at the
north end by the gateway, and this was to be the last refuge,
where all the ammunition and food and no end of chatties of
water were stowed down in the great vault-place, which went
under this part of the building and a good deal of the court.
Then the watch was set, trebled this time, on roof and at
window, and we waited impatiently for the morning. Yes,
we all of us, I believe, waited impatiently for the morning,
when I think if we had known all that was to come, we
should have knelt down and prayed for the darkness to keep
on hour after hour, for days, and weeks, and months, sooner

than the morning should have broke as it did upon a rabble of black faces, some over white clothes, some over the British uniform that they had disgraced; and as I, who was on the west roof, heard the first hum of their coming, and caught the first glimpse of the ragged column, I gave the alarm, setting my teeth hard as I did so; for, after many years of soldiering, I was now for the first time to see a little war in earnest.

Captain Dyer's first act on the alarm being given was to double the guard over the three blacks, now secured in the strongest room he could find, the black nurse being well looked after by the women. Then, quick almost as thought, every man was at the post already assigned to him; the women and children were brought into the corner rooms by the gates, and then we waited excitedly for what should follow. The captain now ordered me out of the little party under a sergeant, and made me his orderly, and so it happened that always being with or about him, I knew how matters were going on, and was always carrying the orders, now to Lieutenant Leigh, now to this sergeant or that corporal; but at the first offset of the defence of the old place, there was a dispute between captain and lieutenant; and I'm afraid it was maintained by the last out of obstinacy, and just at a time when there should have been nothing but pulling together for the sake of all concerned. I must say, though, that there was right on both sides.

Lieutenant Leigh put it forward as his opinion that, short of men as we were, it was folly to keep four enemies under the same roof, who were likely at any time to overpower the one or two sentries placed over them; while, if there was nothing to fear in that way, there was still the necessity of shortening our defensive forces by a couple of valuable men.

'What would you do with them, then?' said Captain Dyer.

' Set them at liberty,' said Lieutenant Leigh.

' I grant all you say, in the first place,' said the captain ; ' but our retaining them is a sheer necessity.'

' Why ?' said Lieutenant Leigh, with a sneer ; and I must say that at first I held with him.

' Because,' said the captain sternly, ' if we set them at liberty, we increase our enemies' power, not merely with three men, but with scoundrels who can give them the fullest information of our defences, over and above that of which I am afraid they are already possessed. The matter will not bear further discussion.—Lieutenant Leigh, go now to your post, and do your duty to the best of your power.'

Lieutenant Leigh did not like this, and he frowned ; but Captain Dyer was his superior officer, and it was his duty to obey, so of course he did.

Now, our position was such, that, say, a hundred men with a field-piece could have knocked a wing in, and then carried us by assault with ease ; but though our enemies were full two hundred and fifty, and many of them drilled soldiers, pieces you may say of a great machine, fortunately for us, there was no one to put that machine together, and set it in motion. We soon found that out, for, instead of making the best of things, and taking possession of buildings —sheds and huts—here and there, from which to annoy us, they came up in a mob to the gate, and one fellow on a horse —a native chief, he seemed to be—gave his sword a wave, and half-a-dozen sowars round him did the same, and then they called to us to surrender.

Captain Dyer's orders were to act entirely on the defensive, and to fire no shot till we had the word, leaving them to commence hostilities.

' For,' said he, speaking to all the men, ' it may be a cowardly policy with such a mutinous set in front of us, but we have the women and children to think of ; therefore, our duty is to hold the foe at bay, and when we do fire, to make every shot tell. Beating them off is, I fear, impossible, but we may keep them out till help comes.'

'Wouldn't it be advisable, sir, to try and send off another despatch ?' I said ; 'there's the trooper's horse.'

'Where ?' said Captain Dyer, with a smile. 'That has already been thought of, Smith ; and Sergeant Jones, the only good horseman we have, went off at two o'clock, and by this time is, I hope, out of danger.—Good heavens ! what does that mean ?' he said, using his glass.

It was curious that I should have thought of such a thing just then, at a time when four sowars led up Sergeant Jones tied by a piece of rope to one of their saddle-bows, while the trooper's horse was behind.

Captain Dyer would not shew, though, that he was put out by the failure of that hope : he only passed the word for the men to stand firm, and then sent me with a message to Mrs Colonel Maine, requesting that every one should keep right away from the windows, as the enemy might open fire at any time.

He was quite right, for just as I knocked at Mrs Maine's door, a regular squandering, scattering fire began, and you could hear the bullets striking the wall with a sharp pat, bringing down showers of white lime-dust and powdered stone.

I found Mrs Maine seated on the floor with her children, pale and trembling, the little things the while laughing and playing over some pictures. Miss Ross was leaning over her sister, and Lizzy Green was waiting to give the children something else when they were tired.

As the rattle of the musketry began, it was soon plain enough to see who had the stoutest hearts ; but I seemed to be noticing nothing, though I did a great deal, and listened to Mrs Bantem's voice in the next room, bullying and scolding a woman for crying out loud and upsetting everybody else.

I gave my message, and then Miss Ross asked me if any one was hurt, to which I answered as cheerfully as could be that we were all right as yet; and then, taking myself off, Lizzy Green came with me to the door, and I held out my hand to say 'Good-bye,' for I knew it was possible I might never see her again. She gave me her hand, and said 'Good-bye,' in a faltering sort of way, and it seemed to me that she shrank from me. The next instant, though, there was the rattling crash of the firing, and I knew now that our men were answering.

CHAPTER XII.

As I went down into the court-yard, I found the smoke rising in puffs as our men fired over the breastwork at the mob coming at the gate. Captain Dyer in the thick of it the while, going from man to man, warning them to keep themselves out of sight, and to aim low.

'Take care of yourselves, my lads. I value every one of you at a hundred of those black scoundrels.—Tut, tut, who's that down?'

'Corporal Bray,' says some one.

'Here, Emson, Smith, both of you lend a hand here: we'll make Bantem's quarters hospital.—Now then, look alive, ambulance party.'

We were about lifting the poor fellow, who had sunk down behind the breastwork, all doubled up like, hands and knees; and head down; but as we touched him, he straightened himself out, and looked up at Captain Dyer.

'Don't touch me yet,' he says in a whisper. 'My stripes for some one, captain. Do for Isaac Smith there. Hooray!' he says faintly; and he took off his cap with one hand, gave it a bit of a wave—'God save the Quee'——

'Bear him carefully to the empty ground floor, south side,' says Captain Dyer sternly; 'and make haste back, my lads: moments are precious.'

'I'll do that, with Private Manning's wife,' says a voice; and turning as we were going to lift our dead comrade, there was big, strapping Mrs Bantem, and another soldier's wife, and she then said a few words to the captain.

'Gone?' says Captain Dyer.

'Quarter of an hour ago, sir,' says Mrs Bantem; 'and then to me: 'Poor trooper, Isaac!'

'Another man here,' says Captain Dyer.—'No, not you, Smith.—Fill up here, Bantem.'

Joe Bantem waved his hand to his wife, and took the dead corporal's place, but not easily, for Measles, who was next man, was stepping into it, when Captain Dyer ordered him back.

'But there's such a much better chance of dropping one of them mounted chaps, sir,' says Measles grumbling.

'Hold your tongue, sir, and go back to your own loophole,' says Captain Dyer; and the way that Measles kept on loading and firing, ramming down his cartridges viciously, and then taking long and careful aim, ah! and with good effect too, was a sight to see.

All the while we were expecting an assault, but none came, for the mutineers fell fast, and did not seem to dare to make a rush while we kept up such practice.

Then I had to go round and ask Lieutenant Leigh to send six more men to the gate, and to bring news of what was going on round the other sides.

I found the lieutenant standing at the window where I caught Chunder, and there was a man each at all the other four little windows which looked down at the outside—all the others, as I have said, looking in upon the court.

The lieutenant's men had a shot now and then at any one who approached; but the mutineers seemed to have deter-

E

mined upon forcing the gate, and, so far as I could see, there was very little danger to fear from any other quarter.

I knew Lieutenant Leigh was not a coward, but he seemed very half-hearted over the defence, doing his duty but in a sullen sort of way; and of course that was because he wanted to take the lead now held by Captain Dyer; and perhaps it was misjudging him, but I'm afraid just at that time he'd have been very glad if a shot had dropped his rival, and he could have stepped into his place.

Captain Dyer's plan to keep the rabble at bay till help could come, was of course quite right; and that night it was an understood thing, that another attempt should be made to send a messenger to Wallahbad, another of our corporals being selected for the dangerous mission.

The fighting was kept on, in an on-and-off way, till evening, we losing several men, but a good many falling on the other side, which made them more cautious, and not once did we have a chance of touching a man with the bayonet. Some of our men grumbled a little at this, saying that it was very hard to stand there hour after hour to be shot down; and could they have done as they liked, they'd have made a sally.

Then came the night, and a short consultation between the captain and Lieutenant Leigh. The mutineers had ceased firing at sundown, and we were in hopes that there would be a rest till daylight, but all the same the strictest watch was kept, and only half the men lay down at a time.

Half the night, though, had not passed, when a hand was laid upon my shoulder, and in an instant I was up, piece in hand, to find that it was Captain Dyer.

'Come here,' he said quietly; and following him into the room underneath where the women were placed, he told 'me to listen, and I did, to hear a low, grating, tearing noise, as

of something scraping on stone. 'That's been going on,'
he said, 'for a good hour, and I can't make it out, Smith.'

'Prisoners escaping,' I said quietly.

'But they are not so near as that. They were confined
in the next room but one,' he said in a whisper.

'Broke through, then,' I said.

Then we went—Captain Dyer and I—quietly up on to
the roof, answered the challenge, and then walked to the
edge, where, leaning over, we could hear the dull grating
noise once more ; then a stone seemed to fall out on to the
sandy way by the palace walls.

It was all plain enough : they had broken through from
one room to another, where there was a window no bigger
than a loophole, and they were widening this.

'Quick, here, sentry,' says the captain.

The next minute the sentry hurried up, and we had a
man posted as nearly over the window as we could guess,
and then I had my orders in a minute : 'Take two men and
the sentry at their door, rush in, and secure them at once.
But if they have got out, join Sergeant Williams, and follow
me to act as reserve, for I am going to make a sally by the
gate to stop them from the outside.'

I roused Harry Lant and Measles, and they were with
me in an instant. We passed a couple of sentries, and gave
the countersign, and then mounted to the long stone passage
which led to where the prisoners had been placed.

As we three privates neared the door, the sentry there
challenged ; but when we came up to him and listened,
there was not a sound to be heard, neither had he heard
anything, he said. The next minute the door was thrown
open, and we found an empty room ; but a hole in the wall
shewed us which way the prisoners had gone.

We none of us much liked the idea of going through that
hole to be taken at a disadvantage, but duty was duty, and
running forward, I made a sharp thrust through with my

piece in two or three directions; then I crept through, followed by Harry Lant, and found that room empty too; but they had not gone by the doorway which led into the women's part, but enlarged the window, and dropped down, leaving a large opening—one that, if we had not detected it then, would no doubt have done nicely for the entrance of a strong party of enemies.

'Sentry here,' I said; and leaving the man at the window, followed by Harry Lant and Measles, I ran back, got down to the court-yard, crossed to where Sergeant Williams with half-a-dozen men waited our coming, and then we were passed through the gate, and went along at the double to where we could hear noise and shouting.

We had the narrow alley to go through—the one I have before mentioned as being between the place we had strengthened and the next building; and no sooner were we at the end, than we found we were none too soon, for there, in the dim starlight, we could see Captain Dyer and four men surrounded by a good score, howling and cutting at them like so many demons, and plainly to be seen by their white calico things.

'By your left, my lads, shoulder to shoulder—double,' says the sergeant.

Then we gave a cheer, and with hearts bounding with excitement, down we rushed upon the scoundrels to give them their first taste of the bayonet, cutting Captain Dyer and two more men out, just as the other two went down.

It was as fierce a fight that as it was short; for we soon found the alarm spread, and enemies running up on all sides. It was bayonet-drill then, and well we shewed the practice, till we retired slowly to the entrance of the alley; but the pattering of feet and cries told that there were more coming to meet us that way; when, following Captain Dyer's orders we retreated in good form in the other direction, so as to get round to the gate by the other alley, on the south side.

And now for the first time we gave them a volley, checking the advance for a few seconds, while we retreated loading, to turn again, and give them another volley, which checked them again; but only for a few seconds, when they came down upon us like a swarm of bees, right upon our bayonets; and as fast as half-a-dozen fell, half-a-dozen more were leaping upon the steel.

We kept our line, though, one and all, retiring in good order to the mouth of the second court, which ran down by the south side of the palace; when, as if maddened at the idea of losing us, a whole host of them came at us with a rush, breaking our line, and driving us anyhow, mixed up together, down the alley, which was dark as pitch; but not so dark but that we could make out a turban or a calico cloth, and those bayonets of ours were used to some purpose.

Half-a-dozen times over I heard the captain's voice cheering us on, and shouting: 'Gate, gate!' Then I saw the flash of his sword once, and managed to pin a fellow who was making at him, just as we got out at the other end with a fierce rush. Then I heard the captain shout 'Rally!' and saw him wave his sword; and then I don't recollect any more, for it was one wild fierce scuffle—stab and thrust, in the midst of a surging, howling, maddened mob, forcing us towards the gateway.

I thought it was all over with us, when there came a cheer, and the gate was thrown open, a dozen men formed, and charged down, driving the niggers back like sheep; and then, somehow or another, we were cut out, and, under cover of the new-comers, reached the gate.

A ringing volley was then given into the thick of the mutineers as they came pouring on again; but the next moment all were safely inside, and the gate was thrust to and barred; and, panting and bleeding, we stood, six of us, trying to get our breath.

'This wouldn't have happened,' says a voice, 'if my advice had been taken. I wish the black scoundrels had been shot. Where's Captain Dyer?'

There was no answer, and a dead chill fell on me as I seemed to realise that things had come now to a bad pass.

'Where's Sergeant Williams?' said Lieutenant Leigh again; but it seemed to me that he spoke in a husky voice.

'Here!' said some one faintly, and, turning, there was the sergeant seated on the ground, and supporting himself against the breastwork.

'Any one know the other men who went out on this mad sally?' says the lieutenant.

'Where's Harry Lant?' I says.

There was no answer here either, and this time it was my turn to speak in a queer husky voice as I said again: 'Where's Measles? I mean Sam Bigley.'

'He's gone too, poor chap,' says some one.

'No, he ain't gone neither,' says a voice behind me, and, turning, there was Measles tying a handkerchief round his head, muttering the while about some black devil. 'I ain't gone, nor I ain't much hurt,' he growled; 'and if I don't take it out of some on 'em for this chop o' the head, it's a rum un; and that's all I've got to say.'

'Load!' says Lieutenant Leigh shortly; and we loaded again, and then fired two or three volleys at the niggers as they came up towards the gate once more; when some one calls out: 'Ain't none of us going to make a sally party, and bring in the captain?'

'Silence there, in the ranks!' shouts Lieutenant Leigh; and though it had a bad sound coming from him as it did, and situated as he was, no one knew better than I did how that it would have been utter madness to have gone out again; for even if he were alive, instead of bringing in

Captain Dyer, now that the whole mob was roused, we should have all been cut to pieces.

It was as if in answer to the lieutenant's order that silence seemed to fall then, both inside and outside the palace—a silence that was only broken now and then by the half-smothered groan of some poor fellow who had been hurt in the sortie—though the way in which those men of ours did bear wounds, some of them even that were positively awful, was a something worth a line in history.

Yes, there was a silence fell upon the place for the rest of that night, and I remember thinking of the wounds that had been made in two poor hearts by that bad hour's work; and I can say now, faithful and true, that there was not a selfish thought in my heart as I remembered Lizzy Green, any more than there was when Miss Ross came uppermost in my mind, for I knew well enough that they must have soon known of the disaster that had befallen our little party.

CHAPTER XIII.

WHATEVER those poor women suffered, they took care it should not be seen by us men, and indeed we had little time to think of them the next day. We had given ourselves the task to protect them, and we were fighting hard to do it, and that was all we could do then; for the enemy gave us but little peace; not making any savage attack, but harassing us in a cruel way, every man acting like for himself, and all the discipline the sepoys had learned seeming to be forgotten.

As for Lieutenant Leigh, he looked cold and stern, but there was no flinching with him now : he was in command, and he shewed it; and though I never liked the man, I must say that he shewed himself now a brave and clever officer ; and but for his skilful arrangement of the few men under his charge, that place would have fallen half-a-dozen times over.

We had taken no prisoners, so that there was no chance of talking of exchange ; though I believe to a man all thought that the captain and files missing from our company were dead.

The women now lent us their help, bringing down spare muskets and cartridges, loading too for us ; so that when the mutineers made an attack, we were able to keep up a much sharper fire than we should have done under other circumstances.

It was about the middle of the afternoon, when, hot and exhausted, we were firing away, for the bullets were coming thick and fast through the gateway, flying across the yard, and making a passage in that direction nearly certain death, when I felt a strange choking feeling, for Measles says to me all at once : 'Look there, Ike.'

I looked and I could hardly believe it, and rubbed my eyes, for just in the thickest of the firing there was the sound of merry laughter, and those two children of the colonel's came toddling out, right across the line of fire, turned back to look up at some one calling to them from the window, and then stood still, laughing and clapping their hands.

I don't know how it was, I only know that it wasn't to look brave, but, dropping my piece, I rushed to catch them, just at the same moment as did Miss Ross and Lizzy Green ; while, directly after, Lieutenant Leigh rushed from where he was, caught Miss Ross round the waist, and dragged her away, as I did Lizzy and the children.

How it was that we were none of us hit, seems strange to me, for all the time the bullets were pattering on the wall beyond us. I only know I turned sick and faint as I just

said to Lizzy : ' Thank God for that ! ' and she led off the
children ; Miss Ross shrinking from Lieutenant Leigh with
a strange mistrustful look, as if she were afraid of him ; and
the next minute they were under cover, and we were back
at our posts.

' Poor bairns ! ' says Measles to me, ' I ain't often glad of
anything, Ike Smith, but I am glad they ain't hurt. Now
my soul seemed to run and help them myself, but my legs
seemed as if they couldn't move. You need not believe it
without you like,' he added in his sour way.

' But I do believe it, old fellow,' I said warmly, as I held
out my hand. ' Chaff's chaff, but you never knew me make
light of a good act done by a true-hearted comrade.'

' All right,' says Measles gruffly. ' Now, see me pot that
sowar.—Missed him, I declare ! ' he exclaimed, as soon
as he had fired. ' These pieces ain't true. No ! hit him !
He's down ! That's one bairn-killer the less.'

' Sam,' I said just then, ' what's that coming up between
the huts yonder ? '

' Looks like a wagin,' says Measles. ' 'Tis a wagin,
ain't it ? '

' No,' I said, feeling that miserable I didn't know what to
do ; ' it isn't a wagon, Sam ; but—— Why, there's
another. A couple of field-pieces ! '

' Nine-pounders, by all that's unlucky,' said Measles,
slapping his thigh. ' Then I tell you what it is, Ike Smith
—it's about time we said our prayers.'

I didn't answer, for the words would not come ; but it
was what had always been my dread, and it seemed now
that the end was very near.

Troubles were coming upon us thick ; for being relieved
a short time after, to go and have some tea that Mrs Bantem
had got ready, I saw something that made me stop short,
and think of where we should be if the water-supply was
run out, for though we had the chatties down below in the

vault under the north end, we wanted what there was in the tank, while there was *Nabob*, the great elephant, drawing it up in his trunk, and cooling himself by squirting it all over his back !

I went to Lieutenant Leigh, and pointed it out to him; and the great beast was led away; when, there being nothing else for it, we opened a way through our breast-work, watched an opportunity, threw open the gate, and he marched out right straight in amongst the mutineers, who cheered loudly, after their fashion, as he came up to them.

There was no more firing that night, and taking it in turns, we, some of us, had a sleep, I among the rest, all dressed as I was, and with my gun in my hand, ready for use at a moment's notice ; and I remember thinking what a deal depended on the sentries, and how thoroughly our lives were in their hands ; and then my next thought was how was it possible for it to be morning, for I had only seemed to close my eyes, and then open them again on the light of day.

But morning it was ; and with a dull, dead feeling of misery upon me, I got up and gave myself a shake, ran the ramrod down my piece, to see that it was charged all right, looked to the cap, and then once more prepared for the continuation of the struggle, low-spirited and disheartened, but thankful for the bit of refreshing rest I had had.

A couple of hours passed, and there was no movement on the part of the enemy ; the ladies never stirred, but we could hear the children laughing and playing about, and how one did seem to envy the little light-hearted, thoughtless things ! But my thoughts were soon turned into another direction, for Lieutenant Leigh ordered me up into one of the rooms commanding the gateway, and looking out on the square where the guns were standing, and came up with me himself.

'You'll have a good look-out from here, Smith,' he said; 'and being a good shot'——

He didn't say any more, for he was, like me, taken up with the movement in the square—a lot of the mutineers running the two guns forward in front of the gate, and then closing round them, so that we could not see what was going on; but we knew well enough that they were charging them, and there seemed nothing for it but to let them fire, unless by a bold sally we could get out and spike them.

Just then, Lieutenant Leigh looked at me, and I at him, when, touching my cap in salute, I said : 'Two good nails, sir, and a tap on each would do it.'

'Yes, Smith,' he said grimly ; 'but who is to drive those two nails home ?'

I didn't answer him for a minute, I should think, for I was thinking over matters, about life, and about Lizzy, and now that Harry Lant was gone, it seemed to me that there might be a chance for me ; but still duty was duty, and if men could not in such a desperate time as this risk something, what was the good of soldiers ?

'I'll drive 'em home, sir,' I says then quietly, 'or they shall drive me home !'

He looked at me for an instant, and then nodded.

'I'll get the men ready,' he says ; 'it's our only chance ; and with a bold dash we may do it. I'll see to the armourer's chest for hammers and spikes. I'll spike one, Smith, and you the other ; but, mind, if I fail, help me, as I will you, if you fail ; and God help us ! Keep a sharp look-out till I come back.'

He left the room, and I heard a little movement below, as of the men getting ready for the sally; and all the while I stood watching the crowd in front, which now began hurraing and cheering ; and there was a motion which shewed that the guns were being run in nearer, till they stopped about fifty yards from the gate.

'What makes him so long ?' I thought, trembling with

excitement; 'another minute, perhaps, and the gate will be battered down, and that mob rushing in.'

Then I thought that we ought all who escaped from the sortie, in case of failure, to be ready to take to the rooms adjoining where I was, which would be our last hope; and then I almost dropped my piece, my mouth grew dry, and I seemed choked, for, with a loud howl, the crowd opened out, and I saw a sight that made my blood run cold—those two nine-pounders standing with a man by each breech, smoking linstock in hand; while bound, with their backs against the muzzles, and their white faces towards us, were Captain Dyer and Harry Lant!

One spark—one touch of the linstock on the breech—and those two brave fellows' bodies would be blown to atoms; and, as I expected that every moment such would be the case, my knees knocked together; but the next moment I was down on those shaking knees, my piece made ready, and a good aim taken, so that I could have dropped one of the gunners before he was able to fire.

I hesitated for a moment before I made up my mind which to try and save, and the thought of Lizzy Green came in my mind, and I said to myself: 'I love her too well to give her pain,' when, giving up Captain Dyer, I aimed at the gunner by poor Harry Lant.

'Don't fire,' said a voice just then, and, turning, there was Lieutenant Leigh. 'The black-hearted wretches!' he muttered. 'But we are all ready; though now, if we start, it will be the signal for the death of those two.—But what does this mean?'

What made him say that, was a chief, all in shawls, who rode forward and shouted out in good English, that they gave us one hour to surrender; but, at the end of that time, if we had not marched out without arms, they would blow their prisoners away from the mouth of the guns.

Then, for fear we had not heard it, he spurred his horse

up to within ten yards of the gate, and shouted it out again, so that every one could hear it through the place ; and, though I could have sent a bullet through and through him, I could not help admiring the bold daring fellow, riding up right to the muzzles of our pieces.

But all the admiration I felt was gone the next moment, as I thought of the cruelties practised, and of those bound there to those gun-muzzles.

There was nothing said for a few minutes, for I expected the lieutenant to speak ; but as he did not, I turned to him and said : 'If all was ready, sir, I could drop one gunner ; and I'd trust Measles—Sam Bigley—to drop the other, when a bold dash might do it. You see they've retired a good thirty yards, and we should only have twenty more to run than they ; while the surprise would give us that start. A good sharp jack-knife would set the prisoners free, and a covering-party would perhaps check the pursuit while we got in.'

'We shall have to try it, Smith,' he said, his breath coming thick and fast with excitement ; and then he seemed to turn white, for Miss Ross and Lizzy came into the room.

CHAPTER XIV.

I should think it must have been the devil tempting Lieutenant Leigh, or he would never have done as he did ; for, as he looked at Miss Ross, the change that came over him was quite startling. He could read all that was passing in her heart ; there was no need for her to lay her hand upon his arm, and point with the other out of the window, as in a voice that I didn't know for hers, she said : 'Will you leave those two brave men there to die, Lieutenant Leigh ?'

He didn't answer for a moment, but seemed to be

struggling with himself; then, speaking as huskily as she did, he said: 'Send away that girl!' and before I could go to her—for I should have done it then, I know—and whisper a few words of hope, poor Lizzy went out, mourning for Harry Lant, wringing her hands; and I stood at my post, a sentry by my commander's orders, so that it was no spying on my part if I heard what followed.

I believe Lieutenant Leigh fancied he was speaking in an undertone, when he led Miss Ross away to a corner, and spoke to her; but this was perhaps the most exciting moment in his life, and his voice rose in spite of himself, so that I heard all; while she, poor thing, I believe forgot all about my presence; and, as a sentry—a machine almost—placed there, what right had I to speak?

'Will you leave him?' said Miss Ross again. 'Will you not try to save him?'

Lieutenant Leigh did not answer for a bit, for he was making his plans, and I felt quite staggered as I saw through them.

'You see how he is placed: what can I do?' said Lieutenant Leigh. 'If I go, it is the signal for firing. You see the gunners waiting. And why should I risk the lives of my men, and my own, to save him?—He is a soldier, and it is the fortune of war: he must die.'

'Are you a man, or a coward?' said Miss Ross angrily.

'No coward,' he said fiercely; 'but a poor slighted man, whom you have wronged, jilted, and ill-used; and now you come to me to save your lover's life—to give mine for it. You have robbed me of all that is pleasant between you; and now you ask more. Is it just?'

'Lieutenant Leigh, you are speaking madly. How can you be so unjust?' she cried, holding tightly by his arm, for he was turning away, while I felt mad with him for torturing the poor girl, when it was decided that the attempt was to be made.

'I am not unjust,' he said. 'The hazard is too great; and what should I gain if I succeeded? Pshaw! Why, if he were saved, it would be at the expense of my own life.'

'I would die to save him!' she said hoarsely.

'I know it, Elsie; but you would not give a loving word to save me. You would send me out to my death without compunction—without a care; and yet you know how I have loved you.'

'You—you loved me; and yet stand and see my heart torn—see me suffer like this!' cried Miss Ross, and there was something half wild in her looks as she spoke.

'Love you!' he cried; 'yes, you know how I have loved you'——

His voice sank here; but he was talking in her ear excitedly, saying words that made her shrink from him up to the wall, and look at him as if he were some object of the greatest disgust.

'You can choose,' he said bitterly, as he saw her action; and he turned away from her.

The next moment she was bending down before him, holding up her hands as if in prayer.

'Promise me,' he said, 'and I will do it.'

'Oh, some other way—some other way!' she cried piteously, her face all drawn the while.

'As you will,' he said coldly.

'But think—oh, think! You cannot expect it of me. Have mercy! Oh, what am I saying?'

'Saying!' he cried, catching her hands in his, and speaking excitedly and fast—'saying things that are sending him to his death! What do I offer you? Love, devotion, all that man can give. He would, if asked now, give up all for his life; and yet you, who profess to love him so dearly, refuse to make that sacrifice for his sake! You cannot love him. If he could hear now, he would implore you to do it.

Think. I risk all. Most likely, my life will be given for
his; perhaps we shall both fall. But you refuse. Enough:
I must go; I cannot stay. There are many lives here under
my charge; they must not be neglected for the sake of one.
As I said before, it is the fortune of war; and, poor fellow,
he has but a quarter of an hour or so to live, unless help
comes.'

'Unless help comes,' groaned Miss Ross frantically, when,
as Lieutenant Leigh reached the door, watching me over his
shoulder the while, Miss Ross went down on her knees,
stretched out her hands towards where Captain Dyer was
bound to the gun, and then she rose, cold, and hard, and
stern, and turned to Lieutenant Leigh, holding out her hand.
'I promise,' she said hoarsely.

'On your oath, before God?' he exclaimed joyfully, as
he caught her in his arms.

'As God is my judge,' she faltered with her eyes
upturned; and then, as he held her to his breast, kissing
her passionately, she shivered and shuddered, and, as he
released her, sank in a heap on the floor.

'Smith,' cried Lieutenant Leigh; 'right face—forward!'
and as I passed Miss Ross, I heard her sob in a tone I shall
never forget: 'O Lawrence, Lawrence!' and then a groan
rose from her breast, and I heard no more.

CHAPTER XV.

'This is contrary to rule. As commandant, I ought to
stay in the fort; but I've no one to give the leadership to,
so I take it myself,' said Lieutenant Leigh; 'and now, my
lads, make ready—present! That's well. Are all ready?
At the word "Fire!" Privates Bigley and Smith fire at
the two gunners. If they miss, I cry fire again, and Privates

Bantem and Grainger try their skill; then, at the double, down on the guns. Smith and I spike them, while Bantem and Grainger cut the cords. Mind this: those guns must be spiked, and those two prisoners brought in; and if the sortie is well managed, it is easy, for they will be taken by surprise. Hush! Confound it, men; no cheering.'

He only spoke in time, for in the excitement the men were about to hurray.

' Now, then, is that gate unbarred?'

' Yes, sir.'

' Is the covering-party ready?'

' Yes, sir.'

My hand trembled as he spoke; but the next instant it was of a piece with my gunstock. There was the dry square, with the sun shining on the two guns that must have been hot behind the poor prisoners' backs; there stood the two gunners in white, with their smoking linstocks, leaning against the wheels, for discipline was slack; and there, thirty or forty yards behind, were the mutineers, lounging about, and smoking many of them. For all firing had ceased, and judging that we should not risk having the prisoners blown away from the guns, the mutineers came boldly up within range, as if defying us, and it was pretty safe practice at some of them now.

I saw all this at a glance, and while it seemed as if the order would never come; but come it did, at last.

' FIRE!'

Bang! the two pieces going off like one; and the gunner behind Captain Dyer leaped into the air, while the one I aimed at seemed to sink down suddenly beside the wheel he had leaned upon. Then the gate flew open, and with a rush and a cheer, we, ten of us, raced down for the guns.

Double-quick time? I tell you it was a hard race; and being without my gun now—only my bayonet stuck in my trousers' waist-band—I was there first, and had driven my spike into the touch-hole before Lieutenant Leigh reached his; but the next moment his was done, the cords were cut, and the prisoners loose from the guns. But now we had to get back.

The first inkling I had of the difficulty of this was seeing Captain Dyer and Harry Lant stagger, and fall forward; but they were saved by the men, and we saw directly that they must be carried.

No sooner thought of than done.

'Hoist Harry on my back,' says Grainger; and he took him like a sack; Bantem acting the same part by Captain Dyer; and those two ran off, while we tried to cover them.

For don't you imagine that the mutineers were idle all this while; not a bit of it. They were completely taken by surprise, though, at first, and gave us time nearly to get to the guns before they could understand what we meant; but the next moment some shouted and ran at us, and some began firing; while by the time the prisoners were cast loose, they were down upon us in a hand-to-hand fight.

But in those fierce struggles there is such excitement, that I've now but a very misty recollection of what took place; but I do recollect seeing the prisoners well on the way back, hearing a cheer from our men, and then, hammer in one hand, bayonet in the other, fighting my way backward along with my comrades. Then all at once a glittering flash came in the air, and I felt a dull cut on the face, followed directly after by another strange, numbing blow, which made me drop my bayonet, as my arm fell uselessly to my side; and then with a lurch and a stagger, I fell, and was trampled upon twice, when as I rallied once, a black savage-looking sepoy raised his clubbed musket to knock out my brains, but a voice I well knew cried: 'Not this time, my fine fellow. That's number three, that is, and well home ;' and I saw Measles drive his bayonet with a crash through the fellow's breast-bone, so that he fell across my legs.—'Now, old chap, come along,' he shouts, and an arm was passed under me.

'Run, Measles, run!' I said as well as I could. 'It's all over with me.'

'No; 'taint,' he said; 'and don't be a fool. Let me do as I like, for once in a way.'

I don't know how he did it, nor how, feeling sick and faint as I did, I managed to get on my legs; but old Measles stuck to me like a true comrade, and brought me in. For one moment I was struggling to my feet; and the next, after what seemed a deal of firing going over my head, I was inside the breastwork, listening to our men cheering and firing away, as the mutineers came howling and raging up almost to the very gate.

'All in?' I heard Lieutenant Leigh ask.

'To a man, sir,' says some one; 'but Private Bantem is hurt.'

'Hold your tongue, will you!' says Joe Bantem. 'I ain't killed, nor yet half. How would you like your wife frightened if you had one?'

'How's Private Lant?'

'Cut to pieces, sir,' says some one softly.

'I'm thankful that you are not wounded, Captain Dyer,' then says Lieutenant Leigh.

'God bless you, Leigh!' says the captain faintly: 'it was a brave act. I've only a scratch or two when I can get over the numbness of my limbs.'

I heard all this in a dim sort of fashion, just as if it was a dream in the early morning; for I was leaning up against the wall, with my face laid open and bleeding, and my left arm smashed by a bullet, and nobody just then took any notice of me, because they were carrying in Captain Dyer and Harry Lant; while the next minute, the fire was going

on hard and fast; for the mutineers were furious, and I
suppose they danced round the guns in a way that shewed
how mad they were about the spiking.

As for me, I did not seem to be in a great deal of pain; but
I got turning over in my mind how well we had done it that
morning; and I felt proud of it all, and glad that Captain
Dyer and Harry Lant were brought in; but all the same
what I had heard lay like a load upon me; and knowing, as
I did, that poor Miss Ross had, as it were, sold herself to
save the captain's life, and that she had, in a way of
speaking, been cheated into doing so, I felt that when the
opportunity came, I must tell the captain all I knew. When
I had got as far as that with my thoughts, the dull numbness
began to leave me, and everything else was driven out of my
mind by the thought of my wound; and I got asking myself
whether it was going to be very bad, for I thought it was, so
getting up a little, I began to crawl along in the shade
towards the ruined south end of the palace, nobody seeming
to notice me.

CHAPTER XVI.

I DARESAY you who read this don't know what the sensation
is of having one arm-bone shivered, and the dead limb
swinging helplessly about in your sleeve, whilst a great
miserable sensation comes over you that you are of no more
use—that you are only a cracked pitcher, fit to hold water no
more, but only to be broken up to mend the road with.
There were all those women and children wanting my help,
and the help of hundreds more such as me, and instead of
being of use, I knew that I must be a miserable burden to
everybody, and only in the way.

Now, whether man—as some of the great philosophers say
—did gradually get developed from the beast of the field,

I'm not going to pretend to know; but what I do know is this—that, leave him in his natural state, and when he, for some reason or another, forgets all that has been taught him, he seems very much like an animal, and acts as such.

It was something after this fashion with me then, for feeling like a poor brute out of a herd that has been shot by the hunters, I did just the same as it would—crawled away to find a place where I might hide myself and lie down and die.

You'll laugh, I daresay, when I tell you my sensations just then, and I'm ready to laugh at them now myself; for, in the midst of my pain and suffering, it came to me that I felt precisely as I did when I was a young shaver of ten years old. One Sunday afternoon, when everybody but mother and me had gone to church, and she had fallen asleep, I got father's big clay-pipe, rammed it full of tobacco out of his great lead box, and then took it into the back kitchen, feeling as grand as a churchwarden, and set to and smoked it till I turned giddy and faint, and the place seemed swimming about me.

Now, that was just how I felt when I crawled about in that place, trying not to meet anybody, lest the women should see me all covered with blood; and at last I got, as I thought, into a room where I should be all alone.

I say I crawled; and that's what I did do, on one hand and my knees, the fingers of my broken arm trailing over the white marble floor, with each finger making a horrible red mark, when all at once I stopped, drew myself up stiffly, and leaned trembling and dizzy up against the wall, trying hard not to faint. For I found that I wasn't alone, and that in place of getting away—crawling into some hole to lie down and die, I was that low-spirited and weak—I had come to a place where one of the women was, for there, upon her knees, was Lizzy Green, sobbing and crying, and tossing her hands about in the agony of her poor heart.

I was misty, and faint, and confused, you know; but perhaps it was something like instinct made me crawl to Lizzy's favourite place, for it was not intended. She did not see me, for her back was my way; and I did not mean her to know I was there; for in spite of my giddiness, I seemed to feel that she had learned all the news about our sortie, and that she was crying about poor Harry Lant.

'And he deserves to be cried for, poor chap,' I said to myself, for I forgot all about my own pains then; but all the same something very dark and bitter came over me, as I wished that she had been crying instead for poor me.

'But then he was always so bright, and merry, and clever,' I thought, 'and just the man who would make his way with a woman; while I—— Please God, let me die now!' I whispered to myself directly after, 'for I'm only a poor, broken, helpless object, in everybody's way.'

It seemed just then as if the hot weak tears that came running out of my eyes made me clearer, and better able to hear all that the sobbing girl said, as I leaned closer and closer to the wall; while, as to the sharp pain every word she said gave me, the dull dead aching of my broken arm was nothing.

'Why—why did they let him go?' the poor girl sobbed: 'as if there were not enough to be killed without him; and him so brave, and stout, and handsome, and true. My poor heart's broken. What shall I do?'

Then she sobbed again; and I remember thinking that unless help soon came, if poor Harry Lant died of his wounds, she would soon go to join him in that land where there was to be no more suffering and pain.

Then I listened, for she was speaking again.

'If I could only have died for him, or been with, or—— Oh, what have I done, that I should be made to suffer so?'

I remember wondering whether she was suffering more

then than I was; for, in spite of my jealous despairing feeling, there was something of sorrow mixed up with it for her.

For she had always seemed to like poor Harry's merry ways, when I never could get a smile from her; and she'd go and sit with Mrs Bantem for long enough when Harry was there, while if by chance I went, it seemed like the signal for her to get up, and say her young lady wanted her, when most likely Harry would walk back with her; and I went and told it all to my pipe.

'If he'd only known how I'd loved him,' she sobbed again, 'he'd have said one kind word to me before he went, have kissed me, perhaps, once; but no, not a look nor a sign! Oh! Isaac, Isaac! I shall never see you more!'

What—what? What was it choking me? What was it that sent what blood I had left gushing up in a dizzy cloud over my eyes, so that I could only gasp out once the one word 'Lizzy!' as I started to my feet, and stood staring at her in a helpless, half-blind fashion; for it seemed as though I had been mistaken, and that it was possible after all that she had been crying for me, believing me to be dead; but the next moment I was shrinking away from her, hiding my wounded face with my hand for fear she should see it, for leaping up, hot and flush-cheeked, and with those eyes of hers flashing at me, she was at my side with a bound.

'You cowardly, cruel, bad fellow!' she half-shrieked; 'how dare you stand in that mean deceitful way, listening to my words? Oh, that I should be such a weak fool, with a stupid, blabbing, chattering tongue, to keep on kneeling and crying there, telling lies, every one of them, and—— Get away with you!'

I think it was a smile that was on my face then, as she gave me a fierce thrust on the wounded arm, when I staggered towards her. I know the pain was as if a red-hot hand had grasped me; but I smiled all the same, and then, as I fell, I heard her cry out two words, in a wild, agonised way, that went right to my heart, making it leap before all was blank; for I knew that those words meant that, in spite of all my doubts, I was loved.

'O Isaac!' she cried, in a wild frightened way, and then, as I said, all was blank and dark for I don't know how long; but I seemed to wake up to what was to me then like heaven, for my head was resting on Lizzy's breast, and, half-mad with fear and grief, she was kissing my pale face again and again.

'Try—try to forgive me for being so cruel, so unfeeling,' she sobbed; and then for a moment, as she saw me smile, she was about to fly out again, fierce-like, at having betrayed herself, and let me know how she loved me. Even in those few minutes I could read it all: how her passionate little heart was fighting against discipline, and how angry she'was with herself; but I saw it all pass away directly, as she looked down at my bleeding face, and eagerly asked me if I was very much hurt.

I tried to answer, but I could not; for the same deathly feeling of sickness came on again, and I saw nothing.

I suppose, though, it only lasted a few minutes, for I woke like again to hear a panting hard breathing, as of some one using great exertion, and then I felt that I was being moved; but, for the life of me, for a few moments I could not make it out, till I heard the faint buzz of voices, when I found that Lizzy, the little fierce girl, who seemed to be as nothing beside me, was actually, in her excitement, carrying me to where she could get help, struggling along panting, a few feet at a time, beneath my weight, and me too helpless and weak to say a word.

'Good heavens! look!' I heard some one say the next moment, and I think it was Miss Ross; but it was some

time before I came to myself again enough to find that I
was lying with a rolled-up cloak under my head, and Lizzy
bathing my lips from time to time, with what I afterwards
learned was her share of the water.

But what struck me most now was the way in which she
was altered : her sharp, angry way was gone, and she seemed
to be changed into a soft gentle woman, without a single
flirty way or thought, but always ready to flinch and shrink
away until she saw how it troubled me, when she 'd creep
back to kneel down by my side, and put her little hand
in mine ; when, to make the same comparison again that
I made before, I tell you that there, in that besieged
and ruined place, half-starved, choked with thirst, and
surrounded by a set of demons thirsting for our blood—I
tell you that it seemed to me like being in heaven.

CHAPTER XVII.

I DON'T know how time passed then ; but the next thing I
remember is listening to the firing for a while, and then,
leaning on Lizzy, being helped to the women's quarters,
where, in spite of all they could do, those children would
keep escaping from their mother to get to Harry Lant, who
lay close to me, poor fellow, smiling and looking happy
whenever they came near him ; and I smiled too, and felt
as happy when Lizzy, after tending me with Mrs Bantem as
long as was necessary, got bathing Harry's forehead with
water and moistening his lips.

‘ Poor fellow,’ I thought, ‘ it will do him good ;’ and I lay
watching Lizzy moving about afterwards, and then I think
I must have gone to sleep, or have fallen into a dull numb
state, from which I was wakened by a voice I knew ; and
opening my eyes, I saw that Miss Ross, pale and scared-

looking, was on her knees by the side of Harry Lant, and
that Captain Dyer was there.

'Not one word of welcome,' he said, with a strange drawn
look on his face, which deepened as Miss Ross rose and
went close to him.

'Yes,' she said; 'thank God you have returned safe.—
No, no; don't touch me,' she cried hoarsely. 'Here, take
me away—lead me out of this!' she said, for at that
moment Lieutenant Leigh came quietly in, and she put her
hands in his. 'Take me out,' she said again hoarsely; and
then like some one muttering in a dream: 'Take me away
—take me away.'

I said that drawn strange look on Captain Dyer's face
seemed to deepen as he stood watching whilst those two
went out together; then he passed his hand over his eyes,
as if to ask himself whether it was a dream; and then, with
a groan, he leaned one hand against the wall, feeling his
way out from the room, and something seemed to hinder me
from calling out to him, and telling him what I knew. For
I was reasoning with myself, what ought I to do? and then,
sick and faint, I seemed to sleep again.

But this time I was waked up by a loud shrieking, and a
rush of feet, and, confused as I was, I knew what it
meant: the hole where the blacks escaped—Chunder and
his party—had not been properly guarded, and the mutineers
had climbed up and made an entrance.

The alarm spread fast enough, but not quick enough to
save life; for, with a howl, half-a-dozen sepoys, with their
scarlet and white coatees open, dashed in with fixed bayonets,
and two women were borne to the ground in an instant,
while a couple of wretches made a dash at those two
children—Little Cock Robin and Jenny Wren, as we called
them—standing there, wondering like, by Harry Lant's bed
on the floor, whilst the golden light of the setting sun filled
the room, and lit up their little angels' faces.

But with a howl, such as I never heard woman give, Mrs Bantem rushed between them and the children, caught a bayonet in each hand, and held them together, letting them pass under one arm, then with a spring forward she threw those great arms of hers round the black fellows' necks as they hung together, and held them in such a hug as they never suffered from before.

The next moment they were all rolling together on the floor; but that incident saved the lives of those poor children, for there came a cheer now, and Measles and a dozen more were led in by Lieutenant Leigh, and——

There, I am telling you too many horrors. They beat them back step by step, at the point of the bayonet; and a fierce struggle it was, a long fight kept up from room to room, for our men were fierce now as the mutineers, and it was a genuine death-struggle; and the broken window being guarded, not a man of about a dozen mutineers who gained entrance lived to go back and relate their want of success.

And can you wonder, when two of those who fought had found their wives bayoneted: Grainger was one of them; and when the fight was over, during which, raging like a demon, he had bayoneted four men, the poor fellow sat down by his dead wife, took her head first in his lap, then to his breast, and rocked himself to and fro, crying like a child, till there was a bugle-call in the court-yard, when he laid her gently in a corner, carrying her like as if she had been a child, kneeled down, and said 'Our Father' right through by her side, kissed her lips two or three times, and then covered her face with a bit of an old red handkerchief; and him all the while covered with blood and dust and black of powder. Then, poor fellow, he got up and took his gun, and went out on the tips of his toes, lest he should wake her who would wake no more in this world.

Perhaps it was weakness, I don't know, but my eyes

were very wet just then, and a soft little hand was laid on
my breast, and Lizzy's head leant over me, and her tears,
too, fell very fast on my hot and fevered face.

I felt that I should die, not then, perhaps, but before
very long, for I knew that my arm was so shattered that it
ought to be amputated just below the elbow, while for want
of surgical assistance it would mortify ; but somehow I felt
very happy just then, and my state did not give me much
pain, only that I wanted to have been up and doing; and
at last Lizzy helping me, I got up, my arm being bandaged
and in a sling, to find that I could walk about a little ; and
I made my way down into the court-yard, where I got
near to Captain Dyer, who, better now, and able to limp
about, was talking with Lieutenant Leigh, both officers now,
and forgetful apparently of all but the present crisis.

'What wounded are there?' said Captain Dyer, as I
walked slowly up.

'Nearly every man to some extent,' said Lieutenant
Leigh ; 'but this man and Lant are the worst.'

'The place ought to be evacuated,' said Captain Dyer ;
'it is impossible to hold it another day.'

'We might hold out another day,' said Lieutenant Leigh,
'but not longer. Why not retreat under cover of the
night?'

'It seems the only thing left,' said Captain Dyer. 'We
might perhaps get to some hiding-place or other before our
absence was discovered ; but the gate and that back
window will be watched of course : how are we to get
away with two severely wounded men, the women, and
children?'

'That must be planned,' said Lieutenant Leigh ; and then
the watch was set for the night, as far as could be done, and
another time of darkness set in.

It was that which puzzled me, why a good bold attack
was not made by night ; why, the place must have been

carried again and again; but no, we were left each night entirely at rest, and the attacks by day were clumsy and bad. There was no support; every man fought for himself, and after his own fashion, and I suppose that every man did look upon himself as an officer, and resented all discipline. At all events, it was our salvation, though at this time it seemed to me that the end must be coming on the next day, and I remember thinking, that if it did come to the end, I should like to keep one cartridge left in my pouch.

Then my mind went off wandering in a misty way upon a plan to get away by night, and I tried to make one, taking into consideration, that the quarters on the north side of us now, and only separated by ten feet of alley, were in the hands of the mutineers, who camped in them, the same being the case in the quarters on the south side, separated again by the ten feet of alley through which we returned when Captain Dyer and Harry Lant were taken. While on the east was the market plain or square, and on the west a wilderness of open country with huts and sheds. I felt, do you know, that a good plan of escape at this time was just what I ought to make, every one else being busy with duty, and me not able to either fight or stand sentry, so I worked on hard at it that night, trying to be useful in some way; and after a fashion, I worked one out.

But I have not told you what I meant to do with that last cartridge in my pouch; I meant that to be pressed to my lips once before I contrived with one hand to load my rifle, and then if the worst came to the very worst, and when I had waited to the last to see if help would come, then, when it seemed that there was no hope, I meant to do what I told myself it would be my duty, as a man and a soldier, to do, if I loved Lizzy Green—do what more than one man did, during the mutiny, by the woman for whom he had been shedding his heart's best blood; and in the dead of that night I did load that gun, after kissing the bullet; and a deal of pain that gave me, mental as well as bodily, but I don't think that I need to tell you what that last cartridge was for.

CHAPTER XVIII.

I THINK by this time you pretty well understand the situation of our palace, and how our stronghold was on the north side, close to which was the gate, so hardly fought for: if you don't, I'm afraid it is my fault, and not yours.

At all events, being at liberty, I went over it here and there, and from floor to roof, as I tried to make out which would be the best way for trying to escape; but somehow I couldn't see it then. To go out from the gate was impossible; and the same related to the broken-out window, as both places were thoroughly watched.

As for the other windows about the place, they were such slips, that without they were widened, any escaping by them was impossible. To have let ourselves down, one by one, from the flat roof by a rope, might have done, but it was a clumsy unsuitable way, with all those children and women, so I gave that up, and then sat down as I was by a little window looking out on to the north alley.

Wearied out at last, I suppose that a sort of stupor came over me, from which I did not wake till morning, to find myself suffering a dull numb pain; but when I opened my eyes I forgot that, because of her who was kneeling beside me, driving away the flies that were buzzing about, as if they knew that I was soon to be for them to rest on, without a hand to sweep them away.

At last, though, as I lay there wondering what could be

done to save us, the thought came all at once, and struggling to my feet, I held Lizzy to my heart a minute, and then went off to find Captain Dyer.

It quite took me aback to see his poor haggard face, and the way in which he took the trouble, for it was plain enough to see how he was cut to the heart by Miss Ross's treatment of him. But for all that, he was the officer and the gentleman ; he had his duty to do, and he was doing it ; so that, if even now, after losing so many men, and with so many more half disabled, if the enemy had made a bold assault now, they would have won the place dearly, though win it they must.

That did not seem their way, though they wanted the place for the sake of the great store of arms and ammunition it contained, but all the same they wanted to buy it cheap.

I found Captain Dyer ready enough to listen to my plan, though he shook his head, and said it was desperate. But after a little thought, he said : ' There are some hours now between this and night—help may come before then ; if not, Smith, we must try it. My hands are full, so I leave the preparations with you : let every one carry food and a bottle of water—nothing more—all we want now is to save life.'

I promised I'd see to it ; and I went and spoke cheerfully to the women, but Mrs Maine seemed quite hysterical. Miss Ross listened to what I had to say in a hard strange way ; and really, if it had not been for Mrs Bantem putting a shoulder first to one wheel and then the other, nothing would have been done.

The next person I went to was Measles, who, during a cessation of the firing, was sitting, black and blood-smeared, with his head tied up, wiping out his gun with pieces he tore off the sleeves of his shirt.

' Well, Ike, mate,' he says, ' not dead yet, you see. If we get out of this, I mean to have my promotion ; but I don't see how we're going to manage it. What bothers me most is, letting these black fellows get all this powder and stuff we have here. Blow my rags if we shall ever use it all! I've been firing away till my old Bess has been so hot that I've been afraid to charge her; and I'll swear I've used twice as many cartridges as any other man. But I say, Ike, old fellow, do you think it's wrong to pot these niggers?'

'No,' I said—'not in a case like this.'

'Glad of it,' he says sincerely; 'because, do you know, old man, I've polished off such a thundering lot, that I've got to be quite narvous about getting killed myself. Only think having forty or fifty black-looking beggars rising up against you in kingdom come, and pointing at you, and saying: "That's the chap as shot me!"'

'I don't think any soldier, acting under orders, who does his duty in defence of women and children, need fear to lie down and die,' I said.

I never saw Measles look soft but that once, as, laying down his ramrod, he took my hand in his, and looked in my face for a bit; then he shook my hand softly, and nodded his head several times.

'How's Harry Lant?' he says at last.

'Very bad,' I said.

'Poor old chap. But tell him I've paid some of the beggars out for it. Mind you tell him—it'll make him feel comfortable like, and ease his mind.'

I nodded, and then told him about the plan.

'Well,' he said, as he slowly and thoughtfully polished his gun-barrel, 'it might do, and it mightn't. Seems a rum dodge; but, anyhow, we might try.'

'I shall want you to help make the bridge,' I says.

'All right, matey; but I don't, somehow, like leaving the beggars all that ammunition;' and then he loaded his piece very thoughtfully, but only to rouse up directly after, for the mutineers began firing again; and Captain Dyer giving the

order, our men replied swift and fast at every black face
that shewed itself for an instant.

That was a day : hot, so that everything you went near
seemed burning. The walls even sent forth a heat of their
own ; and if it hadn't been for the chatties down below, we
should have had to give up, for the tank was now completely
dried, and the flies buzzing about its mud-caked bottom.
But the women went round from man to man with water and
biscuit, so that no one left his post, and every time the black
scoundrels tried to make a lodgment near the gate, half were
shot down, and the rest glad enough to get back into
shelter.

Towards that weary slow-coming evening, though, after we
had beaten them back—or, rather, after my brave comrades
had beaten them back half a score of times—I saw that
something was up ; and as soon as I saw what that something was, I knew that it was all over, for our men were
too much cut up and disheartened for any more gallant
sorties.

I've not said any more about the guns, only that we
spiked them, and left them standing in the market plain,
about fifty yards from the gates. I may tell you now,
though, that the next morning they were gone, and we
forgot all about them till the night I'm telling you of, when
they were dragged out again, with a lot of noise and
shouting, from a building in the far corner of the square.

We didn't want telling what that meant.

It was plain enough to all of us that the scoundrels had
drilled out the touch-holes again, and that during the night
they would be planted, and the first discharge would drive
down all our defences, and leave us open to a rush.

'We must try your plan, Smith,' says Captain Dyer
with a quiet stern look. 'It is time to evacuate the place
now.'

Then he knelt down and took a look at the guns with his

glass, and I knew he must have been thinking of how he stood tied to the muzzle of one of them, for he gave a sort of shudder as he closed his glass with a snap.

Just then, Miss Ross came round with Lizzy and Mrs Bantem, with wine and water, and I saw a sort of quiet triumph in Lieutenant Leigh's face, as, avoiding Captain Dyer, Miss Ross went up to him, as he half-beckoned to her, and stood by him like a slave, giving him bottle and glass, and then standing by his side with her eyes fixed and strange-looking; while, though he fought against it bravely, and tried to be unmoved, Captain Dyer could not bear it, but walked away.

I was just then drinking some water given me by Lizzy, whose pale troubled little face looked up so lovingly in mine that I felt half-ashamed for me, a poor private, to be so happy—for I forgot my wounds then—while my captain was in pain and suffering. And then it was that it struck me that Captain Dyer was just in that state in which men feel despairing, and go and do desperate things. I felt that I ought before now to have told him all about what I had heard, but I was in hopes that things would right themselves, and always came to the conclusion that it was Miss Ross's duty to have given the captain some explanation of her treatment; anyhow, it did not seem to be mine; but when I saw the poor smitten fellow go off like he did, I followed him softly till I came up with him, my heart beating the while with a curious sense of fear.

There was nothing to fear, though: he had only gone up to the roof, and when I came up with him he was evidently calculating about our escape, for he finished off by pulling out his telescope, and looking right across the plain, towards where there was a tank and a small station.

'I think that ought to be our way, Smith,' he said. 'We could stay there for half an hour's rest, and then on again towards Wallahbad, sending a couple of the stoutest

men on for help. By the way, we'll try and start a man
off to-night, as soon as it's dark. Who will you have to
help you?'

'I should like to have Bigley, sir,' I said.

'Will one be sufficient?'

'Quite, sir,' I said; for I thought Measles and I could
manage it between us.

Half an hour after, Measles was busy at work, fetching
up muskets, with bayonets fixed, from down in the store,
and laying them in order on the flat roof, taking care the
while to keep out of sight; and I went to the room where
the women were, under Mrs Bantem's management, getting
ready for what was to come, for they had been told that we
might leave the place all at once.

CHAPTER XIX.

I suppose it was my wound made me do things in a
sluggish dreamy way, and made me feel ready to stop and
look at any little thing which took my attention. Anyhow,
that's the way I acted; and going inside that room, I
stopped short just inside the place, for there were those two
little children of the colonel's sitting on the floor, with a
whole heap of those numbers of the Bible—those that people
take in shilling parts—and with two or three large pictures
in each. Some one had given them the parts to amuse
themselves with; and, as grand and old-fashioned as could
be, they were shewing these pictures to the soldiers'
children.

As I went in they'd got a picture open, of Jacob lying
asleep, with his dream spread before you, of the great flight
of steps leading up into heaven, and the angels going up and
down.

'There,' says little Jenny Wren to a boy half as old again as herself; 'those are angels, and they're coming down from heaven, and they've got beautiful wings like birds.'

'Oh,' says little Cock Robin thoughtfully, and he leaned over the picture. Then he says quite seriously: 'If they've dot wings, why don't they fly down?'

That was a poser; but Jenny Wren was ready with her answer, old-fashioned as could be, and she says: 'I should think it's toz they were moulting.'

I remember wishing that the poor little innocents had wings of their own, for it seemed to me that they would be a sad trouble to us to get away that night, just at the time when a child's most likely to be cross and fretful.

Night at last, dark as dark, save only a light twinkling here and there, in different parts where the enemy had made their quarters. There was a buzzing in the camp where the guns were, and as we looked over, once there came the grinding noise of a wheel, but only once.

We made sure that the gate and the broken window opening were well watched, for there was the white calico of the sentries to be seen; but soon the darkness hid them, and we should not have known that they were there but for the faint spark now and then which shewed that they were smoking, and once I heard, quite plain in the dead stillness, the sound made by a 'hubble-bubble' pipe.

We waited one hour, and then, with six of us on the roof, the plan I made began to be put into operation.

My idea was that if we could manage to cross the north alley, which as I told you was about ten feet wide, we might then go over the roof of the quarters where the mutineers were; then on to the next roof, which was a few feet lower; and from there get down on to some sheds, from which it would be easy to reach the ground, when the way would be open to us, to escape, with perhaps some hours before we were missed.

The plan was, I know, desperate, but it seemed our only chance, and, as you well know, desperate ventures will sometimes succeed when the most carefully arranged plots fail. At all events, Captain Dyer took it up, and the men under my directions, a couple of muskets were taken at a time, and putting them muzzle to muzzle, the bayonet of each was thrust down the other's barrel, which saved lashing them together, and gave us a sort of spar about ten feet long, and this was done with about fifty.

Did I tell you there was a tree grew up in the centre of the alley—a stunty, short-boughed tree, and to this Measles laid one of the double muskets, feeling for a bough to rest it on in the darkness, after listening whether there was any one below ; then he laid more and more, till, with a mattress laid upon them, he formed a bridge, over which he boldly crept to the tree, where, with the lashings he had taken, he bound a couple more muskets horizontal, and then shifted the others? He arranged them all so that the butts of one end rested on the roof of the palace ; the butts at the other end were across those he had bound pretty level in the tree. Then more and more were laid across, and a couple of thin straw mattresses on them; and though it took a tremendously long time, through Measles fumbling in the dark, it was surprising what a firm bridge that made as far as the tree.

The other half was made in just the same fashion, and much more easily. Mattresses were laid on it ; and there, thirty feet above the ground, we had a tolerably firm bridge, one that, though very irregular, a man could cross with ease, creeping on his hands and knees ; but then there were the women, children, and poor Harry Lant.

Captain Dyer thought it would be better to say nothing to them about it, but to bring them all quietly up at the last minute, so as to give them no time for thought and fear ; and then, the last preparation being made, and a rough, short

ladder, eight feet long, Measles and I had contrived, being
carried over and planted at the end of the other quarters,
reaching well down to the next roof, we prepared for a
start.

Measles and Captain Dyer went over with the ladder, and
reported no sentries visible, the bridge pretty firm, and
nothing apparently to fear, when it was decided that Harry
Lant should be taken over first—Measles volunteering to
take him on his back and crawl over—then the women and
children were to be got over, and we were to follow.

I know it was hard work for him, but Harry Lant never
gave a groan, but let them lash his hands together with a
handkerchief, so that Measles put his head through the poor
fellow's arms, for there was no trusting to Harry's feeble
hold.

'Now then, in silence,' says Captain Dyer; 'and you,
Lieutenant Leigh, get up the women and children. But
each child is to be taken by a man, who is to be ready to
gag the little thing if it utters a sound. Recollect, the lives
of all depend on silence.—Now, Bigley, forward!'

'Wait till I spit in my hands, captain,' says Measles,
though what he wanted to spit in his hands for, I don't
know, without it was from use, being such a spitting
man.

But spit in his hands he did, and then he was down on
his hands and knees, crawling on to the mattress very
slowly, and you could hear the bayonets creaking and
gritting, as they played in and out of the musket-barrels;
but they held firm, and the next minute Measles was as far
as the tree, but only to get his load hitched somehow in a
ragged branch, when there was a loud crack as of dead-wood
snapping, a struggle, and Measles growled out an oath—he
would swear, that fellow would, in spite of all Mrs Bantem
said, so you mustn't be surprised at his doing it then.

We all stood and crouched there, with our hearts beating

horribly ; for it seemed that the next moment we should hear a dull, heavy crash ; but instead, there came the sharp fall of a dead branch, and at the same moment there were voices at the end of the alley.

If Captain Dyer dared to have spoken, he would have called 'Halt!' but he was silent ; and Measles must have heard the voices, for he never moved, while we listened minute after minute, our necks just over the edge of the roof, till what appeared to be three of the enemy crept cautiously along through the alley, till one tripped and fell over the dead bough that must have been lying right in their way.

Then there was a horrible silence, during which we felt that it was all over with the plan—that the enemy must look up and see the bridge, and bring down those who would attack us with renewed fury.

But the next minute, there came a soft whisper or two, a light rustling, and directly after we knew that the alley was empty.

It seemed useless to go on now ; but after five minutes' interval, Captain Dyer determined to pursue the plan, just as Measles came back panting to announce Harry Lant as lying on the roof beyond the officers' quarters.

'And you've no idee what a weight the little chap is,' says Measles to me.—'Now, who's next?'

No one answered ; and Lieutenant Leigh stepped forward with Miss Ross. He was about to carry her over ; but she thrust him back, and after scanning the bridge for a few moments, she asked for one of the children, and so as to have no time lost, the little boy, fast asleep, bless him! was put in her arms, when brave as brave, if she did not step boldly on to the trembling way, and walk slowly across.

Then Joe Bantem was sent, though he hung back for his wife, till she ordered him on, to go over with a soldier's child on his back ; and he was followed by a couple more.

Next came Mrs Bantem, with Mrs Colonel Maine, and
the stout-hearted woman stood as if hesitating for a minute
as to how to go, when catching up the colonel's wife, as if
she had been a child, she stepped on to the bridge, and two
or three men held the butts of the muskets, for it seemed as
if they could not bear the strain.

But though my heart seemed in my mouth, and the
creaking was terrible, she passed safely over, and it was
wonderful what an effect that had on the rest.

'If it'll bear that, it'll bear anything,' says some one close
to me ; and they went on, one after the other, for the most
part crawling, till it came to me and Lizzy Green.

'You'll go now,' I said ; but she would not leave me,
and we crept on together, till a bough of the tree hindered
us, when I made her go first, and a minute after we were
hand-in-hand upon the other roof.

The others followed, Captain Dyer coming last, when,
seeing me, he whispered: 'Where's Bigley ?' of course
meaning Measles.

I looked round, but it was too dark to distinguish one
face from another. I had not seen him for the last quarter
of an hour—not since he had asked me if I had any
matches, and I had passed him half-a-dozen from my
tobacco-pouch.

I asked first one, and then another, but nobody had seen
Measles ; and under the impression that he must have
joined Harry Lant, we cautiously walked along the roof,
right over the heads of our enemies ; for from time to time
we could hear beneath our feet the low buzzing sound of
voices, and more than once came a terrible catching of the
breath, as one of the children whispered or spoke.

It seemed impossible, even now, that we could escape, and
I was for proposing to Captain Dyer to risk the noise, and
have the bridge taken down, so as to hold the top of the
building we were on as a last retreat ; but I was stopped

from that by Measles coming up to me, when I told him Captain Dyer wanted him, and he crept away once more.

We got down the short ladder in safety, and then crossed a low building, to pass down the ladder on to another, which fortunately for us was empty ; and then, with a little contriving and climbing, we dropped into a deserted street of the place, and all stood huddled together, while Captain Dyer and Lieutenant Leigh arranged the order of march.

And that was no light matter ; but a litter was made of the short ladder, and Harry Lant laid upon it ; the women and children placed in the middle ; the men were divided ; and the order was given in a low tone to march, and we began to walk right away into the darkness, down the straggling street ; but only for the advance-guard to come back directly, and announce that they had stumbled upon an elephant picketed with a couple of camels.

'Any one with them ?' said Captain Dyer.

'Could not see a soul, sir,' said Joe Bantem, for he was one of the men.

'Grenadiers, half-left,' said Captain Dyer ; 'forward !' and once more we were in motion, tramp, tramp, tramp, but quite softly ; Lieutenant Leigh at the rear of the first party, so as to be with Miss Ross, and Captain Dyer in the rear of all, hiding, poor fellow, all he must have felt, and seeming to give up every thought to the escape, and that only.

CHAPTER XX.

I COULD just make out the great looming figure of an elephant, as we marched slowly on, when I was startled by a low sort of wimmering noise, followed directly after by a grunting on my right.

'What's that?' says Captain Dyer. Then in an instant: 'Threes right!' he cried to the men, and they faced round, so as to cover the women and children.

There was no further alarm, though, and all seemed as silent as could be; so once more under orders, the march was continued till we were out from amidst the houses, and travelling over the sandy dusty plain; when there was another alarm—we were followed—so said the men in the rear; and sure enough, looming up against the darkness— a mass of darkness itself—we could see an elephant.

The men were faced round, and a score of pieces were directed at the great brute; but when within three or four yards, it was plain enough that it was alone, and Measles says aloud: 'Blest if it isn't old *Nabob !*'

The old elephant it was; and passing through, he went up to where Harry Lant was calling him softly, knelt down to order; and then climbing and clinging on as well as they could, the great brute's back was covered with women and children—the broad shallow howdah pretty well taking the lot—while the great beast seemed as pleased as possible to get back amongst his old friends, rubbing his trunk first on this one and then on that; and thankful we were for the help he gave us, for how else we should have got over that desert plain I can't say.

I should think we had gone a good eight miles, when Measles ranges up close aside me as I walked by the elephant, looking up at the riding-party from time to time, and trying to make out which was Lizzy, and pitying them too, for the children were fretful, and it was a sad time they had of it up there.

'They'll have it hot there some time to-morrow morning, Ike,' says Measles to me.

'Where?' I said faintly, for I was nearly done for, and I did not take much interest in anything.

'Begumbagh,' he says. And when I asked him what he meant, he said : ' How much powder do you think there was down in that vault?'

'A good five hundredweight,' I said.

'All that,' says Measles. 'They'll have it hot, some of 'em.'

'What do you mean?' I said, getting interested.

'Oh, nothing pertickler, mate ; only been arranging for promotion for some of 'em, since I can't get it myself. I took the head out of one keg, and emptied it by the others, and made a train to where I've set a candle burning ; and when that candle's burnt out, it will set light to another ; and that will have to burn out, when some wooden chips will catch fire, and they'll blaze a good deal, and one way and another there'll be enough to burn to last till, say, eight o'clock this morning, by which time the beauties will have got into the place ; and then let 'em look out for promotion, for there's enough powder there to startle two or three of 'em.'

'That's what you wanted the matches for, then?' I said.

'That's it, matey ; and what do you think of it, eh?'

'You've done wrong, my lad, I'm afraid, and'—— I didn't finish ; for just then, behind us, there was a bright flashing light, followed by a dull thud ; and looking back, we could see what looked like a little fire-work ; and though plenty was said just then, no one but Measles and I knew what that flash meant.

'That's a dead failure,' growled Measles to me as we

went on. 'I believe I am the unluckiest beggar that ever breathed. That oughtn't to have gone off for hours yet, and now it 'll let 'em know we 're gone, and that's all.'

I did not say anything, for I was too weak and troubled, and how I kept up as I did, I don't know to this day.

The morning broke at last with the knowledge that we were three miles to the right of the tank Captain Dyer had meant to reach. For a few minutes, in a quiet stern way, he consulted with Lieutenant Leigh as to what should be done—whether to turn off to the tank, or to press on. The help received from old *Nabob* made them determine to press on; and after a short rest, and a better arrangement for those who were to ride on the elephant, we went on in the direction of Wallahbad, I, for my part, never expecting to reach it alive. Many a look back did I give to see if we were followed, but it was not until we were within sight of a temple by the roadside, that there was the news spread that there were enemies behind; and though I was ready enough to lay the blame upon Measles, all the same they must have soon found out our flight, and pursued us.

The sun could never have been hotter, nor the ground more parched and dusty than it was now. We were struggling on to reach that temple, which we might perhaps be able to hold till help came; for two men had been sent on to get assistance; though of all those sent, one and all were waylaid and cut down, long before they could reach our friends. But we did not know that then; and in the full hope that before long we should have help, we crawled on to the temple, but only to find it so wide and exposed, that in our weak condition it was little better than being in the open. There was a building, though, about a hundred yards farther on, and towards that we made, every one rousing himself for what was really the last struggle, for not a quarter of a mile off, there was a yelling crowd of blood-hounds in eager pursuit.

It was with a panting rush that we reached the place, to find it must have been the house of the collector of the district; but it was all one wrack and ruin—glass, tables, and chairs smashed; hangings and carpets burnt or ragged to pieces, and in one or two places, blood-stains on the white floor, told a terrible tale of what had taken place not many days before.

The elephant stopped and knelt, and the women and children were passed in as quickly as possible; but before all could be got in, about a dozen of the foremost mutineers were down upon us with a savage rush—I say *us*, but I was helpless, and only looking on from inside—two of our fellows were cut down in an instant, and the others borne back by the fierce charge. Then followed a desperate struggle, ending in the black fellows dragging off Miss Ross and one of the children that she held.

They had not gone many yards, though, before Captain Dyer and Lieutenant Leigh seemed to see the peril together, and shouting to our men, sword in hand they went at the black fiends, well supported by half-a-dozen of our poor wounded chaps.

There was a rush, and a cloud of dust; then there was the noise of yells and cheers, and Captain Dyer shouting to the men to come on; and it all acted like something intoxicating on me, for, catching up a musket, I was making for the door, when I felt an arm holding me back, and I did what I must have done as soon as I got outside— reeled and fainted dead away.

CHAPTER XXI.

It was a couple of hours after when I came to, and became sufficiently sensible to know that I was lying with my head in Lizzy's lap, and Harry Lant close beside me. It was very dim, and the heat seemed stifling, so that I asked Lizzy where we were, and she told me in the cellar of the house—a large wide vault, where the women, children, and wounded had been placed for safety, while the noise and firing above told of what was taking place.

I was going to ask about Miss Ross, but just then I caught sight of her trying to support her sister, and to keep the children quiet.

As I got more used to the gloom, I made out that there was a small iron grating on one side, through which came what little light and air we got; on the other, a flight of stone steps leading up to where the struggle was going on. There was a strong wooden door at the top of this, and twice that door was opened for a wounded man to be brought down; when, coolly as if she were in barracks, there was that noble woman, Mrs Bantem, tying up and binding sword-cuts and bayonet-thrusts as she talked cheerily to the men.

The struggle was very fierce still, the men who brought down the wounded hurrying away, for there was no sign of flinching; but soon they were back with another poor fellow, who was now whimpering, now muttering fiercely. ' If I 'd only have had—confound them !—if I 'd only had another cartridge or two, I wouldn't have cared,' he said as they laid him down close by me; ' but I always was the unluckiest beggar on the face of the earth. They 've most done for me, Ike, and no wonder, for it 's all fifty to one up there, and I don't believe a man of ours has a shot left.'

Again the door closed on the two men who had brought down poor Measles, hacked almost to pieces; and again it was opened, to bring down another wounded man, and this one was Lieutenant Leigh. They laid him down, and were off back up the steps, when there was a yelling, like as if some evil spirits had broken loose, and as the door was opened, Captain Dyer and half-a-dozen more were beaten back, and I thought they would have been followed down— but no; they stood fast in that doorway, Captain Dyer and the six with him, while the two fellows who had been down leaped up the stairs to support them, so that, in that narrow opening, there were eight sharp British bayonets, and the captain's sword, making such a steel hedge as the mutineers could not pass.

They could not contrive either to fire at our party, on account of the wall in front, and every attempt at an entrance was thwarted; but we all knew that it was only a question of time, for it was impossible for man to do more.

There seemed now to be a lull, and only a buzzing of voices above us, mingled with a groan and a dying cry now and then, when I quite forgot my pain once more on hearing poor Harry Lant, who had for some time been quite off his head, and raving, commence talking in a quiet sort of way.

'Where's Ike Smith?' he said. 'It's all dark here; and I want to say good-bye to him.'

I was kneeling by his side the next minute, holding his hand.

'God bless you, Ike,' he said; 'and God bless her. I'm going, old mate; kiss her for me, and tell her that if she hadn't been made for you, I could have loved her very dearly.'

What could I do or say, when the next minute Lizzy was kneeling on his other side, holding his hand?

'God bless you both,' he whispered. 'You'll get out of the trouble after all; and don't forget me.'

We promised him we would not, as well as we could, for we were both choked with sorrow ; and then he said, talking quickly : 'Give poor old Sam Measles my tobacco-box, Ike, the brass one, and shake hands with him for me ; and now I want Mother Bantem.'

She was by his side directly, to lift him gently in her arms, calling him her poor gallant boy, her brave lad, and no end of fond expressions.

'I never had a bairn, Harry,' she sobbed ; 'but if I could have had one, I'd have liked him to be like you, my own gallant, light-hearted soldier boy ; and you were always to me as a son.'

'Was I?' says Harry softly. 'I'm glad of it, for I never knew what it was to have a mother.'

He seemed to fall off to sleep after that, when, no one noticing them, those two children came up, and the first I heard of it was little Clive crying : 'Ally Lant—Ally Lant, open eyes, and come and play wis elfant.'

I started, and looked up to see one of those little innocents —his face smeared, and his little hands all dabbled with blood, trying to open poor Harry Lant's eyes with his tiny fingers.

'Why don't Ally Lant come and play with us?' says the other ; and just then he opened his eyes, and looked at them with a smile, when in a moment I saw what was happening, for that poor fellow's last act was to get those two children's hands in his, as if he felt that he should like to let his last grasp in this world be upon something innocent ; and then there was a deepening of that smile into a stern look, his lips moved, and all was over ; while I was too far off to hear his last words.

But there was one there who did hear them, and she told me afterwards, sobbing as though her heart would break.

'Poor Harry, poor light-hearted Harry,' Mother Bantem

said. 'And did you see the happy smile upon his face as he
passed away, clasping those two poor children's hands—so
peaceful, so quiet, after all his suffering; forgetting all then,
but what seemed like two angels' faces by his dying pillow,
for he said, Ike, he said'——

Poor Mother Bantem broke down here, and I thought
about what Harry's dying pillow had been—her faithful,
old, motherly breast. But she forced back her sobs, and
wiped the tears from her rough, plain face, as she said in
low, reverent tones: 'Poor Harry! His last words: "Of
such is the kingdom of Heaven."'

Death was very busy amongst our poor company, and one
—two—three more passed away there, for they were riddled
with wounds; and then I saw that, in spite of all that could
be done, Lieutenant Leigh would be the next. He had
received his death-wound, and he knew it too; and now he
lay very still, holding tightly by Miss Ross's hand, while she
knelt beside him.

Captain Dyer, with his eight men, all left, were still
keeping the door; but of late they had not been interfered
with, and the poor fellows were able to do one another a
good turn in binding up wounds. But what all were now
suffering for want of, was water; and beyond a few drops in
one or two of the bottles carried by the women, there was
none to be had.

As for me, I could only lie there helpless, and in a half-
dreamy way, see and listen to all that was going on. The
spirit in me was good to help; but think of my state—going
for days with that cut on the face, and a broken arm, and in
that climate.

I was puzzling myself about this time as to what was going
to happen next, for I could not understand why the rebels
were so quiet; but the next minute I was watching Lieutenant Leigh, and thinking about the morning when we saw
Captain Dyer bound to the muzzle of the nine-pounder.

H

Could he have been thinking about the same thing? I say *yes*, for all at once he started right up, looking wild and excited. He had hold of Miss Ross's hand; but he threw it from him, as he called out: 'Now, my lads, a bold race, and a short one. We must bring them in. Spike the guns—cut the cords. Now, then—Elsie or death. Are you ready there? Forward!'

That last word rang through the vault we were in, and Captain Dyer ran down the steps, his hacked sword hanging from his wrist by the knot. But he was too late to take his messmate's hand in his, and say *farewell*, if that had been his intention, for Lieutenant Leigh had fallen back; and that senseless figure by his side was to all appearance as dead, when, with a quivering lip, Captain Dyer gently lifted her, and bore her to where, half stupefied, Mrs Colonel Maine was sitting.

CHAPTER XXII.

I GOT rather confused, and am to this day, about how the time went; things that only took a few minutes seeming to be hours in happening, and what really did take a long time gliding away as if by magic. I think I was very often in a half-delirious state; but I can well remember what was the cause of the silence above.

Captain Dyer was the first to see, and taking a rifle in his hand, he whispered an order or two; and then he, with two more, rushed into the passage, and got the door drawn towards us, for it opened outwards; but in so doing, he slipped on the floor, and fell with a bayonet-thrust through his shoulder, when, with a yell of rage—it was no cheer this time—our men dashed forward, and dragged him in; the door was pulled to, and held close; and then those poor wounded fellows—heroes I call 'em—stood angrily muttering.

I think I got more excited over that scene than over any part of the struggle, and all because I was lying there helpless; but it was of no use to fret, though I lay there with the weak tears running down my cheeks, as that brave man was brought down, and laid near the grating, with Mother Bantem at work directly to tear off his coat, and begin to bandage, as if she had been brought up in a hospital.

The door was forsaken, for there was a new guard there, that no one would try to pass, for the silence was explained to us all: first, there was a loud yelling and shrieking outside; and then there was a little thin blue wreath of smoke beginning to curl under the door, crawling along the top step, and collecting like so much blue water, to spread very slowly; for the fiends had been carrying out their wounded and dead, and were now going to burn us where we lay.

I can recollect all that; for now a maddening sense of horror seemed to come upon me, to think that those few poor souls left were to be slain in such a barbarous way, after all the gallant struggle for life; but what surprised me was the calm, quiet way in which all seemed to take it.

Once, indeed, the men had a talk together, and asked the women to join them in a rush through the passage; but they gave up the thought directly, for they knew that if they could get by the flames, there were more cruel foes outside, waiting to thrust them back.

So they all sat down in a quiet, resigned way, listening to the crackle outside the door, watching the thin smoke filter through the crevices, and form in clouds, or pools, according to where it came through.

And you'd have wondered to see those poor fellows, how they acted : why, Joe Bantem rubbed his face with his handkerchief, smoothed his hair and whiskers, and then got his belts square, as if off out on parade, before going and sitting quietly down by his wife.

Measles lay very still, gently humming over the old child's hymn, *Oh ! that'll be joyful,* but only to burst out again into a fit of grumbling.

Another went and knelt down in a corner, where he stayed ; the rest shook hands all round, and then, seeing Captain Dyer sitting up, and sensible, they went and saluted him, and asked leave to shake hands with him, quite upsetting him, poor fellow, as he called them, in a faint voice, his ' brave lads,' and asked their pardon, if he'd ever been too harsh with them.

' God bless you ! no, sir,' says Joe Bantem, jumping up, and shaking the hand himself, ' which *that* you've never been, but always a good officer as your company loved. Keep a brave heart, my boys, it'll soon be over. We've stood in front of death too many times now to shew the white-feather. Hurray for Captain Dyer, and may he have his regiment in the tother land, and we be some of his men !'

Joe Bantem gave a bit of a reel as he said this, and then he'd have fallen if it hadn't been for his wife ; and though his was rather strong language, you see it must be excused, for, leave alone his wounds, and the mad feeling they'd bring on, there was a wild excitement on the men then, brought on by the fighting, which made them, as you may say, half-drunk.

We must all have been choked over and over again, but for that grating ; for the hotter the fire grew above, the finer current of air swept in. The mutineers could not have known of it, or one of their first acts must have been to seal it up. But it was half-covered by some creeping flower, which made it invisible to them, and so we were able to breathe.

And now it may seem a curious thing, but I'm going to

say a little more about love. A strange time, you'll perhaps say, when those poor people were crouching together in that horrible vault, expecting their death moment by moment. But that's why it was, and not from any want of retiring modesty. I believe that those poor souls wished to shew those they loved how true was that feeling ; and therefore it was that wife crept to husband's side, and Lizzy Green, forgetting all else now, placed her arms round my neck, and her lips to mine, and kissed me again and again.

It was no time for scruples ; and thus it was that, being close to them, I heard Miss Ross, kneeling by the side of Captain Dyer, ask him, sobbing bitterly the while—ask him to forgive her, while he looked almost cold and strange at her, till she whispered to him long and earnestly, when I knew that she must be telling him all about the events of that morning. It must have been, for with a cry of joy I saw him bend towards her, when she threw her arms round him, and clasped his poor bleeding form to her breast.

They were so when I last looked upon them, and every one seemed lost in his or her own suffering, all save those two children, one of whom was asleep on Mrs Maine's lap, and the other playing with the gold knot of Captain Dyer's sword.

Then came a time of misty smoke and heat, and the crackling of woodwork ; but all the while there was a stream of hot pure air rushing in at that grating to give us life.

We could hear the black fiends running round and round the burning building, yelling, and no doubt ready to thrust back any one who tried to get out. But there seemed then to come another misty time, from which I was roused by Lizzy whispering to me : ' Is it very near now ?'

' What ?' I said faintly.

' Death,' she whispered, with her lips close to my ear. ' If it is, pray God that He will never let us part again in the land where all is peace !'

I tried to answer her, but I could not, for the hot, stifling blinding smoke was now in my throat, when the yelling outside seemed to increase. There was a loud rushing sound; the trampling of horses; the jingling of cavalry sabres; a loud English hurray; and a crash; and I knew that there was a charge of horse sweeping by. Then came the hurried beating of feet, the ring of platoon after platoon of musketry, a rapid, squandering, skirmishing fire; more yelling, and more English cheers; the rush, again, of galloping horses; and, by slow degrees, the sound of a fierce skirmish, growing more and more distant, till there came another rapid beating of hoofs, a sudden halt, the jingle and rattle of harness, and a moment after, bim—bom —bom—bom! at regular intervals; and I waved my hand, and gave a faint cheer, for I could mentally see it all: a troop of light-horse had charged twice; the infantry had come up at the double; and now here were the horse-artillery, with their light six-pounders, playing upon the retreating rebels where the cavalry were not cutting them up.

That faint cheer of mine brought out some more; and then there was a terrible silence, for the relief seemed to have come too late; but a couple of our men crawled to the grating, where the air reviving them, they gave another 'Hurray!' which was answered directly.

And then there was a loud shout, the excited buzz of voices, the crashing of a pioneer's axe against the frame-work of the grating; and after a hard fight, from which our friends were beaten back again and again, we poor wretches, nearly all insensible, were dragged out about a quarter of an hour before the burning house fell with a crash. Then there was a raging whirlwind of flame, and smoke, and sparks, and the cellar was choked up with the burning ruin.

CHAPTER XXIII.

How well I remember coming to myself as I lay there on the grass, with our old surgeon, Mr Hughes, kneeling by my side ; for it was our own men that formed the infantry of the column, with a troop of lancers, and one of horse-artillery. There was Colonel Maine kneeling by his wife, who, poor soul, was recovering fast, and him turning from her to the children, and back again ; while it was hard work to keep our men from following up the pursuit, now kept up by the lancers and horse-artillery, so mad and excited were they to find only eight wounded men out of the company they had left.

But, one way and another, the mutineers paid dear for what suffering they caused us. I can undertake to say that, for every life they took, half-a-dozen of their own side fell—the explosion swept away, I suppose, quite fifty, just as they had attempted a surprise, and came over from the south side in a night-attack ; while the way in which they were cut up in the engagement was something awful.

For, anxious beyond measure at not hearing news of the party left in Begumbagh, Colonel Maine had at length obtained permission to go round by that station, reinforce the troops, and then join the general by another route.

They were making forced marches, when they caught sight of the rebels yelling round the burning building, fully a couple of hundred being outside ; when, not knowing of the sore strait of those within, they had charged down, driving the murderous black scoundrels before them like so much chaff.

But you must not think that our pains were at an end. Is it not told in the pages of history how for long enough it

was a hard fight for a standing in India, and how our
troops were in many places sore put to it; while home after
home was made desolate by the most cruel outrages! It
was many a long week before we could be said to be in
safety; but I don't know that I suffered much beyond the
pains of that arm, or rather that stump, for our surgeon, Mr
Hughes, when I grumbled a little at his taking it off, told
me I might be very thankful that I had escaped with life,
for he had never known of such a case before.

But it was rather hard lying alone there in the tem-
porary hospital, missing the tender hands that one loved.

And yet I have no right to say quite alone, for poor old
Measles was on one side, and Joe Bantem on the other,
with Mrs Bantem doing all she could for us three, as well as
five more of our poor fellows.

More than once I heard Mr Hughes talk about the men's
wounds, and say it was wonderful how they could live
through them; but live they all seemed disposed to, except
poor Measles, who was terrible bad and delirious, till one
day, when he could hardly speak above a whisper, he says
to me—being quite in his right mind : 'I daresay some of
you chaps think that I'm going to take my discharge; but
all the same, you're wrong, for I mean to go in now for
promotion!'

He said 'now;' but what he did then was to go in for
sleep—and sleep he did for a good four-and-twenty hours—
when he woke up grumbling, and calling himself the most
unlucky beggar that ever breathed.

Time went on; and one by one we poor fellows got out
of hospital cured; but I was the last; and it was many
months after, that, at his wish, I called upon Captain—then
Major—Dyer, at his house in London. For, during those
many months, the mutiny had been suppressed, and our
regiment had been ordered home.

I was very weak and pale, and I hadn't got used to this empty sleeve, and things looked very gloomy ahead; but, somehow, that day when I called at Major Dyer's seemed the turning-point; for, to a poor soldier there was something very soothing for your old officer to jump up, with both hands outstretched to catch yours, and to greet you as warmly as did his handsome, bonny wife.

They seemed as if they could hardly make enough of me; but the sight of their happiness made me feel low-spirited; and I felt no better when Mrs Dyer—God bless her!—took my hand in hers, and led me to the next room, where she said there was an old friend wanted to see me.

I felt that soft jewelled hand holding mine, and I heard the door close as Mrs Dyer went out again, and then I stood seeing nothing—hearing nothing—feeling nothing, but a pair of clinging arms round my neck, and a tear-wet face pressed to mine.

And did that make me feel happy?

No! I can say it with truth. For as the mist cleared away from my eyes, and I looked down on, to me, the brightest, truest face the sun ever shone on, there was a great sorrow in my heart, as I told myself that it was a sin and a wrong for me, a poor invalided soldier, to think of taking advantage of that fine handsome girl, and tying her down to one who was maimed for life.

And at last, with the weak tears running down my cheeks, I told her of how it could not be: that I should be wronging her, and that she must think no more of me, only as a dear friend; when there is that amount of folly in this world, that my heart swelled, and a great ball seemed rising in my throat, and I choked again and again, as those arms clung tighter and tighter round my neck, and Lizzy called me her hero, and her brave lad who had saved her life again and again; and asked me to take her to my heart, and keep her there; for her to try and be to me a worthy loving wife—one that would never say a bitter word to me as long as she lived.

I said that there was so much folly in this world, so how can you wonder at me catching it of her, when she was so close that I could feel her breath upon my cheeks, my hair, my eyes, as once more, forgetting all in her love, she kissed me again and again. How, then, could I help, but with that one hand press her to my heart, and go the way that weak heart of mine wished.

I know it was wrong; but how can one always fight against weakness. And, to tell you the truth, I had fought long enough—so long that I wished for peace. And I must say this, too, you must not be hard on Lizzy, and think that it would have been better for her to have let me do a little more of the courting: there are exceptional cases, and this was one.

I had a true friend in Major Dyer, and to him I owe my present position—not a very grand one; but speaking honestly as a man, I don't believe, if I had been a general, some one at home could think more of me; while, as to this empty sleeve, she's proud of it, and says that all the country is the same.

Wandering about as a regiment is, one does not often have a chance to see one's old messmates; but Sergeant and Mrs Bantem and Sergeant Measles did have tea and supper with us one night here in London, Mrs Bantem saying that Measles was as proud of his promotion as a dog with two tails, though Measles did say he was an unlucky beggar, or he'd have been a captain. And, my! what a night we did have of that, without one drawback, only Measles would spit on my wife's Brussels carpet; and so we did have a night last year when the old regiment was stationed at Edinburgh, and the wife and me had a holiday, and went down and saw Colonel and Mrs Maine, and those children grown up a'most into a man and woman. But Colonel Dyer had exchanged into another regiment, and they say he is going to retire on half-pay, on account of his wound troubling him.

We fought our old battles over again on those nights; and we did not forget the past and gone; for Mrs Bantem stood up after supper, with her stiff glass of grog in her hand—a glass into which I saw a couple of tears fall—as she spoke of the dead—the brave men who fell in defence of the defenceless and innocent, hoping that the earth lay lightly on the grave of Lieutenant Leigh, while she proposed the memory of brave Harry Lant.

We drank that toast in silence; and more than one eye was wet as the old scenes came back—scenes such as I hope may never fall to the lot of men again to witness; for if there is ever a fervent prayer sent up to the Maker of All, by me, an old soldier, who has much to answer for, it is contained in those words, so familiar to you all:

'PEACE ON EARTH!' *Amen.*

THE GOLDEN INCUBUS.

CHAPTER I.

SIR JOHN DRINKWATER IS ECCENTRIC.

'YOU'RE an old fool, Burdon, and it's all your fault.'

That's what Sir John said, as he shook his Malacca cane at me; and I suppose it was my fault; but then, how could I see what was going to happen?

It began in 1851. I remember it so well because that was the year of the Great Exhibition, and Sir John treated me to a visit there; and when I'd been and was serving breakfast next morning, he asked me about it, and laughed and asked me if I'd taken much notice of the goldsmiths' work. I said I had, and that it was a great mistake to clean gold plate with anything but rouge.

'Why?' he said.

Because, I told him, if any of the plate-powder happened to be left in the cracks, if it was rouge it gave a good effect; but if it was a white preparation, it looked dirty and bad.

'Then we'll have all the chests open to-morrow, James Burdon,' he said; 'and you shall give the old gold plate a good clean up with rouge, and I'll help you.'

'You, Sir John?'

He nodded. And the very next day he sent all the other servants to the Exhibition, came down to my pantry, opened the plate-room, and put on an apron just like a servant would, and helped me to clean that gold plate. He got tired by one o'clock, and sat down upon a chair and looked at it all glistening as it was spread out on the dresser and shelves—some bright with polishing, some dull and dead and ancient-looking. Cups and bowls and salvers and round dishes covered with coats of arms; some battered and bent, and some as perfect as on the day it left the goldsmith's hands.

I 'd worked hard—as hard as I could, for sneezing, for I was doing that half the time, just as if I had a bad cold. For every cup or dish was kept in a green baize bag that fitted in one of the old ironbound oak chests, and these chests were lined with green baize. And all this being exceedingly old, the moths had got in; and pounds and pounds of pepper had been scattered about the baize, to keep them away.

'I 'll have a glass of wine, Burdon,' Sir John says at last; 'and we 'll put it all away again. It 's very beautiful. That 's Cellini work—real,' he says, as he took up a great golden bowl, all hammered and punched and engraved. 'But the whole lot of it is an incubus, for I can't use it, and I don't want to make a show.'

'Take a glass yourself, my man,' he said, as I got him the sherry—a fresh bottle from the outer cellar. 'Ha! at a moderate computation that old gold plate is worth a hundred thousand pounds; and a hundred thousand pounds at only three per cent. in the funds, Burdon, would be three thousand a year. So you see I lose that income by letting this heap of old gold plate lie locked up in those chests.—Now, what would you do with it, if it were yours?'

'Sell it, Sir John, and put it in houses,' I said sharply.

'Yes, James Burdon; and a sensible thing to do. But you are a servant, and I'm a baronet; though I don't look one,‑do I?' he said, holding up his red hands and laughing.

'You always look a gentleman, Sir John,' I said; 'and that's what you are.'

'Please God, I try to be,' he said sadly. 'But I don't want the money, James; and these are all old family heirlooms that I hold in trust for my life, and have to hand over—bound in honour to do so—to my son.— Look!' he said, 'at the arms and crest of the Boileaus on every piece.'

'Boileau, Sir John?'

'Well, Drinkwater, then. We translated the name when we came over to England. There; let's put it all away. It's a regular incubus.'

So it was all packed up again in the chests; for he wouldn't let me finish cleaning it, saying it would take a week; and that it was more for the sake of seeing and going over it, than anything, that he had had it out. So we locked it all up again in the plate-room. And it took five waters hot as he could bear 'em to wash his hands; and even then there was some rouge left in the cracks, and in the old signet ring with the coat of arms cut in the stone—same as that on the plate.

I don't know how it was; perhaps I was out of sorts, but from that day I got thinking about gold plate and what Sir John said about its worth. I knew what 'incubus' meant, for I went up in the library and looked out the word in the big dictionary; and that plate got to be such an incubus to me that I went up to Sir John one morning and gave him warning.

'But what for?' he said. 'Wages?'

'No, Sir John. You're a good master, and her ladyship was a good mistress before she was took up to heaven.'

'Hush, man, hush!' he says sharply.

'And it'll break my heart nearly not to see young Master Barclay when he comes back from school.'

'Then why do you want to go?'

'Well, Sir John, a good home and good food and good treatment's right enough; but I don't want to be found some morning a-weltering in my gore.'

'Now, look here, James Burdon,' he says, laughing. 'I trust you with the keys of the wine-cellar, and you've been at the sherry.'

'You know better than that, Sir John. No, sir. You said that gold plate was an incubus, and such it is, for it's always a-sitting on me, so as I can't sleep o' nights. It's killing me, that's what it is. Some night I shall be murdered, and all that plate taken away. It ain't safe, and it's cruel to a man to ask him to take charge of it.'

He did not speak for a few minutes.

'What am I to do, then, Burdon?'

'Some people send their plate to the bank, Sir John.'

'Yes,' he says; 'some people do a great many things that I do not intend to do.—There; I shall not take any notice of what you said.'

'But you must, please, Sir John; I couldn't stay like this.'

'Be patient for a few days, and I'll have something done to relieve you.'

I went down-stairs very uneasy, and Sir John went out; and next day, feeling quite poorly, after waking up ten times in the night, thinking I heard people breaking in, as there'd been a deal of burglary in Bloomsbury about that time, I got up quite thankful I was still alive; and directly after breakfast, the wine-merchant's cart came from

St James's Street with fifty dozen of sherry, as we really didn't want. Sir John came down and saw to the wine being put in bins; and then he had all the wine brought from the inner cellar into the outer cellar, both being next my pantry, with a door into the passage just at the foot of the kitchen stairs.

'That's a neat job, Burdon,' said Sir John, as we stood in the far cellar all among the sawdust, and the place looking dark and damp, with its roof like the vaults of a church, and stone flag floor, but with every bin empty.

'Going to lay down some more wine here, Sir John?' I said; but he didn't answer, only stood with a candle in the arched doorway, which was like a passage six feet long, opening from one cellar into the other. Then he went up-stairs, and I locked up the cellar and put the keys in my drawer.

'He always was eccentric before her ladyship died,' I said to myself; 'and now he's getting worse.'

I saw it again next morning, for Sir John gave orders, sudden-like, for everybody to pack off to the country-house down by Dorking; and of course everybody had to go, cook and housekeeper and all; and just as I was ready to start, I got word to stay.

Sir John went off to his club, and I stayed alone in that old house in Bloomsbury, with the great drops of perspiration dripping off me every time I heard a noise, and feeling sometimes as if I could stand it no longer; but just as it was getting dusk, he came back, and in his short abrupt way, he says: 'Now, Burdon, we'll go to work.'

I'd no idea what he meant till we went down-stairs, when he had the strong-room door opened and the cellar too; and then he made me help him carry the old plate-chests right through my pantry into the far wine-cellar, and range them one after the other along one side.

I wanted to tell him that they would not be so safe there; but I daren't speak, and it was not till what followed that I began to understand; for, as soon as we had gone through the narrow arched passage back to the outer cellar, he laughed, and he says: 'Now, we'll get rid of the incubus, Burdon. Fix your light up there, and I'll help.'

He did help; and together we got a heap of sawdust and hundreds of empty wine-bottles; and these we built up at the end of the arched entrance between the cellars from floor to ceiling, just as if it had been a wine-bin, till the farther cellar was quite shut off with empty bottles. And then, if he didn't make me move the new sherry that had just come in and treat that the same, building up full bottles in front of the empty ones till the ceiling was reached once more, and the way in to the chests of gold plate shut up with wine-bottles two deep, one stack full, the other empty.

He saw me shake my head, as if I didn't believe in it; and he laughed again in his strange way, and said: 'Wait a bit.'

Next morning I found he'd given orders, for the men came with a load of bricks and mortar, and they set to work and built up a wall in front of the stacked-up bottles, regularly bricking up the passage, just as if it was a bin of wine that was to be left for so many years to mature; after which the wall was white-washed over, the men went away, and Sir John clapped me on the shoulder. 'There, Burdon!' he said; 'we've buried the incubus safely. Now you can sleep in peace.'

CHAPTER II.

WHY EDWARD GUNNING LEFT.

IT's curious how things get forgotten by busy people. In a few weeks I left off thinking about the hiding-place of all that golden plate; and after a time I used to go into that first cellar for wine with my half-dozen basket in one hand, my cellar candlestick in the other, and never once think about there being a farther cellar; while, though there was the strong-room in my pantry with quite a thousand pounds-worth of silver in it—perhaps more—I never fancied anybody would come for that.

Master Barclay came, and went back to school, and Sir John grew more strange; and then an old friend of his died and left one little child, Miss Virginia, and Sir John took her and brought her to the old house in Bloomsbury, and she became—bless her sweet face!—just like his own.

Then, all at once I found that ten years had slipped by, and it set me thinking about being ten years nearer the end, and that the years were rolling on, and some day another butler would sleep in my pantry, while I was sleeping—well, you know where, cold and still—and that then Sir John would be taking his last sleep too, and Master Barclay be, as it says in the Scriptures, reigning in his stead.

And then it was that all in a flash something seemed to say to me : Suppose Sir John has never told his lawyers about that buried gold plate, and left no writing to show where it is. I felt quite startled, and didn't know what to think. As far as I could tell, nobody but Sir John and I knew the secret. Young Master Barclay certainly didn't, or else, when I let him carry the basket for a treat, and went into the cellar to fetch his father's port, he, being a talking, lively, thoughtless boy, would have been sure to say something. His father ought certainly to tell him some day; but suppose the master was taken bad suddenly with apoplexy and died without being able— what then?

I didn't sleep much that night, for once more that gold plate was being an incubus, and I determined to speak to Sir John as an old family servant should, the very next day.

Next day came, and I daren't; and for days and days the incubus seemed to swell and trouble me, till I felt as if I was haunted. But I couldn't make up my mind what to do, till one night, just before going to bed, and then it came like a flash, and I laughed at myself for not thinking of it before. I didn't waste any time, but getting down my ink-bottle and pens, I took a sheet of paper, and wrote as plainly as I could about how Sir John Drinkwater and his butler James Burdon had hidden all the chests of valuable old gold cups and salvers in the inner wine-cellar, where the entrance was bricked up; and to make all sure, I put down the date as near as I could remember in 1851, and the number of the house, 19 Great Grandon Street, Bloomsbury, because, though it was not likely, Sir John might move, and if that paper was found after I was dead, people might go on a false scent, find nothing, and think I was mad.

I locked that paper up in my old desk, feeling all the while as if I ought to have had it witnessed; but people don't like to put their names to documents unless they know what they're about, and of course I couldn't tell anybody the contents of that.

I felt satisfied as a man should who feels he has done his duty; and perhaps that's what made the time glide away so fast without anything particular happening. Sir John bought the six old houses like ours opposite, and gave twice as much for them as they were worth, because some one was going to build an Institution there, which might very likely prove to be a nuisance.

I don't remember anything else in particular, only that the houses would not let well, because Sir John grew close and refused to spend money in doing them up. But there was the trouble with Edward Gunning, the footman, a clever, good-looking young fellow, who had been apprenticed to a bricklayer and contractor, but took to service instead. He did no good in that; for, in spite of all I could say, he would take more than was good for him, and then Sir John found him out.

So Edward Gunning had to go; and I breathed more freely, and felt less nervous.

CHAPTER III.

MR BARCLAY THINKS FOR HIMSELF.

So another ten years had slipped away; and the house opposite, which had been empty for two years, was getting in very bad condition—I mean as to paper and paint.

'Nobody will take it as it is, Sir John,' the agent said to him in my presence.

'Then it can be left alone,' he says, very gruffly. 'Good-morning.'

'Well, Mr Burdon,' said the agent, as I gave him a glass of wine in my pantry, 'it's a good thing he's so well off; but it's poison to my mind to see houses lying

empty.' Which no doubt it was, seeing he had five per
cent. on the rents of all he let.

Then Mr Barclay spoke to his father, and he had to go
out with a flea in his ear; and when, two days later, Miss
Virginia said something about the house opposite looking
so miserable, and that it was a pity there were no bills
up to say it was to let, Sir John flew out at her, and
that was the only time I ever heard him speak to her
cross.

But he was so sorry for it, that he sent me to the bank
with a cheque directly after, and I was to bring back
a new fifty-pound note; and I know that was in the
letter I had to give Miss Virginia, and orders to have
the carriage round, so that she might go shopping.

Now, I'm afraid you'll say that Mr Barclay Drinkwater
was right in calling me Polonius, and saying I was as prosy
as a college don; but if I don't tell you what brought all
the trouble about, how are you to understand what
followed? Old men have their own ways; and though
I'm not very old, I've got mine, and if I don't tell
my story my way, I'm done.

Well, it wasn't a week after Mr Bodkin & Co., the
agent, had that glass of wine in the pantry, that he came
in all of a bustle, as he always was, just as if he must
get everything done before dark, and says he has let
the house, if Sir John approves.

Not so easily done as you'd think, for Sir John wasn't,
he said, going to have anybody for an opposite neigh-
bour; but the people might come and see him if they
liked.

I remember it as well as if it was yesterday. Sir John
was in a bad temper with a touch of gout—bin 27—'25
port, being rather an acid wine, but a great favourite of
his. Miss Virginia had been crying. The trouble had

been about Mr Barclay going away. He'd finished his schooling at college, and was now twenty-seven, and a fine strong handsome fellow, as wanted to be off and see the world; but Sir John told him he couldn't spare him.

'No, Bar,' he says in my presence, for I was bathing his foot—'if you go away—I know you, you dog—you'll be falling in love with some smooth-faced girl, and then there'll be trouble. You'll stop at home, sir, and eat and drink like a gentleman, and court Virginia like a gentleman; and when she's twenty-one, you'll marry her; and you can both take care of me till I die, and then you can do as you like.'

Then Mr Barclay, looking as much like his father as he could with his face turned red, said what he ought not to have said, and refused to marry Miss Virginia; and he flung out of the room; while Miss Virginia—bless her for an angel!—must have known something of the cause of the trouble—I'm afraid, do you know, it was from me, but I forget—and she was in tears, when there was a knock and ring, and a lady's card was sent in for Sir John: 'Miss Adela Mimpriss.'

It was about the house; and I had to show her in—a little, slight, elegantly dressed lady of about three-and-twenty, with big dark eyes, and a great deal of wavy hair.

Sir John sent for Mr Barclay and Miss Virginia, to see if they approved of her; and it was settled that she and her three maiden sisters were to have the opposite house; and when the bell rang for me to show her out, Mr Barclay came and took the job out of my hands.

'I'm very glad,' I heard him say, 'and I hope we shall be the best of neighbours;' and his face was flushed, and he looked very handsome; while, when they shook hands on the door-mat, I could see the bright-eyed thing smiling in his face and looking pleased; and that shaking of the hands took a deal longer than it ought, while she gave him a look that made me think if I'd had a daughter like that, she'd have had bread-and-water for a week.

Then the door was shut, and Mr Barclay stood on the mat, smiling stupid-like, not knowing as I was noticing him; and then he turned sharply round and saw Miss Virginia on the stairs, and his face changed.

'James Burdon,' I said to myself, 'these are girls and boys no longer, but grown-up folk, and there's the beginning of trouble here.'

CHAPTER IV.

A LITTLE SKIRMISH.

I DIDN'T believe in the people opposite, in spite of their references being said to be good. You may say that's because of what followed; but it isn't, for I didn't like the looks of the stiff elderly Miss Mimprisses; and I didn't like the two forward servants, though they seemed to keep themselves to themselves wonderfully, and no man ever allowed in the house. Worst of all, I didn't like that handsome young Miss Adela, sitting at work over coloured worsted at the dining-room or drawing-room window, for young Mr Barclay was always looking across at her; and though he grew red-faced, my poor Miss Virginia grew every day more pale.

They seemed very strange people over the way, and it was only sometimes on a Sunday that any one at our place caught a glimpse of them, and then one perhaps would come to a window for a few minutes and sit and talk to Miss Adela—one of the elder sisters, I mean; and when I caught sight of them, I used to think that it was no wonder they had taken to dressing so primly and so plain, for they must have given up all hope of getting husbands long before.

Mr Barclay suggested to Sir John twice in my hearing that he should invite his new tenants over to dinner; and once, in a hesitating way, hinted something about Miss Virginia calling. But Sir John only grunted; while I saw my dear young lady dart such an indignant look at Mr Barclay as made him silent for the rest of the evening, and seem ashamed of what he had said.

I talked about it a good deal to Tom as I sat before my pantry fire of an evening; and he used to leap up in my lap and sit and look up at me with his big eyes, which were as full of knowingness at those times as they were stupid and slit-like at others. He was a great favourite of mine was Tom, and had been ever since I found him, a half-starved kitten in the area, and took him in and fed him till he grew up the fine cat he was.

'There's going to be trouble come of it, Tom,' I used to say; and to my mind, the best thing that could have happened for us would have been for over-the-way to have stopped empty; for, instead of things going on smoothly and pleasantly, they got worse every day. Sir John said very little, but he was a man who noticed a great deal. Mr Barclay grew restless and strange, but he never said a word now about going away. While, as for Miss Virginia, she seemed to me to be growing older and more serious in a wonderful way; but when she was spoken to, she had always a pleasant smile and a bright look, though it faded away again directly, just as the sunshine does when there are clouds. She used to pass the greater part of her time reading to Sir John, and she kept his accounts for him and wrote his letters; and one morning as I was clearing away the breakfast things, Mr Barclay being there, reading the paper, Sir John says sharply: 'Those people opposite haven't paid their first quarter's rent.'

No one spoke for a moment or two, and then in a fidgety sharp way, Mr Barclay says: 'Why, it was only due yesterday, father.'

'Thank you, sir,' says Sir John, in a curiously polite way; 'I know that; but it was due yesterday, and it ought to have been paid.—'Ginny, write a note to the Misses Mimpriss with my compliments, and say I shall be obliged by their sending the rent.'

Miss Virginia got up and walked across to the writing-table; and I went on very slowly clearing the cloth, for Sir John always treated me as if I was a piece of furniture; but I felt uncomfortable, for it seemed to me that there was going to be a quarrel.

I was right; for as Miss Virginia began to write, Mr Barclay crushed the newspaper up in his hands and said hotly: 'Surely, father, you are not going to insult those ladies by asking them for the money the moment it is due.'

'Yes, I am, sir,' says the old gentleman sharply; 'and you mind your own business. When I'm dead, you can collect your rents as you like; while I live, I shall do the same.'

Miss Virginia got up quickly and went and laid her hand upon Sir John's breast without saying a word; but her pretty appealing act meant a deal, and the old man took the little white hand in his and kissed it tenderly. 'You go and do as I bid you, my pet,' he said; 'and you, Burdon, wait for the note, take it over, and bring an answer.'

'Yes, Sir John,' I said quietly; and I heard Miss Virginia give a little sob as she went and sat down and began writing. Then I saw that the trouble was coming, and that there was to be a big quarrel between father and son.

'Look here, father,' says Mr Barclay, getting up and walking about the room, 'I never interfere with your affairs '——

'I should think not, sir,' says the old man, very sarcastic-like.

'But I cannot sit here patiently and see you behave in so rude a way to those four ladies who honour you by being your tenants.'

'Say I feel greatly surprised that the rent was not sent over yesterday, my dear,' says Sir John, without taking any notice of his son.

'Yes, uncle,' says Miss Virginia. She always called him 'uncle,' though he wasn't any relation.

'It's shameful!' cried Mr Barclay. 'The result will be that they will give you notice and go.'

'Good job, too,' said Sir John. 'I don't like them, and I wish they had not come.'

'How can you be so unreasonable, father?' cried the young man hotly.

'Look here, Bar,' says Sir John ('Fold that letter and seal it with my seal, 'Ginny')—'look here, Bar.'

I glanced at the young man, and saw him pass his hand across his forehead so roughly that the big signet ring he wore—the old-fashioned one Sir John gave him many years before, and which fitted so tightly now that it wouldn't come over the joint—made quite a red mark on his brow.

'I don't know what you are going to say, father,' cried Mr Barclay quickly; 'but, for Heaven's sake, don't treat me

as a boy any longer, and I implore you not to send that
letter.'

There was a minute's silence, during which I could hear
Mr Barclay breathing hard. Then Sir John began again.
'Look here, sir,' he said. 'Over and over again, you've
wanted to go away and travel, and I've said I didn't want
you to go. During the past three months you've altered
your mind.'

'Altered my mind, sir?' says the young man sharply.

'Yes, sir; and I've altered mine. That's fair. Now,
you don't want to go, and I want you to.'

'Uncle!'

'Have you done that letter, my pet?—Yes? That's
well. Now, you stand there and take care of me, for fear
Mr Barclay should fly in a passion.'

'Sir, I asked you not to treat me like a boy,' says Mr
Barclay bitterly.

'I'm not going to,' says Sir John, as he sat playing with
Miss Virginia's hand, while I could see that the poor
darling's face was convulsed, and she was trying to hide
the tears which streamed down. 'I'm going to treat you
as a man. You can have what money you want. Be off
for a year's travel. Hunt, shoot, go round the world, what
you like; but don't come back here for a twelvemonth.—
Burdon, take that letter over to the Misses Mimpriss, and
wait for an answer.'

I took the note across, wondering what would be said
while I was gone, and knowing why Sir John wanted his
son to go as well as he did, and Miss Virginia too, poor
thing. The knocker seemed to make the house opposite
echo very strangely, as I thumped; but when the door was
opened in a few minutes, everything in the hall seemed
very proper and prim, while the maid who came looked as
stiff and disagreeable as could be.

'For Miss Mimpriss, from Sir John Drinkwater,' I said;
'and I 'll wait for an answer.'

'Very well,' says the woman shortly.

'I 'll wait for an answer,' I said, for she was shutting
the door.

'Yes; I heard,' she says, and the door was shut in my
face.

'Hang all old maids!' I said. 'They needn't be afraid
of me;' and there I waited till I heard steps again and the
door was opened; and the ill-looking woman says in a
snappish tone: 'Miss Adela Mimpriss's compliments, and
she 'll come across directly.'

'Any one would think I was a wild beast,' I said to
myself, as I went back and gave my message, finding all
three in the room just as I had left them when I went
away.

CHAPTER V.

JAMES BURDON SMELLS FIRE.

MR BARCLAY followed me out, and as soon as we were
in the hall, 'Burdon,' he says, 'you have a bunch of small
keys, haven't you?'

'Yes, Master Barclay, down in my pantry.'

'Lend them to me: I want to try if one of them will fit
a lock of mine.'

He followed me down; and I was just handing them to
him, when there was a double knock and a ring, and I saw
him turn as red as a boy of sixteen found out at some
trick.

I hurried up to open the door, leaving him there, and
found that it was Miss Adela Mimpriss.

'Will you show me in to Sir John?' she says, smiling; and I did so, leaving them together; and going down-stairs, to see Mr Barclay standing before the fire and looking very strange and stern. He did not say anything, but walked up-stairs again; and I could hear him pacing up and down the hall for quite a quarter of an hour before the bell rang; and then I got up-stairs to find him talking very earnestly to Miss Adela Mimpriss, and she all the time shaking her head and trying to pull away her hand.

I pretended not to see, and went into the dining-room slowly, to find Miss Virginia down on her knees before Sir John, and him with his two hands lying upon her bent head, while she seemed to be sobbing.

'I did not ring, Burdon,' he said huskily.

'Beg pardon, Sir John; the bell rang.'

'Ah, yes. I forgot—only to show that lady out.'

I left the room; and as I did so, I found the front door open, and Mr Barclay on the step, looking across at Miss Adela Mimpriss, who was just tripping up the steps of the house opposite; and I saw her use a latchkey, open the door, and look round as she was going in, to give Mr Barclay a laughing look; and then the door was closed, and my young master shut ours.

That day and the next passed quietly enough; but I could see very plainly that there was something wrong, for there was a cold way of speaking among our people in the dining-room, the dinner going off terribly quiet, and Sir John afterwards not seeming to enjoy his wine; while Miss Virginia sat alone in the drawing-room over her tea; and Mr Barclay, after giving me back my keys, went up-stairs, and I know he was looking out, for Miss Adela Mimpriss was sitting at the window opposite, and I saw her peep up twice.

This troubled me a deal, for, after all those years, I

never felt like a servant, but as if I was one of them; and it made me so upset, that, as I lay in my bed in the pantry that night wondering whether Mr Barclay would go away and forget all about the young lady opposite, and come back in a year and be forgiven, and marry Miss Virginia, I suddenly thought of my keys.

'That's it,' I said. 'It was to try the lock of his portmanteau. He means to go, and it will be all right, after all.'

But somehow, I couldn't sleep, but lay there pondering, till at last I began to sniff, and then started up in bed, thinking of Edward Gunning.

'There's something wrong somewhere,' I said to myself, for quite plainly I could smell burning—the oily smell as of a lamp, a thing I knew well enough, having trimmed hundreds.

At first I thought I must be mistaken; but no—there it was, strong; and jumping out of bed, I got a light; and to show that I was not wrong, there was my cat Tom looking excited and strange, and trotting about the pantry in a way not usual unless he had heard a rat.

I dressed as quickly as I could, and went out into the passage. All dark and silent, and the smell very faint. I went up-stairs and looked all about; but everything was as I left it; and at last I went down again to the pantry, thinking and wondering, with Tom at my heels, to find that the smell had passed away. So I sat and thought for a bit, and then went to bed again; but I didn't sleep a wink, and somehow all this seemed to me to be very strange.

CHAPTER VI.

A SUDDEN CHANGE.

IF any one says I played spy, I am ready to speak up pretty strongly in my self-defence, for my aim always was to do my duty by Sir John my master; but I could not help seeing two or three things during the next fortnight, and they all had to do with a kind of telegraphing going on from our house to the one over the way, where Miss Adela generally appeared to be on the watch; and her looks always seemed to me to say: 'No; you mustn't think of such a thing,' and to be inviting him all the time. Then, all at once I thought I was wrong, for I went up as usual at half-past seven to take Mr Barclay's boots and his clothes which had been brought down the night before, after he had dressed for dinner. I tapped and went in, just as I'd always done ever since he was a boy, and went across to the window and drew the curtains. 'Nice morning, Master Barclay,' I said. 'Half-past'—— There I stopped, and stared at the bed, which all lay smooth and neat, as the housemaid had turned it down, for no one had slept in it that night. I was struck all of a heap, and didn't know what to think. To me it was just like a silver spoon or fork being missing, and setting one's head to work to think whether it was anywhere about the house.

He hadn't stopped to take his wine with Sir John after dinner; but that was nothing fresh, for they'd been very cool lately. Then I hadn't seen him in the drawing-room; but that was nothing fresh neither, for he had avoided Miss Virginia for some little time.

'It is very strange,' I thought, for I had not seen him go out; and then, all at once I gave quite a start, for I felt that he must have done what Sir John had told him to do—gone.

'That won't do,' I said directly after. 'He wouldn't have gone like that;' and I went straight to Sir John's room and told him, as in duty bound, what I had found out, for Mr Barclay was not the young man to be fast and stop out of nights and want the servants to screen him. There was something wrong, I felt sure, and so I said.

'No,' said the old gentleman, as he sat up in bed, and then began to dress; 'he wouldn't go at my wish; but that girl over the way is playing with him, and he is too proud to stand it any longer, besides being mortified at making such an ass of himself. There's nothing wrong, Burdon. He has gone, and a good job too.'

Of course, I couldn't contradict my master; but I went up and examined Mr Barclay's room, to find nothing missing, not so much as a shirt or a pair of socks, only his crush-hat, and the light overcoat from the brass peg in the front hall; and I shook my head.

Miss Virginia looked paler than ever at breakfast; but nothing more was said up-stairs. Of course, the servants gossiped; and as it was settled that Mr Barclay had done what his father had told him, a week passed away, and matters settled down with Miss Adela Mimpriss sitting at the window just as usual, doing worsted-work, and the old house looking as grim as ever, and as if a bit of paint and a man to clean the windows would have been a blessing to us all.

Every time the postman knocked, Miss Virginia would start; and her eyes used to look so wild and large, that when I'd been to the little box and found nothing from

Mr Barclay, I used to give quite a gulp; and many's the time I've stood back in the dining-room and shook my fist at Miss Adela sitting so smooth and handsome at the opposite house, and wished she'd been at the world's end before she came there.

CHAPTER VII.

A TERRIBLE DISCOVERY.

MR BARCLAY had been gone three weeks, and no news from him; and I was beginning to think that he had gone off in a huff all at once, though I often wondered how he would manage for want of money, when one night, as I sat nursing Tom, I thought I'd look through my desk, that I hadn't opened for three or four years, and have a look at a few old things I'd got there—a watch Sir John gave me, but which I never wore; six spade-ace guineas; and an old gold pin, beside a few odds and ends that I'd had for a many years; and some cash. Tom didn't seem to like it, and he stared hard at the desk as I took it on my knees, opened it, lifted one of the flaps, and put my hand upon the old paper which contained the statement about the old gold plate. No; I did not. I put my hand on the place where it ought to have been; but it wasn't there.

'I must have put it in the other side,' I said to myself; and I opened the other lid.

Then I turned cold, and ran my hand here and there, wild-like, to stop at last with my mouth open, staring. The paper was gone! So was the money, and every article of value that I had hoarded up.

J

For a few minutes I was too much stunned even to think; and when at last I could get my brain to work, I sat there, feeling a poor, broken, weak old man, and I covered my face with my hands and cried like a child.

'To think of it!' I groaned at length—'him so hand-some and so young—him whom I'd always felt so proud of—proud as if he'd been my own son. Why, it would break his father's heart if he knew. It's that woman's doing,' I cried savagely. 'She turned his head, or he'd never have done such a cruel, base, bad act as to rob a poor old man like me.' For I'd recollected lending Mr Barclay my keys, and I felt that sooner than ask his father for money, he had taken what he could find, and gone. 'Let him!' I said savagely at last. 'But he needn't have stolen them. I'd have given him everything I'd got. I'd have sold out the hundred pounds I've got in the bank and lent him that. But he didn't know what he was doing, poor boy. That woman has turned his brain.'

'Ah, well!' I said at last bitterly, 'it's my secret. Sir John shall never know. He trusted me with one, and now his son'—— I stopped short there, for I recollected the paper, and fell all of a tremble, thinking of that gold plate, and that some one else knew of its hiding-place now; and I asked myself what I ought to do. For a long time I struggled; but at last I felt that, much as I wanted to hide Mr Barclay's cruelly mean act, I must not keep this thing a secret. 'It's my duty to tell my master,' I said at last, 'and I must.' So I went up to where Sir John was sitting alone, pretending to enjoy his wine, but looking very yellow and old and sunken of face. 'He's fretting about Master Barclay,' I said to myself, and I felt that I could not tell him that the lad had taken my little treasures, but that he must know about the paper, so I up and told him only this at once; and that's why he said I was an old fool, and that it was all my fault.

'You old fool!' he cried excitedly, 'what made you write such a paper? It was like telling all the world.'

'I thought it would be so shocking, Sir John, if we were both to die and the things were forgotten.'

'Shocking? Be a good job,' he cried. 'A man who has a lot of gold in his care is always miserable.—Taken out of your desk, you say. When?'

'Ah, that I can't tell, Sir John. It might have been done years ago, for aught I know.'

'And the old gold plate all stolen and melted down, and spent. Here have I been thinking you a trustworthy man. There; we must see to it at once. I shan't rest till I know it is safe.'

It seemed to me then that he snatched at the chance of finding something to do to take his attention off his trouble, for when I asked him if I should get a bricklayer to come in, he turned upon me like a lion. 'Burdon,' he said, 'we'll get this job done, and then I shall have to make arrangements for you to go into an imbecile ward.'

'Very good, Sir John,' I said patiently.

'Very good!' he cried, laughing now. 'There; be off, and get together what tools you have, and as soon as the servants have gone to bed, we'll go and open the old cellar ourselves.'

CHAPTER VIII.

THE SIGNET RING.

IT was exactly twelve o'clock by the chiming timepiece in the hall. Just the hour for such a task, I felt with a sort of shiver, as Sir John came down to the pantry, where I had candles ready, and a small crowbar used for opening packing-cases, and a screw-driver.

'Everybody seems quiet up-stairs, Burdon,' says Sir John, 'so let's get to work at once.—But, hillo! just put out a lamp?'

'No, Sir John,' I said. 'I often smell that now; but I've never been able to make out what it is.'

'Humph! Strange,' he says; and then we went straight to the cellar, the great baize door at the top of the kitchen steps being shut; and directly after we were standing on the damp sawdust with the bins of wine all round.

'It hasn't been touched, apparently, and there seems to be no need; but I should like to see if it is all right. But we shall never get through there, Burdon,' he says, looking at the bricked-up wall, across the way to the inner cellar.

'I don't know,' I said, taking off my coat and rolling up my sleeves, to find that though the highest price had been paid for that bricklaying, the cheat of a fellow who had the job had used hardly a bit of sand and bad lime, so that, after I had loosened one brick and levered it out, all the others came away one at a time quite clear of the mortar.

'Never mind,' says Sir John. 'Out of evil comes good. I'll try that sherry too, Burdon, and we'll put some fresh in its place. But if that's left twenty years, we shall never live to taste it, eh?'

I shook my head sadly as I worked away in that arch, easily reaching the top bricks, which were only six feet from the sawdust; and, as is often the case, what had seemed a terrible job proved to be easy.

'There,' he says; 'the place will be sweeter now. We'll just have a glance at the old chests, and then we must build up the empty bottles again. To-morrow, I'll order in some more wine—for my son.'

He said that last so solemnly that I looked up at him as he stood there with the light shining in his eyes.

'As'll come back some day, sorry for the past, Sir John,' I said, 'and ready to do what you wish.'

'Please God, Burdon!' he says, bowing his head for a bit. Then he looked up quite sharply, and took a candle, and I the other. 'Come along,' he says in his old, quiet, stern way; and I was half afraid I had offended him, as he stepped in at the opening and stood at the mouth of the inner cellar. Then I heard him give a sharp sniff, and I smelt it too—that same odour of burnt oil. We neither of us spoke as we walked over the damp black sawdust, both thinking of the likelihood of foul air being in the place; but we found we could breathe all right; and as we held up the candles, the light shone on the black-looking old chests, every one with its padlocks and seals all right, just as we had left them all those years before.

I looked up at Sir John, and he gave me a satisfied nod as he tried one of the seals, and then we both stood as if turned to stone, for from just at my feet there came a dull knocking sound, and as I looked down, I could see the black sawdust shake.

What I wanted to do was to run, for I felt that the place was haunted; but I couldn't move, and when I looked at Sir John, he was holding up his right hand, as if to order me to be silent. Then he held his candle down, for there was another sound, but this time more of a grinding cracking in a dull sort of way, just as if some one was forcing an iron chisel in between the joints of the stones. Then there was a long pause, and I half thought it had been fancy; but soon after, as I stood there hardly able to breathe, the sawdust just in one place was heaved up about an inch.

I was terribly alarmed, not knowing what to think; but Sir John was brave as brave, and he signed to me not to speak, and stood watching till there was a dull cracking sound, the sawdust was heaved up again, and all at once I seemed to get a hot puff of that burnt oily smell right in my nose. Then I began to understand, and felt afraid in a different fashion, as I knew that we had only got there just in time.

The next minute Sir John made a movement toward me, took my candle and turned it upside down, so that it went out, and then pointed back toward the outer cellar, as he put his lips to my ear:

'Iron bar!'

I stepped back softly, and got the iron bar from where it lay on the edge of a bin, and I was about to pick up the screw-driver, when I remembered where the wooden mallet lay, and I picked up that before stepping softly back to where Sir John was watching the floor; and now I could see that the sawdust was higher in one place, as if a flagstone had been heaved up a little at one end.

There was no doubt about it, for, as I handed the crowbar, the end of the stone was wrenched up a little higher and then stuck; for it was tightly held by those on either side; but it was up far enough to let a thin ray of dull light come up through the floor and shine on the side of one of the old chests.

It was a curious scene there, in that gloomy cellar: Sir John standing on one side, candle in his left, the iron bar in his right hand, and me on the other bending down ready with the mallet to hit over the head the first that should come up through the floor. For, though horribly alarmed, I could understand now what it all meant—an attempt to steal the gold in the chests, though how those who were working below had managed to get there was more than I could have said.

As we watched, the smell of the burnt oil came through, and I knew that it must have been going on for a long time.

All at once we could hear a low whispering, and then there was a grinding noise of iron against stone; the flag gritted and gave a little, but it held fast all along; and I could understand that the man who was trying to wrench it up had no room to work, and therefore no power to wrench up the stone. Then came the faint whispering again, and it seemed to sound hollow. Then another grinding noise, and the end of the flag was moved a trifle higher, so that the line of light on the old chest looked two or three inches broad.

I stepped softly to Sir John and put my lips to his ear as the whispering could be heard again, and I said softly: ' Shall I fetch the police ?'

Sir John for answer set his candle down upon the top of one of the chests and put it out with the bar as he whispered to me in turn: ' Wait a few moments.' And then—'Look!' He pointed with the iron bar; and as I stared hard at the faint light shining up from below the edge of the stone, I could see just the tips of some one's fingers come through and sweep the sawdust away to right and left. Then they came through a little more, and were drawn back, while directly after came the low whispering again, and the hand now was thrust right through as far as the wrist.

'Yes,' said Sir John then, as he grasped my arm—'the police!' Just then he uttered a gasp, and I turned to look at him; but we were in the dark, and I could not see his face, but he gripped my arm more tightly, and I looked once more toward the broad ray, to see the hand resting now full in the light, and I turned cold with horror, for there was something shining quite brightly, and I could see that it was a signet ring, and what was more, the old ring Mr Barclay used to wear—the one he had worn since he was quite a stripling, and beyond which the joint had grown so big that he could never get the jewel off.

I should have bent down there, staring at that ring for long enough, fascinated, as you may say, only all at once I felt my arm dragged, and I was pushed softly into the outer cellar, and from there into the passage beyond, Sir John closing and locking the door softly, before tottering into the pantry and sinking into a chair, uttering a low moan.

'Oh, don't take on, sir,' I whispered; but he turned upon me roughly.

'Silence, man!' he panted, 'and give me time to think;' and then I heard him breathe softly, in a voice so full of agony that it was terrible to hear: 'Oh, my son!—my son!'

'No, no, sir,' I said—for I couldn't bear it. 'He wouldn't; there's some mistake.'

'Mistake? Then you saw it too, Burdon? No; there is no mistake.'

I couldn't speak, for I remembered about the keys, and something seemed to come up in my throat and choke me, for it seemed so terrible for my young master to have done this thing.

'What are you going to do, sir?' I said at last, and it was me now who gripped his arm.

'Do?' he said bitterly. 'All that is a heritage: mine to hold in trust for my son—his after my death to hold in trust for the generations to come. Burdon, it is an incubus—a curse; but I have my duty to do: that old gold shall not be wasted on a '——

CHAPTER IX.

MR BARCLAY GOES TOO FAR.

When young Mr Barclay——

Stop! How do I know all this?

Why, it was burned into my memory, and I heard every word from him.

When young Mr Barclay left the dining-room on the night he disappeared, he went up to his own room, miserable at his position with his father, and taking to himself the blame for the unhappiness that he had brought upon the girl who loved him with all her sweet true heart. 'But it's fate—it's fate,' he said, as he went up to his room; and then, unable to settle himself there, he lit a cigar, came down, and went out just as he was dressed in his evening clothes, only that he had put on a light overcoat, and began to walk up and down in front of our house and watch the windows opposite, to try and catch a glimpse of Miss Adela.

Ten o'clock, eleven, struck, but she did not show herself at the window; and feeling quite sick at heart, he was thinking of going in again, when he suddenly heard a faint cough, about twenty yards away; and turning sharply, he saw the lady he was looking for crossing the road, having evidently just come back from some visit.

' Adela—at last,' he whispered as he caught her hand.

' Mr Drinkwater !' she cried in a startled way. ' How you frightened me !'

' Love makes men fools,' said Mr Barclay, as he slipped into her home ere she could close the door. ' Now take me in and introduce me to your sisters.'

' Adela, is that you ? Here, for goodness' sake. Why don't you answer ?'

' Is she there ?'

The first was a rough man's voice, the next that of a woman, and as they were heard in the passage, another voice cried hoarsely : ' It's of no use : the game's up.'

' Hist ! Hide ! Behind that curtain ! Anywhere !' panted Adela, starting up in alarm. ' Too late !'

Barclay had sprung to his feet, and stood staring in amazement, and perfectly heedless of the girl's appeal to him to hide, as two rough bricklayer-like men came in, followed by a woman.

' Will you let me pass ?' cried Mr Barclay.—' Miss Mimpriss, I beg your pardon for this intrusion. Forgive me, and good-night.'

One man gave the other a quick look, and as Mr Barclay tried to pass, they closed with him, and, in spite of his struggles, bore him back from the door. The next moment, though, he recovered his lost ground, and would have shaken himself free, but the sour-looking woman who had entered with the two men watched her opportunity, got behind, flung her arms about the young man's neck, and he was dragged heavily to the floor, where, as he lay half stunned, he saw Adela gazing at him with her brows knit; and then, without a word of protest, she hurried from the room.

Mr Barclay heaved himself up, and tried to rise; but one of his adversaries sat upon his chest while the other bound him hand and foot, an attempt at shouting for help being met by a pocket-handkerchief thrust into his mouth.

A minute later, as Mr Barclay lay staring wildly, the rough woman, whom he recalled now as one of the servants, and who had hurried from the room, returned, helping Adela to support a pallid-looking man, whose hands, face, and rough working clothes were daubed with clayey soil.

'Confound you! why didn't you bring down the brandy?' he said harshly.—'Gently, girls, gently. That's better. I'm half crushed.—Who's that?'

'Visitor,' said one of Mr Barclay's captors sourly. 'What's to be done?'

Mr Barclay looked wildly from one to the other, asking himself whether all this was some dream. Who were these men? Where the elderly Misses Mimpriss? And what was the meaning of Adela Mimpriss being on such terms with the injured man, who looked as if he had been working in some mine?

Their eyes met once, but she turned hers away directly, and held a glass of brandy to the injured man's lips.

'That's better,' he said. 'I can talk now. I thought I was going to be smothered once.—Well, lads, the game's up.'

'Why?' said one of the others sharply.

'Because it is. You won't catch me there again if I

know it; and here's private inquiry at work from over the way.'

'Hold your tongue!' said the first man of the party. 'There; he can't help himself now. You watch him, Bell; and if he moves, give warning.'

The rough woman seated herself beside Mr Barclay and watched him fiercely. The two men crossed over to their companion; while Adela, still looking cold and angry, with brow wrinkled up, drew back to stand against the table and listen.

The men spoke in a low tone; but Mr Barclay caught a word now and then, from which he gathered that, while the man who had in some way been hurt was for giving up, the other two angrily declared that a short time would finish it now, and that they would go on with it at all hazards.

'And what will you do with him?' said the injured man grimly.

Mr Barclay could not help looking sharply at Adela, who just then met his eye, but it was with a look more of curiosity than anything else; and as she realised that he was gazing at her reproachfully, she turned away and watched the three men.

'Very well,' said the one who was hurt, 'I wash my hands of what may follow.'

'All right.'

Mr Barclay turned cold as he wondered what was to happen next. He saw plainly enough now that the house had been let to a gang of men engaged upon some nefarious practice, but what it was he could not guess. Coining seemed to be the most likely thing; but from what he had heard and read, these men did not look like coiners.

Then a curious feeling of rage filled him, and the blood rushed to his brain as he lay reproaching himself for his folly. He had been attracted by this woman, who was evidently thoroughly in league with the man who spoke to her in a way which sent a jealous shudder through him, while the sisters of whom he had once or twice caught a glimpse, seemed to be absent, unless—— The thought which occurred to him seemed to be so wild that he drove it away, and lay waiting for what was to come next.

'Be off, girls!' said the first man suddenly; and without a word, the two women present left the room, Adela not so much as casting a glance in the direction of the prisoner.

The three men whispered together for a few moments, and then Mr Barclay made an effort to get up, but it was useless, for the first two seized him between them, all bound as he was, and dragged him out of the room, along the passage, and down the stone steps to the basement, where they thrust him into the wine-cellar, and half dragged him across there into the inner cellar, the houses on that side being exactly the same in construction as ours.

'Fetch a light,' said one of them; and this was done, when the speaker bent down and dragged the handkerchief from the prisoner's mouth.

'You scoundrel!' cried Mr Barclay.

'Keep a civil tongue in your head, my fine fellow,' he said.

'You shall suffer for this,' retorted Mr Barclay.

'P'r'aps so. But now, listen. If you like to shout, you can do so, only I tell you the truth: no one can hear you when you're shut in here; and if you do keep on making a noise, one of us may be tempted to come and silence you.'

'What do you want?—Money?'

'You to hold your tongue and be quiet. You behave yourself, and no harm shall come to you; but I warn you that if you attempt any games, look out, for you've desperate men to deal with. Now, then, will you take it coolly ?'

'Tell me first what this means,' said Mr Barclay.

'I shall tell you nothing. I only say this—will you take it coolly, and do what we want ?'

'I can't help myself,' says Mr Barclay.

'That's spoken like a sensible lad,' says the second man. —'Now, look here : you've got to stop for some days, perhaps, and you shall have enough to eat, and blankets to keep you warm.'

'But stop here—in this empty cellar ?'

'That's it, till we let you go. If you behave yourself, you shan't be hurt. If you don't behave yourself, you may get an ugly crack on the head to silence you. Now, then, will you be quiet ?'

'I tell you again, that I cannot help myself.'

'Shall I undo his hands ?' said one to the other.

'Yes ; you can loosen them.'

This was done, and directly after Mr Barclay sat thinking in the darkness, alone with as unpleasant thoughts as a man could have for company.

CHAPTER X.

A PECULIAR POSITION.

THE prisoner had been sitting upon the sawdust about an hour, when the door opened again, and the two men entered, one bearing a bundle of blankets and a couple of pillows, the other a tray with a large cup of hot coffee and a plate of bread and butter.

'There, you see we shan't starve you,' said the first man ;

'and you can make yourself a bed with these when you've done.'

'Will you leave me a light?'

'No,' says•the man with a laugh. 'Wild sort of lads like you are not fit to trust with lights. Good-night.'

The door of the inner cellar was closed and bolted, for it was not like ours, a simple arch; and then the outer cellar door was shut as well; and Mr Barclay sat for hours reproaching himself for his infatuation, before, wearied out, he lay down and fell asleep. How the time had gone, he could not tell, but he woke up suddenly, to find that there was a light in the cellar, and the two men were looking down at him.

'That's right—wake up,' says the principal speaker, 'and put on those.'

'But'—— began Mr Barclay, as the man pointed to some rough clothes.

'Put on those togs, confound you!' cried the fellow fiercely, 'or '——

He tapped the butt of a pistol; and there was that in the man's manner which showed that he was ready to use it.

There was nothing for it but to obey; and in a few minutes the prisoner stood up unbound and in regular workman's dress.

'That's right,' said his jailer. 'Now, come along; and I warn you once for all, that if you break faith and attempt to call out, you die, as sure as your name's Barclay Drinkwater!'

Mr Barclay felt as if he was stunned; and, half led, half pushed, he was taken into what had once been the pantry, but was now a curious-looking place, with a bricked round well in the middle, while on one side was fixed a large pair of blacksmith's forge bellows, connected with a zinc pipe which went right down into the well.

'What does all this mean?' he said. 'What are you going to do?'

'Wait, and you'll see,' was all the reply he could get; and he stared round in amazement at the heaps of new clay that had been dug out, the piles of old bricks which had evidently been obtained by pulling down partition walls somewhere in the house, the lower part of which seemed, as it were, being transformed by workmen. Lastly, there were oil-lamps and a pile of cement, the material for which was obtained from a barrel marked 'Flour.'

The man called Ned was better, and joined them there, the three being evidently prepared for work, in which Mr Barclay soon found that he was to participate, and at this point he made a stand.

'Look here,' he said; 'I demand an explanation. What does all this mean?'

'Are you ready for work?' cried the leader of the little gang, seizing him by the collar menacingly.

'You people have obtained possession of this house under false pretences, and you have made the place an utter wreck. I insist on knowing what it means.'

'You do—do you?' said the man, thrusting him back, and holding him with his shoulders against a pile of bricks. 'Then, once for all, I tell you this: you've got to work here along with us in silence, and hard too, or else be shut up in that cellar in darkness, and half-starved till we set you free.'

'The police shall'——

'Oh yes—all right. Tell the police. How are you going to do it?'

'Easily enough. I'll call for help, and'——

'Do,' said the man, taking a small revolver from his breast. 'Now, look here, Mr Drinkwater; men like us don't enter upon such an enterprise as this without being prepared for consequences. They would be very serious for us if they were found out. Nobody saw you come in where you were not asked, and when you came to insult my friend's wife.'

'Wife?' exclaimed Mr Barclay, for the word almost took his breath away.

'Yes, sir, wife; and it might happen that the gallant husband had an accident with you. We can dig holes, you see. Perhaps we might put somebody in one and cover him up.—Now, you understand. Behave yourself, and you shall come to no harm; but play any tricks, and—— Look here, my lads; show our new labourer what you have in your pockets.'

'Not now,' they said, tapping their breasts. 'He's going to work.'

Mr Barclay, as he used to say afterwards, felt as if he was in a dream, and without another word went down the ladder into the well, which was about ten feet deep, and found himself facing the opening of a regular egg-shaped drain, carefully bricked round, and seemingly securely though roughly made.

'Way to Tom Tiddler's ground,' said the man who had followed him. 'Now, then, take that light and this spade. I'll follow with a basket; and you've got to clear out the bricks and earth that broke loose yesterday.'

Mr Barclay looked in at the drain-like passage, which was just high enough for a man to crawl along easily, and saw that at one side a zinc pipe was carried, being evidently formed in lengths of about four feet, joined one to the other, but for what purpose, in his confused state, he could not make out.

What followed seemed like a part of a dream, in which, after crawling a long way, at first downwards, and then, with the passage sloping upwards, he found his farther

K

progress stopped by a quantity of loose stones and crumbled down earth, upon which, by the direction of the man who followed close behind, he set down a strong-smelling oil lamp, filled the basket pushed to him, and realised for the first time in his life what must be the life of a miner toiling in the bowels of the earth.

At first it was intensely hot, and the lamp burned dimly ; but soon after he could hear a low hissing noise, and a pleasant cool stream of air began to fill the place ; the heat grew less, the light burned more brightly, and he understood what was the meaning of the bellows and the long zinc tube.

For a full hour he laboured on, wondering at times, but for the most part feeling completely stunned by the novelty of his position. He filled baskets with the clay and bricks, and by degrees cleared away the heap before him, after which he had to give place to the man who had been injured, but who now crept by both the occupants of the passage, a feat only to be accomplished after they had both lain down upon their faces.

Then the prisoner's task was changed to that of passing bricks and pails of cement, sometimes being forced to hold the light while the man deftly fitted in bricks, and made up what had been a fall, and beyond which the passage seemed to continue ten or a dozen feet.

At intervals the gang broke off work to crawl backwards out of the passage to partake of meals which were spread for them in the library. These meals were good, and washed down with plenty of spirits and water, the two servant-like women and the so-called Adela waiting on the party, everything being a matter of wonder to the prisoner, who stared wildly at the well-dressed, lady-like, girlish creature who busied herself in supplying the wants of the gang of four bricklayer-like men.

At the first meal, Mr Barclay refused food. He said that he could not eat; but he drank heartily from the glass placed at his side—water which seemed to him to be flavoured with peculiar coarse brandy. But he was troubled with a devouring thirst, consequent upon his exertions, and that of which he had partaken seemed to increase the peculiar dreamy nature of the scene. Whether it was laudanum or some other drug, we could none of us ever say for certain; but Mr Barclay was convinced that, nearly all the time, he was kept under the influence of some narcotic, and that, in a confused dreamy way, he toiled on in that narrow culvert.

He could keep no account of time, for he never once saw the light of day, and though there were intervals for food and rest, they seemed to be at various times; and from the rarity with which he heard the faint rattle of some passing vehicle, he often thought that the greater part of the work must be done by night.

At first he felt a keen sense of trouble connected with what he looked upon as his disgrace and the way he had lowered himself; but at last he worked on like some machine, obedient as a slave, but hour by hour growing more stupefied, even to the extent of stopping short at times and kneeling before his half-filled basket motionless, till a rude thrust or a blow from a brickbat pitched at him roused him to continue his task.

The drug worked well for his taskmasters, and the making of the mine progressed rapidly, for every one connected therewith seemed in a state of feverish anxiety now to get it done.

And so day succeeded day, and night gave place to night. The two servant-like women went busily on with their work, and fetched provisions for the household consumption, no tradespeople save milkman and baker being allowed to call, and they remarked that they never once found the area gate unlocked. And while these two women, prim and self-contained, went on with the cooking and housework and kept the doorstep clean, the so-called Miss Adela Mimpriss went on with the woolwork flowers at the dining-room window, where she could get most light, and the world outside had no suspicion of anything being wrong in the staid, old-fashioned house opposite Sir John Drinkwater's. Even the neighbours on either side heard no sound.

'What does it all mean?' Mr Barclay used to ask himself, and at other times, 'When shall I wake?' for he often persuaded himself that this was the troubled dream of a bad attack of fever, from which he would awaken some day quite in his right mind. Meanwhile, growing every hour more machine-like, he worked on and on always as if in a dream.

CHAPTER XI.

CONCLUSION.

I STOOD watching Sir John, who seemed nearly mad with grief and rage, and a dozen times over my lips opened to speak, but without a sound being heard. At last he looked up at me and saw what I wanted to do, but which respect kept back.

'Well,' he said, 'what do you propose doing?'

I remained silent for a moment, and then, feeling that even if he was offended, I was doing right, I said to him what was in my heart.

'Sir John, I never married, and I never had a son. It's all a mystery to me.'

'Man, you are saved from a curse!' he cried fiercely.

'No, dear master, no,' I said, as I laid my hand upon his arm. 'You don't believe that. I only wanted to say that if I had had a boy—a fine, handsome, brave lad like Mr Barclay'——

'Fine!—brave!' he says contemptuously.

'Who had never done a thing wrong, or been disobedient in any way till he fell into temptation that was too strong for him'——

'Bah! I could have forgiven that. But for him to have turned thief!'

I was silent, for his words seemed to take away my breath.

'Man, man!' he cried, 'how could you be such an idiot as to write that document and leave it where it could be found?'

'I did it for the best, sir,' I said humbly.

'Best? The worst,' he cried. 'No, no; I cannot forgive. Disgrace or no disgrace, I must have in the police.'

'No, no, no!' I cried piteously. 'He is your own son, Sir John, your own son; and it is that wretched woman who has driven him mad.'

'Mad? Burdon, mad? No; it is something worse.'

'But it is not too late,' I said humbly.

'Yes, too late—too late! I disown him. He is no longer son of mine.'

'And you sit there in that dining-room every night, Sir John,' I said, 'with all us servants gathered round, and read that half a chapter and then say, "As we forgive them that trespass against us." Sir John—master—he is your own son, and I love him as if he was my own.'

There wasn't a sound in that place for a minute, and then he drew his breath in a catching way that startled

me, for it was as if he was going to have a fit. But his
face was very calm and stern now, as he says to me gently:
'You are right, old friend'—and my heart gave quite a
bound—'old friend.'

'Let's go to him and save him, master, from his sin.'

'Two weak old men, Burdon, and him strong, desperate,
and taken by surprise. My good fellow, what would
follow then?'

'I don't know, Sir John. I can only see one thing,
and that is, that we should have done our duty by the
lad. Let's leave the rest to Him.'

He drew a long deep breath.

'Yes,' he says. 'Come along.'

We went back in the darkness to the cellar door and
listened; but all seemed very still, and I turned the key
in the patent Bramah lock without a sound. We went
in, and stood there on the sawdust, with that hot smell
of burnt oil seeming to get stronger, and there was a faint
light in the inner cellar now, and a curious rustling, panting
sound. We crept forward, one on each side of the opening;
and as we looked in, my hand went down on one of the
sherry bottles in the bin by my arm, and it made a faint
click, which sounded quite loud.

I forgot all about Sir John; I didn't even know that
he was there, as I stared in from the darkness at the
scene before me. They—I say they, for the whispering
had taught me that there was more than one—had got
the stone up while we had been away. It had been pushed
aside on to the sawdust, and a soft yellow light shone up
now out of the hole, showing me my young master, looking
so strange and staring-eyed and ghastly, that I could hardly
believe it was he. But it was, sure enough, though dressed
in rough workman's clothes, and stained and daubed with
clay.

It wasn't that, though, which took my attention, but
his face; and as I looked, I thought of what had been
said a little while ago in my place, and I felt it was true,
and that he was mad. He had just crept up out of the
hole, when he uttered a low groan and sank down on his
knees, and then fell sidewise across the hole in the floor.
He was not there many moments before there was a low
angry whispering; he seemed to be heaved up, and a big
workman-looking fellow came struggling up till he sat on
the sawdust with his legs in the hole, and spoke down to
some one.

'It's all right,' he said. 'The chests are here; but the
fool has fainted away. Quick! the lamp, and then the
tools.'

He bent down and took a smoky oil lamp that was
handed to him, and I drew a deep breath, for the sound
of his voice had seemed familiar; but the light which
shone on his face made me sure in spite of his rough
clothes and the beard he had grown. It was Edward
Gunning, our old servant, who was discharged for being
too fond of drink, turned bricklayer once again.

As he took the lamp, he got up, held it above his head,
looked round, and then, with a grin of satisfaction at
the sight of the chests, stepped softly toward the opening
into the outer cellar, where Sir John and I were watching.

It didn't take many moments, and I hardly know now
how it happened, but I just saw young Mr Barclay lying
helpless on the sawdust, another head appearing at the
hole, and then, with the light full upon it, Edward
Gunning's face being thrust out of the opening into the
cellar where we were, and his eyes gleaming curiously
before they seemed to shut with a snap. For, all at once—
perhaps it was me being a butler and so used to wine—my
hand closed upon the neck of one of those bottles, which

rose up sudden-like above my head, and came down with a crash upon that of this wretched man.

There was a crash; the splash of wine; the splintering of glass; the smell of sherry—fine old sherry, yellow seal— and I stood for a moment with the bottle neck and some sawdust in my hand, startled by the yell the man gave, by the heavy fall, and the sudden darkness which had come upon us.

Then—I suppose it was all like a flash—I had rushed to the inner cellar and was dragging the slab over the hole, listening the while to a hollow rustling noise which ended as I got the slab across and sat on it to keep it down.

'Where are you, Burdon?' says Sir John.

'Here, sir!—Quick! A light!'

I heard him hurry off; and it seemed an hour before he came back, while I sat listening to a terrible moaning, and smelling the spilt sherry and the oily knocked-out lamp. Then Sir John came in, quite pale, but looking full of fight, and the first thing he did was to stoop down over Edward Gunning and take a pistol from his breast. 'You take that, Burdon,' he said, 'and use it if we are attacked.'

'Which we sha'nt be, Sir John, if you help me to get this stone back in its place.'

He set the lamp on one of the chests and lent a hand, when the stone dropped tightly into its place; and we dragged a couple of chests across, side by side, before turning to young Mr Barclay, who lay there on his side as if asleep.

'Now,' says Sir John, as he laid his hand upon the young man's collar and dragged him over on to his back, 'I think we had better hand this fellow over to the police.'

'The doctor, you mean, sir. Look at him.'

I needn't have bade him look, for Sir John was already doing that.

It was a doctor that I fetched, and not the police, for Mr Barclay lay there quite insensible, and smelling as if he had taken to eating opium, while Ned Gunning had so awful a cut across his temple that he would soon have bled to death.

The doctor came and dressed the rascal's wounds as he was laid in my pantry; but he shook his head over Mr Barclay, and with reason; for two months had passed away before we got him down to Dorking, and saw his pale face beginning to get something like what it was, with Miss Virginia, forgiving and gentle, always by his side.

But I'm taking a very big jump, and saying nothing about our going across to the house opposite as soon as it was daylight, to find the door open and no one there; while the state of that basement and what we saw there, and the artfulness of the people, and the labour they had given in driving that passage right under the road as true as a die, filled me with horror, and cost Sir John five hundred pounds.

Why, their measurements and calculations were as true as true; and if it hadn't been for me missing that paper— which, of course, it was Edward Gunning who stole it— those scoundrels would have carried off that golden incubus as sure as we were alive. But they didn't get it; and they had gone off scot-free, all but our late footman, who had concussion of the brain in the hospital where he was took, Sir John saying that he would let the poor wretch get well before he handed him over to the police.

'But, bless you, he never meant to. He was too pleased to get Mr Barclay back, and to find that he hadn't the least idea about the golden incubus being in the cellar; while as to the poor lad's sorrow about his madness and that wretched woman, who was Ned Gunning's wife, it was pitiful to see.

The other scoundrels had got away; and all at once we found that Gunning had discharged himself from the hospital; and by that time the house over the way was put straight, the builder telling me in confidence that he thought Sir John must have been mad to attempt to make such a passage as that to connect his property without consulting a regular business man. That was the morning when he got his cheque for the repairs, and the passage—which he called 'Drinkwater's Folly'—had disappeared.

Time went on, and the golden incubus went on too—that is, to a big bank in the Strand, for we were at Dorking now, where those young people spent a deal of time in the open air; and Mr Barclay used to say he could never forgive himself; but his father did, and so did some one else.

Who did?

Why, you don't want telling that. Heaven bless her sweet face! And bless him, too, for a fine young fellow! as strong—ay, and as weak, too, of course—as any man.

Dear, dear, dear! I'm pretty handy to eighty now, and Sir John just one year ahead; and I often say to myself, as I think of what men will do for the sake of a pretty face—likewise for the sake of gold: 'This is a very curious world.'

IN A GOWT.

LOOKS ominous, don't it, to see nearly every gate-post and dyke-bridge made of old ships' timber? Easy enough to tell that, from its bend, and the tree-nail holes. Ours is a bad coast, you see; not rocky, but with long sloping sands; and when the sea's high, and there's a gale on shore, a vessel strikes, and there she lies, with the waves lifting her bodily, and then letting her fall again upon the sands, shaking her all to pieces: first the masts go, then a seam opens somewhere in her sides, and as every wave lifts her and lets her down, she shivers and loosens, till she as good as falls all to pieces, and the shore gets strewn with old wreck.

Good wrecks used to be little fortunes to the folk along shore, but that's all altered now; the coastguard look out too sharp. Things are wonderfully changed to what they were when I was a boy. Fine bit of smuggling going on in those days; hardly a farmer along the coast but had a finger in it, and ran cargoes right up to the little towns inland. The coast was not so well watched, and people were bribed easier, I suppose; but, at all events, that sort of thing has almost died out now.

Never had a brush with the coastguard or the cutter in my time, for we were all on the cut-and-run system: but I had a narrow escape for my life once, when a boat's crew came down upon us, and I'll tell you how it was.

We were a strong party of us down on the shore off our point here at Merthorpe, busy as could be; night calm, and still, and dark, and one of those fast-sailing French boats—*chasse-marées*, they call them—landing a cargo. Carts, and packhorses, and boats were all at it; and the kegs of brandy, and barrels of tobacco, and parcels of lace were coming ashore in fine style; I and another in a little boat kept making trips backwards and forwards between the shore and the *chasse-marée*, landing brandy-tubs—nice little brandy-kegs, you know, with a V.C.—*Vieux Cognac* —branded on each.

I don't know how many journeys I had made, when all at once there was an alarm given, and as it were right out of the darkness, I could see a man-of-war's boat coming right down upon us, while, before I quite got over the first fright, there was another in sight.

Such a scrimmage—such a scamper; boats scattering in all directions; the French boat getting up a sail or two, and all confusion; whips cracking, wheels ploughing through the soft sand, and horses galloping off to get to the other side of the sandbank. We were close aside the long, low *chasse-marée*, in our bit of a skiff thing, when the alarm was given, and pushed off hard for the shore, which was about two hundred yards distant, while on all sides there were other boats setting us the example, or following in our wake; in front of us there was a heavy cart backed as far out into the sea as she would stand, with the horses turned restive and jibbing, for there was a heavy load behind them, and the more the driver lashed them, the more the brutes backed out in the shallow water, while every moment the wheels kept sinking farther into the sand.

I saw all this as the revenue cutter's boats separated, one

making for the *chasse-marée*, and the other dashing after
the flying long-shore squadron ; and as I dragged at my oar,
I had the pleasure of seeing that we must either be soon
overhauled, or else leap out into the shallow water, and run
for it, and I said so to my companion.

'Oh, hang it, no,' he cried ; 'pull on. They 'll stave in
the boat, and we shall lose all the brandy.'

I did pull on, for I was so far from being loyal, that I
was ready to run any risk sooner than lose the little cargo
we had of a dozen brandy-kegs, and about the same number
of packages ; but there seemed not the slightest prospect of
our getting off, unless we happened to be unobserved in the
darkness. However, I pulled on, and keeping off to the
right, we had the satisfaction of seeing the revenue boat
row straight on, as if not noticing us.

'Keep off a little now,' I whispered, 'or we shall be
ashore.'

'No, no—it 's all right,' was the reply ; 'we are just over
the swatch ;' which is the local term given to the long
channels washed out in the sand by the tide, here and
there forming deep trenches along the coast, very dangerous
for bathers.

'They see us,' I whispered ; when my companion backed
water, and the consequence was, that the boat's head
turned right in-shore, and we floated between the piles,
and were next moment, with shipped oars, out of sight in
the outlet of the gowt.

Now, I am not prepared to give the derivation of the
word 'gowt,' but I can describe what it is—namely, the
termination, at the sea-coast, of the long Lincolnshire land-
drains, in the shape of a lock with gates, which are opened
at certain times, to allow the drainage to flow under the
sand into the sea, but carefully closed when the tide is up,
to prevent flooding of the marsh-lands, protected by the

high sea-bank, which runs along the coast, and acts the part of cliffs. From these lock-gates, a square woodwork tunnel is formed by means of piles driven into the shore, and crossed with stout planks; and this covered water-way in some cases runs for perhaps two hundred yards right beneath the sandbank, then beneath the sand, and has its outlet some distance down the shore; while, to prevent the air blowing the tunnel up when the sea comes in, a couple of square wooden pipes descend at intervals of some fifty yards through the sand into the water-way; at high water, when the mouth is covered, and the lock-gates closed, the air comes bellowing and roaring up these pipes as every wave comes in; and at times, when the tunnel is pretty full, the water will, after chasing the air, rush out after it, and form a spray fountain; while, as the waves recede, the wind rushes back with a strange whistling sound, and a draught that draws anything down into the tunnel with a fierce rush. But there was another peculiarity of the hollow way that was strangely impressed upon my memory that night—namely, its power of acting as a vast speaking-tube, for if a person stood at one of the escape-pipes and whispered, his words were distinctly audible to another at the other pipe some fifty yards off, who could as easily respond.

Well, it was into the mouth of the gowt tunnel that we had now run the boat, where we were concealed from view certainly; and thrusting against the piles with his hands, my companion worked the boat farther into the darkness, until the keel touched the soft sand.

'That's snug,' he whispered : 'they'll never find us here.'

'No,' I said, as a strange fear came upon me. 'But isn't the tide rising?'

'Fast,' he said.

'Then we shall be stopped from getting out.'

'Nonsense!' he said. 'It will take an hour to rise above the tunnel-mouth, and if it did, we could run her head up higher and higher. Plenty of fresh air through the pipes.'

'If we 're not drowned,' I said.

'There, if you want to lose the cargo, we 'll pull out at once, and give up,' he said.

'But I don't,' I replied; 'I am staunch enough; only I don't want to risk my life.'

'Well, who does?' he said. 'Only keep still, and we shall be all right.'

The few minutes we had been conversing had been long enough for the tide to float the boat once more, and this time I raised my hand to the roof, and thrusting against the tunnel-covered, weed-hung, slimy woodwork, soon had the boat's keel again in the sand, so as to prevent her being sucked out by the reflux of the tide. At times we could hear shouts, twice pistol-shots, and then we were startled by the dull, heavy report of a small cannon.

'That 's after the *chasse-marée*,' whispered my companion; 'but she sails like a witch. She 's safe unless they knock a spar away.'

'I wish *we* were,' I said, for I did not feel at all comfortable in our dark hole, up which we were being forced farther and farther by the increasing tide; while more than once we had to hold on tightly by the horrible slimy piles, to keep from being drawn back.

'Just the place to find dead bodies,' whispered my companion, evidently to startle me.

'Just so,' I said coldly. 'Perhaps they 'll find two to-morrow.'

'Don't croak,' was the polite rejoinder; and then he was silent; but I could hear a peculiar boring noise being made, and no further attempts at a joke issued from my friend's lips.

'Suppose we try and get out now?' I whispered, after another quarter of an hour's listening in the darkness, and hearing nothing but the soft rippling, and the 'drip, drip' of water beyond us; while towards the mouth came the 'lap, lap' of the waves against the sides of the tunnel, succeeded by a rushing noise, and the rattling of the loose mussels clustering to the woodwork, now loudly, now gently; while every light rustle of the seaweed seemed to send a shiver through me.

The noise as of boring had ceased some time, and my friend now drew my attention to one of the kegs, which he had made a hole through with his knife; and never before did spirits come so welcome as at that moment.

'Better try and get out now,' whispered my companion.

'They must be somewhere handy, though one can't see even their boat,' said a strange voice, which seemed hollow and echoing along the tunnel, while the rattling of the shells and lapping of the water grew louder.

All at once I raised my head, as if to feel for the hole down which the sound of the voice came, when, to my alarm, I struck it heavily against the top of the tunnel, making it bleed against the shelly surface.

'Wait a bit,' said my companion thickly; 'they're on the look-out yet; it's madness to go out.' And I then heard a noise which told me that he was trying to drown consciousness in the liquor to which he had made his way.

However, it seemed to me madness to stay where we were, to be drowned like rats in a hole; and taking advantage of the next receding wave, I gave the boat a start, and she went down towards the mouth of the tunnel for a little way, when a coming current would have driven her back, only I clung to the roof, now very low down, and rather close to which the boat now floated. Another thrust, and I pushed her some distance down ; but with the next wave that came in, my hand was jammed against the slimy roof, and, unnerved with horror, I gasped : 'Rouse up, Harry ! the mouth's under water !'

Hollowly sounded my voice as the wave sank, and I felt once more free, and in sheer despair forced the boat lower down the tunnel ; but this time, when the tide came in again, I had to lie right back, the boat rose so high, and I felt the dripping seaweed hanging from the roof sweep coldly and slimily over my face ; when, before the next wave could raise us, I thrust eagerly at the side, forcing the boat inward again, but in the fear and darkness, got her across the tunnel, so that head and stern were wedged, and as the next rush of water came, it smote the boat heavily, and made her a fixture, so that in spite of my efforts, I could not move her either way.

Wash came the water again and again, and at every dash a portion came into the boat, drenching me to the skin ; while I now became aware that Harry Hodson was lying stupefied across the kegs, and breathing heavily.

I made one more effort to move the boat, but it was tighter than ever ; and after conquering an insane desire to dive out, and try and swim to the mouth, I let myself cautiously down on the inner side, and stood, with the water breast-high, clinging to the gunwale. The next moment it rose above my mouth, lifting me from my feet, and as it rushed back, sucked my legs beneath the boat ; but I gained my feet again, and began to wade inward.

Yet strong upon me as was the desire for life, I could not leave my companion to his fate in so cowardly a way ; so I turned back, and this time swimming, I reached the boat, now nearly full of water ; and half dragging, half lifting, I got his body over the side, and holding on by his collar, tried once more for bottom.. But it was a horrible time there in the dense black darkness—a darkness that, in my distempered brain, seemed to be peopled with hideous forms, swimming, crawling, and waiting to devour us, or fold us in their slimy coils. The dripping water sounded hollow and echoing; strange whispers and cries seemed floating around; the mussels rustled together: and ever louder and louder came the 'lap, lap, lapping' of the water as it rushed in and dashed against the sides and ceiling of the horrible place.

I was now clinging with one hand to the boat's side, while with the other I held tightly by Hodson's collar; but though I waited till the wave receded before I tried the bottom, it was not to be touched; so, shuddering and horror-stricken, I waited the coming wave, and struck off, swimming with all my might. It was only a minute's task; but when, after twice trying, my feet touched the bottom, I was panting heavily, and so nervous, that I had to lean, trembling and shaking, against the side. But I had a tight hold of Hodson, whose head I managed to keep above water; and it was not until warned of my danger by the rising tide, and the difficulty I found in keeping my feet, that I again essayed to press forward.

Just then, something cold and wet swept across my face, and dashing out my arms to keep off some monster of the deep, my hands came in contact with a round body which beat against my breast, and in my horror, as I dashed away, I was some paces ere the dragging at my limb told me that I had left my comrade to his fate. The next moment, however, he was swept up to me; and once more clutching his collar, and keeping his head above water, I waded slowly along the tunnel, when again I nearly lost my hold, for the same wet slimy body swept across my face; but raising my hand, I only dashed away one of the long strands of bladder-weed which hung thickly from the cross timbers of the roof.

It was no hard matter to bear my companion along with me, for I had only to keep his head up, his body floating along the surface, but my foothold was uncertain, for now the bottom was slimy, and my feet sunk in the ooze deeper and deeper, for I was nearing the gates through which the fresh water of the marshes was let in; and though the water was now only to my middle, I made my way with difficulty, for there was a perceptible current against me.

Breathing would have been easy, had it not been for my excitement; and now a horrid dread seemed to check the very act, for all at once I heard a heavy reverberating noise, and the thought struck me that they were opening the gates, and in another instant the fearful rush of fresh water would come bearing all before it—even our lives.

In the agony of the moment I uttered a wild unearthly shriek—so fearful a cry, that I shrank against the side afterwards, and clung to a slimy post, trembling to hear the strange whispering echoes, as the cry reverberated along the place, and mingled with the lapping rush of the water, the dripping from the roof, and a loud sound as of a little waterfall in front.

Now came again the shape of something round swimming up against me, and as it struck my side, I beat at it savagely, though I smiled at my foolish fear the next moment, for it was one of the brandy-kegs washed out of the boat. But horror still seemed to hold me, as I waded on farther and farther, till once more the water began to deepen, and the ooze at the bottom grew softer; so I stopped, listening to the heavy rushing of water in front, where the drainage escaped, and washed heavily down, deepening the tunnel at the foot of the doors; while in that hollow, cavernous place, growing smaller moment by moment, the rushing sound was something hideous. Danger in front, for the great gates might at any time be opened; and danger behind, where the tide was coming in ceaselessly, and deepening the water around me with its regular beating throb, minute by minute. Thoughts of the past and present seemed to surge through my brain, so that I grew bewildered, and had any chance of escape presented itself, I could not have seized it, though I could not but tell myself that escape was impossible. A few minutes—ten, twenty, thirty perhaps, and the black darkness seemed to be growing blacker.

'I must be free,' I muttered; and dragging Hodson's handkerchief from his neck, I bound it to my own, and then making them fast beneath his arms, felt among the woodwork till I could find a place where I could pass them through, so that I could secure him from slipping down, or being swept away by the ebbing and flowing of the water.

I was not long in finding a place; but then the hand-kerchiefs were not long enough, and I had to add one from my pocket; then I left the poor fellow quite insens-ible and half-hanging from one of the timbers. And now I waded about, searching for the mouth of the air-pipe, in the hope of shouting up it for succour, since I felt convinced that the tide would effectually fill the tunnel, while the very thought of the gates being opened half-maddened me; and heedless now of who might hear me, so that they brought succour, I hunted aimlessly about, yelling and shrieking for aid.

It was a fearful struggle between reason and dread; and for ever dread kept getting the upper hand: now it was a floating keg again and again making me dash away; now one of the packages hurried in by the tide; while the strange drippings and hollow whisperings were magnified into an infinity of horrors. Every monster with which imagination has peopled the sea seemed to be there to attack me—strange serpent or lizard like beasts, slimy and scaled, thronging along the ceiling or up the sides, swimming around me, or burrowing through the sand. More than once I actually touched some swimming object, but the contact was momentary, and the stranger darted off. Then reason would gain supremacy for a while; and trying to cool my throbbing brow with the water, I thought of my position, whispered a few prayers, and endeavoured to compose myself. There was even now a doubt: the tide might not rise high enough to cover me; certainly it was now at my breast, and I was standing with difficulty in the shallowest place I could pick. The next moment, as the waves receded, it would fall to my waist; but again it was up to my chest, and in spite of gleams of hope, despair whispered truly that it was now higher up my chest than before. True; but one wave in so many always came higher than the others. The tide might still be at its height, and this be that particular wave.

I moved again and again, but ever with the same result; and at last, despairingly, I was clinging to a shell-covered piece of timber at the side, with the water at my chin.

A noise, a clanking noise as of chains rattling and iron striking iron; and now hope fled, for I knew that this must be the opening of the doors of the gowt; but, to my surprise, no rush of water followed; only a little came, which lapped against my lips, while a rush of air smote my forehead.

Voices, shouts, and Hodson's name uttered; but I could not shout in reply. Then my own name; and I gave some inarticulate cry by way of answer, while once more reason seemed to get the better of the dread, for I knew that the far doors of the gowt had not been opened, and that they kept up the drainage, while the pair nearest to me had only had the pressure upon them of the water escaping from the first. And now a good bold swim, and

I could have been in the big pit-like opening between the two pairs of gates; but the spirit was gone, the nerve was absent, and still clinging to the shelly piece of timber, I closed my eyes, for I felt that, near as rescue seemed, I could do nothing to aid it. As for Hodson, in this time of dread, I had forgotten him—forgotten all but the great horror of the water lap, lap, lapping at my lip, and occasionally receding, its fizzing spray in my nostrils.

Higher and higher, covering my lip; but by a desperate effort I raised myself a few inches, but only to go through the same agonies again, as the water still crept up and up, slowly but surely, while in this my last struggle my head touched the top timbers, the weed washed and swept over it, and as I forced my fingers round the timber to which I clung, my body floated in the water.

Another minute, and I felt that all was over, for the water covered my face once, twice; and half strangled, I waited gasping for the third time; but it came not. Half a minute passed, and then again it washed over my face, seeming as if it would never leave it; but at last it was gone, and too unnerved to hope, I awaited its return, but it came not.

I dared not hope yet, till I felt that the water was perceptibly lower, and then the reaction was so fearful that I could hardly retain my hold till the tide had sunk so that once more I could stand, when my shouts for help brought assistance to me through the gowt, for they lowered down a little skiff with ropes, and I was brought out as nearly dead as my poor companion.

That night's work sprinkled my hair with gray, and was my last experience with the smuggling business. The loss was heavy; but I had escaped with life, while poor Hodson was followed to the grave by some score the following Sunday.

A FIGHT WITH A STORM.

I GOT first to be mate when quite a youngish fellow; the owners were told somehow or other that I'd worked hard on the last voyage, and they made me mate of the ship, and gave me a good silver watch and chain; a watch that went to the bottom of the sea five years after in a wreck off the Irish coast, by Wexford, when I and six more swam ashore, saving our lives, and thankful for them. For the sea swallows up a wonderful store of wealth every season; and it meant to have our ship, too, that year I was made mate, only we escaped it.

It happened like this. We were bound for Cadiz in a large, handsome, new brig, having on board a rich cargo; for besides a heavy value in gold, we had a lot of valuable new machinery, that had been made for the Spanish government by one of our large manufacturers somewhere inland. But besides this, there was a vast quantity of iron, in long, heavy, cast pillars. A huge weight they were, and we all shook our heads at them as they were lowered down into the hold, for we thought of what a nice cargo they would turn out, if we should have a heavy passage. We had about a score of passengers, too, and amongst them was a fine gentlemanly fellow, going out with his wife, and he was to superintend the fitting up of the machinery, several of the other passengers being his men.

She was a new, well-found vessel, and fresh in her paint; and with her clean canvas, and all smart, we were rather proud of that boat. But we'd only just got beyond the Lizard when it came on to blow, just as it can blow off there in February, with rain, and snow, and hail; and we were at last glad to scud before the gale under bare poles.

Night and day, then, night and day following one another fast, with the hatches battened down, and the ship labouring so that it seemed as if every minute must be her last. She was far too heavily laden; and instead of her being a ship to float out the fiercest storms, here we were loaded down, so that she lay rolling and pitching in a way that her seams began to open, and soon every hand had to take his turn at the pumps.

The days broke heavy and cloudy, and the nights came on with the darkness awful, and the gale seeming to get fiercer and fiercer, till at last, worn out, sailors and passengers gave up, the pumps were abandoned, and refusing one and all to stay below, men and women were clustered together, getting the best shelter they could.

'I don't like to see a good new ship go to the bottom like this,' I shouted in one of my mates' ears, and he shouted back something about iron; and I nodded, for we all knew that those great pillars down below were enough to sink the finest vessel that ever floated.

Just then I saw the skipper go below, while the gentleman who was going out to superintend was busy lashing one of the life-buoys to his wife.

'That ain't no good,' I shouted to him, going up on hands and knees, for the sea at times was enough to wash you overboard, as she dipped and rolled as though she would send her masts over the side every moment. But I got to where they were holding on at last; and seeing that, landsman-like, he knew nothing of knotting and lashing, I made the life-buoy fast, just as a great wave leaped over the bows, and swept the ship from stem to stern.

As soon as I could get my breath, I looked round, to find that where the mate and three passengers were standing a minute before, was now an empty space; while on running to the poop, and looking over, there was nothing to be seen but the fierce rushing waters.

I got back to where those two were clinging together, and though feeling selfish, as most men would, I couldn't help thinking how sad it would be for a young handsome couple like them to be lost, for I knew well enough that though she was lashed to the life-buoy, the most that would do would be to keep her afloat till she died of cold and exhaustion.

'Can nothing be done?' Mr Vallance—for that was his name—shouted in my ear.

'Well,' I said, shouting again, 'if I was captain, I should run all risks, and get some of that iron over the side.'

'Why don't he do it, then?' he exclaimed; and of course, being nobody on board that ship, I could only shake my head.

Just then Mrs Vallance turned upon me such a pitiful look, as she took tighter hold of her husband—a look that seemed to say to me: 'Oh, save him, save him!' And I don't know how it was, but feeling that something ought to be done, I crept along once more to the captain's cabin, and going down, there, in the dim light, I could see him sitting on a locker, with a bottle in his hand,

and a horrible wild stupid look on his face, which told me in a moment that he wasn't a fit man to have been trusted with the lives of forty people in a good new ship. Then I stood half-bewildered for a few moments, but directly after I was up on deck, and alongside of Mr Vallance.

'Will you stand by me, sir,' I says, 'if I'm took to task for what I do?'

'What are you going to do?' he says.

'Shy that iron over the side.'

'To the death, my man!'

'Then lash her fast where she is,' I said, nodding to Mrs Vallance; 'and, in God's name, come on.'

I saw the poor thing's arms go tight round his neck, and though I couldn't hear a word she said, I knew it meant: 'Don't leave me;' but he just pointed upwards a moment, kissed her tenderly; and then, I helping, we made her fast, and the next minute were alongside the hatches, just over where I knew the great pillars to lie.

I knew it was a desperate thing to do, but it was our only chance; and after swinging round the fore-yard, and rigging up some tackle, the men saw what was meant, and gave a bit of a cheer. Then they clustered together, passengers and men, while I shouted to Mr Vallance, offering him his choice—to go below with another, to make fast the rope to the pillars, or to stay on deck.

He chose going below; and warning him that we should clap on the hatches from time to time, to keep out the water, I got hold of a marlinespike, loosened the tarpaulin a little, had one hatch off, and then stationed two on each side, to try and keep the opening covered every time a wave came on board.

It seemed little better than making a way in for the
sea to send us to the bottom at once; but I knew that
it was our only hope, and persevered. Mr Vallance and
one of the men went below, the tackle was lowered,
and in less time than I expected, they gave the signal
to haul up. We hauled—the head of the pillar came
above the coamings, went high up, then lowered down
till one end rested on the bulwarks; the rope was cast
off; and then, with a cheer, in spite of the rolling of
the ship, it was sent over the side to disappear in the
boiling sea.

Another, and another, and another, weighing full six
hundredweight apiece, we had over the side, the men
working now fiercely, and with something like hope in
their breasts; and then I roared to them to hold fast:
the tarpaulin was pulled over, and I for one threw myself
upon it, just as a wave came rolling along, leaped the
bows, and dashed us here and there.

But we found to our great joy that hardly a drop had
gone below, the weight of the water having flattened down
the tarpaulin; so seizing the tackle once more, we soon
had another pillar over the side, and another, and another
—not easily, for it was a hard fight each time; and more
than once men were nearly crushed to death. It was
terrible work, too, casting them loose amidst the hurry
and strife of the tempest; but we kept on, till, utterly
worn out and panting, we called on Mr Vallance to come
up, when we once more securely battened down the hatch
and waited for the morning.

We agreed amongst ourselves that the ship did not
roll so much; and perhaps she was a little easier, for
we had sent some tons overboard; but the difference
was very little; and morning found us all numbed with
the cold, and helpless .to a degree. I caught Mr Vallance's

eye, and signalled to him that we should go on again; but it required all we could do to get the men to work, one and all saying that it was useless, and only fighting against our fate.

Seeing that fair words wouldn't do, I got the tackle ready myself, and then with the marlinespike in one hand, I went up to the first poor shivering fellow I came to, and half-led, half-dragged him to his place; Mr Vallance followed suit with another; and one way and another we got them to work again; and though not so quickly as we did the day before, we sent over the side tons and tons of that solid iron—each pillar on being cut loose darting over the bulwark with a crash, and tearing no end of the planking away, but easing the vessel, so that now we could feel the difference; and towards night, though the weather was bad as ever, I began to feel that we might have a chance; for the ship seemed to ride over the waves more, instead of dipping under them, and shuddering from stem to stern. We'd been fortunate, too, in keeping the water from getting into the hold; and one way and another, what with the feeling of duty done, and the excitement, things did not look so black as before; when all at once a great wave like a green mountain of water leaped aboard over the poop, flooded the deck, tore up the tarpaulin and another hatch, and poured down into the hold, followed by another and another; and as I clung to one of the masts, blinded and shaking with the water, I could feel that in those two minutes all our two days' work had been undone.

'God help us!' I groaned, for I felt that I had done wrong in opening the hatches; but there was no time for repining. Directly the waves had passed on, rushing out at the sides, where they had torn away the bulwarks,

I ran to the mouth of the hold, for I felt that Mr Vallance and the poor fellow with him must have been drowned.

I shouted—once, twice, and then there was a groan; when, seizing hold of the tackle that we had used to hoist the pillars, I was lowered down, and began to swim in the rushing water that was surging from side to side, when I felt myself clutched by a drowning man, and holding on to him, we were dragged up together.

But I did not want the despairing look Mrs Vallance gave me to make me go down again, and this time I was washed up against something, which I seized; but there seemed no life in it when we were hauled up, for the poor fellow did not move, and it was pitiful to see the way in which his poor wife clung to him.

Another sea coming on board, it was all we could do to keep from being swept off; and as the water seemed to leap and plunge down the hatch with a hollow roar, a chill came over me again, colder than that brought on by the bitter weather. I was so worn out that I could hardly stir; but it seemed that if I did not move, no one else would; so shouting to one or two to help me, I crawled forward, and got the hatches on again, just as another wave washed over us; but before the next came, with my marlinespike I had contrived to nail down the tarpaulin once more, in the hope that, though waterlogged, we might float a little longer.

It seemed strange, but after a little provision had been served round, I began to be hopeful once more, telling myself that, after all, water was not worse than iron, and that if we lived to the next day, we might get clear of our new enemy without taking off the hatches.

We had hard work, though, with Mr Vallance, who lay for hours without seeming to show a sign of life; but towards morning, from the low sobbing murmur I heard close by me, and the gentle tones of a man's voice, I knew that they must have brought him round. You see, I was at the wheel then, for it had come round to my turn, and as soon as I could get relieved, I went and spoke to them, and found him able to sit up.

As day began to break, the wind seemed to lull a little, and soon after a little more, and again a little more, till, with joyful heart, I told all about me that the worst was over; and it was so, for the wind shifted round to the south and west, and the sea went down fast. Soon, too, the sun came out; and getting a little sail on the ship, I began to steer, as near as I could tell, homewards, hoping before long to be able to make out our bearings, which I did soon after, and then got the passengers and crew once more in regular spells at the pumps.

We were terribly full of water; and as the ship rolled the night before, it was something awful to hear it rush from side to side of the hold, threatening every minute to force up the decks; but now keeping on a regular drain, the scuppers ran well, and hour by hour we rose higher and higher, and the ship, from sailing like a tub, began to answer her helm easily, and to move through the water.

It was towards afternoon that, for the first time, I remembered the captain, just, too, as he made his appearance on deck, white-looking, and ill, but now very angry and important.

I had just sent some of the men aloft, and we were making more sail, when in a way that there was no need for, he ordered them down, at the same time saying something very unpleasant to me. Just then I saw Mr Vallance step forward to where the other passengers were collected, many of them being his own men; and then, after a few words, they all came aft together to where the captain stood, and Mr Vallance acted as spokesman.

'Captain Johnson,' he said, 'I am speaking the wishes of the passengers of this ship when I request you to go below to your cabin, and to stay there until we reach port.'

'Are you mad, sir?' exclaimed the captain.

'Not more so than the rest of the passengers,' said Mr Vallance, 'who, one and all, agree with me that they have no confidence in you as captain ; and that, moreover, they consider that by your conduct you have virtually resigned the command of the ship into Mr Robinson's hands.'

'Are you aware, Mr Passenger, that *Mister* Robinson is one of the apprentices?'

'I am aware, sir, that he has carried this vessel through a fearful storm, when her appointed commander left those men and women in his charge to their fate, while he, like a coward, went below to drown out all knowledge of the present with drink.'

He raved and stormed, and then called upon the crew to help him ; but Mr Vallance told them that he would be answerable to the owners for their conduct, and not a man stirred. I spoke to him till he turned angry, and insisted upon my keeping to the command, and backed up at last by both passengers and crew, who laughed, and seemed to enjoy it ; but I must say that, until we cast anchor in Yarmouth Roads, they obeyed me to a man.

So they made the captain keep for all the world like a prisoner to his cabin till we entered the Tyne, after being detained a few days only in the Roads, where it had been necessary to refit, both of the topmasts being snapped, and the jib-boom being sprung, besides our being leaky, though not so bad but that a couple of hours a day after the first clearance kept the water under.

Before we had passed Harwich very far, we had the beach yawls out, one after another, full of men wanting to board us and take us into harbour, so as to claim salvage. One and all had the same tale to tell us—that we could never get into port ourselves; and more than once it almost took force to keep them from taking possession, for, not content with rendering help when it is wanted, they are only too ready to make their help necessary, and have frightened many a captain before now into giving up his charge into other hands. But with Mr Vallance at my back, I stood firm; and somehow or another I did feel something very much like pride when I took the brig safely into port, and listened to the owners' remarks.

THE END.

Edinburgh :
Printed by W. & R. Chambers, Limited.

BOOKS

SUITABLE FOR PRIZES AND PRESENTATION.

Price 5s.

ROY ROYLAND, or the Young Castellan. By GEORGE MANVILLE FENN. With eight Illustrations by W. Boucher. **5/**

A highly interesting tale of the English Civil War, which relates how the brave lad, Roy Royland, defended the family stronghold while his father was away fighting for the king. There are many exciting situations. A traitor in the camp betrays them, but he eventually falls into the pit he has dug for others.

THE BROTHERHOOD OF THE COAST. By DAVID LAWSON JOHNSTONE. With twenty-one Illustrations by W. Boucher. Large crown 8vo, antique cloth gilt. **5/**

'There is fascination for every healthily-minded boy in the very name of the Buccaneers. . . . Mr D. Lawson Johnstone's new story of adventure is already sure of a warm welcome.'—*Manchester Guardian.*

'A lode of that precious metal which went to the making of *Treasure Island* and *Catriona.*'—*Morning Leader.*

'Another splendid tale of adventure by the author of *The Rebel Commodore.* . . . While the more tragic scenes are remarkable for their sustained strength and dramatic power, many passages culminate in true and unaffected pathos.'—*Brechin Advertiser.*

W. & R. Chambers, Limited, London and Edinburgh.

GIRLS NEW AND OLD. By L. T. Meade. With eight Illustrations by J. Williamson.   **5/**

> This versatile and accomplished authoress is of the opinion that this is one of the best tales of the kind she has ever written. A varied group of girls at Redgarth School is sketched with great realism, in their different lights and shades of character, while many good moral lessons are inculcated, more by example and warning than by precept.

DON. By the author of *Laddie*, &c. With eight Illustrations by J. Finnemore. Large crown 8vo, antique cloth gilt.   **5/**

> 'Written in a bright and sunny manner that is pleasant to read. . . . It may be eminently recommended for young girls, and that of itself in these days is a very desirable quality for a book to possess.'—*Manchester Guardian.*
>
> 'A fresh and happy story . . . told with great spirit . . . it is as pure as spring air.'—*Glasgow Herald.*
>
> 'A brightly-written study of mind and manners . . . No great passions meet us in these pleasant, homely, bantering pages, but there is enough of wholesome love and hate to keep us interested to the last.'—*Morning Leader.*

OLIVIA. By Mrs Molesworth. With eight Illustrations by Robert Barnes.   **5/**

> 'A beautiful story, an ideal gift-book for girls.'—*British Weekly.*
>
> 'A bright story of English provincial life.'—*Daily Chronicle.*
>
> 'Mrs Molesworth maintains her place in the front rank of writers for girls. The story is a good one.'—*Standard.*

BETTY : a School Girl. By L. T. Meade. With eight Illustrations by Everard Hopkins.   **5/**

> 'Mrs L. T. Meade has shown her accustomed skill in delineating girl-life. . . . All the types are true to nature.'—*Dundee Advertiser.*
>
> 'This is an admirable tale of school-girl life : her history involves an excellent moral skilfully conveyed.'—*Glasgow Herald.*

WESTERN STORIES. By William Atkinson. With Frontispiece.   **5/**

> 'These stories touch a very high point of excellence. They are natural, vivid, and thoroughly interesting.'—*Speaker.*

W. & R. Chambers, Limited, London and Edinburgh.

Lady Royland held out her hand for the packet the trooper had taken
from his wallet.

BLANCHE. By Mrs MOLESWORTH, author of *Robin Redbreast, The Next-Door House*, &c. With eight Illustrations by Robert Barnes. **5/**

> 'A story for girls, full of literary grace, and of sustained interest.'
> —*Glasgow Herald.*
>
> 'Eminently healthy . . . pretty and interesting, free from sentimentality.'—*Queen.*

DIAMOND DYKE, or the Lone Farm on the Veldt: a Story of South African Adventure. By GEORGE MANVILLE FENN, author of *The Rajah of Dah, Dingo Boys*, &c. With eight Illustrations by W. Boucher. **5/**

> 'This capital picture of the struggles and trials of settlers in a new country. . . . The interest of the story is well maintained.'—*Standard.*
>
> 'There is not a dull page in the book.'—*Aberdeen Free Press.*
>
> 'A bright, breezy story, full of natural interest.'—*Graphic.*

REAL GOLD : a Story of Adventure. By GEORGE MANVILLE FENN. With eight Illustrations by W. S. Stacey. **5/**

> 'In the author's best style, and brimful of life and adventure. . . . Equal to any of the tales of adventure Mr Fenn has yet written.'—*Standard.*

POMONA. By the author of *Laddie, Rose and Lavender, Zoe, Baby John*, &c. With eight Illustrations by Robert Barnes. **5/**

> 'A pretty story, prettily told, and it makes very good reading for girls, big girls, who like love-stories that are neither mawkish, foolish, nor sentimental.'—*Queen.*
>
> 'A bright, healthy story for girls.'—*Bookseller.*

DOMESTIC ANNALS OF SCOTLAND, from the Reformation to the Rebellion of 1745. By ROBERT CHAMBERS, LL.D. Abridged from the original octavo edition in three volumes. **5/**

ALL ROUND THE YEAR. A Monthly Garland by THOMAS MILLER, author of *English Country Life*, &c. And Key to the Calendar. With Twelve Allegorical Designs by John Leighton, F.S.A., and other Illustrations. **5/**

W. & R. Chambers, Limited, London and Edinburgh.

Running races with Bounce, and bringing him back with a great twist
of bindweed round his soft neck.

Price 3s. 6d.

THE BLUE BALLOON: a Tale of the Shenandoah Valley. By
REGINALD HORSLEY. With six Illustrations by W. S. Stacey. **3/6**

> The author of *The Yellow God* shows even more than his usual
> skill and vivacity in depicting some of the thrilling scenes and
> episodes of the American Civil War, in which his hero and the
> other characters bear a part.

THE WIZARD KING: a Story of the Last Moslem Invasion of
Europe. By DAVID KER. With six Illustrations by W. S.
Stacey. **3/6**

> The hero of this story is John Sobieski, round whose marvellous
> career are woven threads of incident and adventure, many of which
> are historical.

THE REBEL COMMODORE (Paul Jones); being Memoirs of the
Earlier Adventures of Sir Ascott Dalrymple. By D. LAWSON
JOHNSTONE. With six Illustrations by W. Boucher. **3/6**

> '*The Rebel Commodore* is a spirited and well-written story. The
> scenes at sea and on shore are dramatically presented, and strike
> us as wonderfully true to the life.'—*Times.*
>
> 'The story is told with great spirit, and there is genuine literary
> quality about it.'—*Yorkshire Herald.*
>
> 'It is a good story, full of hairbreadth escapes and perilous
> adventures.'—*To-Day.*
>
> 'The picture of the wild life of the smuggling population on the
> shores of the Solway Firth is admirably drawn, and the account of
> the doings of the buccaneering squadrons on the coasts of Scotland
> and Holland is strictly historical.'—*Standard.*

ROBIN REDBREAST. By Mrs MOLESWORTH, author of *Imogen,
Next-Door House, The Cuckoo Clock,* &c. With six original
Illustrations by Robert Barnes. **3/6**

> 'It is a long time since we read a story for girls more simple,
> natural, or interesting.'—*Publishers' Circular.*
>
> 'Equal to anything she has written. . . . Can be heartily recom-
> mended for girls' reading.'—*Standard.*

'Fire, boys! Fire!'

THE WHITE KAID OF THE ATLAS. By J. MACLAREN COBBAN. With six Illustrations by W. S. Stacey.   3/6

> 'Told with unfailing spirit and vivacity.'—*Westminster Gazette.*
>
> 'A well-told tale of adventure and daring in Morocco, in which the late and the present Sultan both figure. . . . A very pleasant book to read.'—*Imperial and Asiatic Quarterly Review.*
>
> 'Full of stirring adventure, and written in a befitting spirited style.'—*Christian World.*

THE YELLOW GOD: a Tale of some Strange Adventures. By REGINALD HORSLEY. With six Illustrations by W. S. Stacey. 3/6

> 'Admirably designed, and set forth with life-like force. . . . A first-rate book for boys.'—*Saturday Review.*
>
> 'The tale is very skilfully told, abounds in pathos as well as humour, and the interest is well sustained to the end.'—*Schoolmaster.*

PRISONER AMONG PIRATES. By DAVID KER, author of *Cossack and Czar, The Wild Horseman of the Pampas,* &c. With six Illustrations by W. S. Stacey.   3/6

> 'A singularly good story, calculated to encourage what is noble and manly in boys.'—*Athenæum.*
>
> 'In point of variety of incident it would be hard to find a book which surpasses it.—*Educational Times.*

JOSIAH MASON: A BIOGRAPHY. With Sketches of the History of the Steel Pen and Electroplating Trades. By JOHN THACKRAY BUNCE.   Portrait and Illustrations.   3/6

IN THE LAND OF THE GOLDEN PLUME: a Tale of Adventure. By DAVID LAWSON JOHNSTONE, author of *The Paradise of the North, The Mountain Kingdom,* &c. With six Illustrations by W. S. Stacey.   3/6

> 'Most thrilling, and excellently worked out.'—*Graphic.*
>
> 'A genuine old-fashioned boys' book of the Kingston-Ballantyne stamp. It merits a place on the same shelf with *The Coral Island* and *King Solomon's Mines.*'—*School Monthly.*

W. & R. Chambers, Limited, London and Edinburgh.

'The Turks are marching upon Vienna!'

FOUR ON AN ISLAND: a Story of Adventure. By L. T. MEADE, author of *Daddy's Boy, Scamp and I, Wilton Chase,* &c. With six original Illustrations by W. Rainey.   3/6

> 'This is a very bright description of modern Crusoes.'—*Graphic.*

THE DINGO BOYS, or the Squatters of Wallaby Range. By GEORGE MANVILLE FENN, author of *The Rajah of Dah, In the King's Name,* &c. With six original Illustrations by W. S. Stacey.   3/6

THE CHILDREN OF WILTON CHASE. By L. T. MEADE, author of *Four on an Island, Scamp and I,* &c. With six Illustrations by Everard Hopkins.   3/6

> 'Both entertaining and instructive.'—*Spectator.*
>
> 'Great skill is shown in the narration; the authoress hits off in the happiest manner characteristics of child life.'—*Leeds Mercury.*

THE PARADISE OF THE NORTH: a Story of Discovery and Adventure around the Pole. By D. LAWSON JOHNSTONE, author of *Richard Tregellas, The Mountain Kingdom,* &c. With fifteen Illustrations by W. Boucher.   3/6

> 'A lively story of adventure, and a decided addition to Polar literature.'—*Spectator.*
>
> 'Marked by a Verne-like fertility of fancy.'—*Saturday Review.*

THE RAJAH OF DAH. By GEORGE MANVILLE FENN, author of *In the King's Name,* &c. With six Illustrations by W. S. Stacey.   3/6

> 'Will be found thoroughly satisfactory as a prize.'—*Journal of Education.*

W. & R. Chambers, Limited, London and Edinburgh.

From THE WHITE KAID OF THE ATLAS, *by J. Maclaren Cobban ;*
price 3s. 6d.

THE KAID REELED IN THE SADDLE.

Price 2s. 6d.

WHITE TURRETS. By Mrs Molesworth, author of *Carrots, Olivia*, &c.   With four Illustrations by W. Rainey.   **2/6**

> 'An admirably told story.'—*Daily Telegraph.*
>
> 'A charming story. . . . a capital antidote to the unrest that inspires young folks that seek for some great thing to do, while the great thing for them is at their hand and at their home.'—*Scotsman.*

HUGH MELVILLE'S QUEST: a Boy's Adventures in the Days of the Armada.   By F. M. Holmes.   With four Illustrations by W. Boucher.   **2/6**

> Contains much stirring incident and adventure, and many hairbreadth escapes, ere Hugh Melville delivers his long-lost brother from captivity amongst the Spaniards.

ELOCUTION, a Book for Reciters and Readers.   Edited by R. C. H. Morison.   **2/6**

> 'No elocutionist's library can be said to be complete without this neatly bound volume of 500 pages. . . . An introduction on the art of elocution is a gem of conciseness and intellectual teaching.'—*Era.*
>
> 'One of the best books of its kind in the English language.'—*Glasgow Citizen.*

THISTLE AND ROSE.   By Amy Walton.   Illustrated by Robert Barnes.   **2/6**

> 'A thoroughly good story for a young girl. . . . . A beautiful and instructive presentation book.'—*Practical Teacher.*
>
> 'Is as desirable a present to make to a girl as any one could wish.'—*Sheffield Daily Telegraph.*

VANISHED, or the Strange Adventures of Arthur Hawkesleigh. By David Ker.   Illustrated by W. Boucher.   **2/6**

> 'I wish every boy's book was as healthy in tone as *Vanished.*'—*To-Day* (J. K. Jerome).
>
> 'It must be ranked high amongst its kind.'—*Spectator.*
>
> 'A quite entrancing tale of adventure.'—*Athenæum.*

W. & R. Chambers, Limited, London and Edinburgh.

'It is quite charming,' she said ; 'just the sort of nest one would
long to have.'

ADVENTURE AND ADVENTURERS; being True Tales of Daring, Peril, and Heroism.   With Illustrations.   2/6

> 'The narratives are as fascinating as fiction.'—*British Weekly.*
>
> 'It very deftly combines the grace and charm of fiction with the reality of fact and direct personal experience.'—*Schoolmaster.*

BLACK, WHITE, AND GRAY: a Story of Three Homes. By AMY WALTON, author of *White Lilac, A Pair of Clogs,* &c.   With four Illustrations by Robert Barnes.   2/6

> 'Told with all the simple charm that Miss Walton knows so well how to use.   There are few more capable writers for the young than the authoress of this handsome book.'—*Schoolmaster.*

OUT OF REACH: a Story.   By ESMÈ STUART, author of *Through the Flood, A Little Brown Girl,* &c.   With four Illustrations by Robert Barnes.   2/6

> 'The story is a very good one, and the book can be recommended for girls' reading.'—*Standard.*

IMOGEN, or Only Eighteen. By Mrs MOLESWORTH.   With four Illustrations by H. A. Bone.   2/6

> 'The book is an extremely clever one.'—*Daily Chronicle.*
>
> 'A readable and very pretty story.'—*Black and White.*

THE LOST TRADER, or the Mystery of the *Lombardy.*   By HENRY FRITH, author of *The Cruise of the 'Wasp,' The Log of the 'Bombastes,'* &c.   With four Illustrations by W. Boucher.   2/6

> 'Mr Frith writes good sea-stories, and this is the best of them that we have read.'—*Academy.*

THE NEXT-DOOR HOUSE.   By Mrs MOLESWORTH.   With six Illustrations by W. Hatherell.   2/6

> 'I venture to predict for it as loving a welcome as that received by the inimitable *Carrots.*'—*Manchester Courier.*

W. & R. Chambers, Limited, London and Edinburgh.

The Moor rose on one arm and looked at him eagerly and
anxiously.

COSSACK AND CZAR. By DAVID KER, author of *The Boy Slave in Bokhara, The Wild Horseman of the Pampas,* &c. With original Illustrations by W. S. Stacey. 2/6

> 'There is not an uninteresting and scarcely a careless line in it.'—*Spectator.*
>
> 'With his own personal knowledge of Cossack life in the Steppes, and so brisk a theme as the struggle between Peter and Charles XII. of Sweden, no wonder that Mr Ker's volume is exciting.'—*Graphic.*

THROUGH THE FLOOD, the Story of an Out-of-the-Way Place. By ESMÈ STUART. With Illustrations. 2/6

> 'A bright story of two girls, and shows how goodness rather than beauty in a face can heal old strifes.'—*Friendly Leaves.*

WHEN WE WERE YOUNG. By Mrs O'REILLY, author of *Joan and Jerry, Phœbe's Fortunes,* &c. With four Illustrations by H. A. Bone. 2/6

> 'A very interesting story suitable for either boys or girls.'—*Standard.*
>
> 'A delightfully natural and attractive story.'—*Journal of Education.*

ROSE AND LAVENDER. By the author of *Laddie, Miss Toosey's Mission,* &c. With four original Illustrations by Herbert A. Bone. 2/6

> 'A brightly-written tale, the characters in which, taken from humble life, are sketched with life-like naturalness.'—*Manchester Examiner.*

BASIL WOOLLCOMBE, MIDSHIPMAN. By ARTHUR LEE KNIGHT, author of *The Adventures of a Midshipmite,* &c. With Frontispiece by W. S. Stacey, and other Illustrations. 2/6

JOAN AND JERRY. By Mrs O'REILLY, author of *Sussex Stories,* &c. With four original Illustrations by Herbert A. Bone. 2/6

> 'An unusually satisfactory story for girls.'—*Manchester Guardian.*

Hawkesleigh grasped the upper rope firmly with both hands, and pushed himself boldly out into the empty air.

THE YOUNG RANCHMEN, or Perils of Pioneering in the Wild West. By CHARLES R. KENYON. With four original Illustrations by W. S. Stacey, and other Illustrations.   **2/6**

MEMOIR OF WILLIAM AND ROBERT CHAMBERS. With Autobiographic Reminiscences of William Chambers, and Supplemental Chapter. 14th edition. With Portraits and Illustrations.   **2/6**

> 'What would be the story of popular education in this island if the names of William and Robert Chambers, and of all that they did, could be cut out? . . . As a matter of social history the book is indispensable; for who can be said to possess a knowledge of the England and the Scotland of the nineteenth century who is not familiar with the story of the brothers Chambers?'— *School Board Chronicle.*

POPULAR RHYMES OF SCOTLAND. By ROBERT CHAMBERS. **2/6**

> A collection of the traditionary verse of Scotland, in which the author has gathered together a multitude of rhymes and short snatches of verse applicable to places, families, natural objects, games, &c., wherewith the cottage fireside was amused in days gone past.

TRADITIONS OF EDINBURGH. By ROBERT CHAMBERS. *New Edition.* With Illustrations.   **2/6**

> 'The work is too well known to need any description here. It is an accepted storehouse of the legendary history of this city.'— *Scotsman.*

HISTORY OF THE REBELLION OF 1745-6. By ROBERT CHAMBERS. *New Edition,* with Index and Illustrations.   **2/6**

> 'There is not to be found anywhere a better account of the events of '45 than that given here.'—*Newcastle Chronicle.*

GOOD AND GREAT WOMEN: a Book for Girls. Comprises brief lives of Queen Victoria, Florence Nightingale, Baroness Burdett-Coutts, Mrs Beecher-Stowe, Jenny Lind, Charlotte Brontë, Mrs Hemans, Dorothy Pattison. Numerous Illustrations.   **2/6**

> 'A brightly written volume, full to the brim of interesting and instructive matter; and either as reader, reward, or library book, is equally suitable.'—*Teachers' Aid.*

LIVES OF LEADING NATURALISTS. By H. ALLEYNE NICHOL-SON, Professor of Natural History in the University of Aberdeen. Illustrated. **2/6**

> 'Popular and interesting by the skilful manner in which notices of the lives of distinguished naturalists, from John Ray and Francis Willoughby to Charles Darwin, are interwoven with the methodical exposition of the progress of the science to which they are devoted.' —*Scotsman.*

BENEFICENT AND USEFUL LIVES. Comprising Lord Shaftesbury, George Peabody, Andrew Carnegie, Walter Besant, Samuel Morley, Sir James Y. Simpson, Dr Arnold of Rugby, &c. By R. COCHRANE. Numerous Illustrations. **2/6**

> 'Nothing could be better than the author's selection of facts setting forth the beneficent lives of those generous men in the narrow compass which the capacity of the volume allows.'—*School Board Chronicle.*

GREAT THINKERS AND WORKERS: being the Lives of Thomas Carlyle, Lord Armstrong, Lord Tennyson, Charles Dickens, Sir Titus Salt, W. M. Thackeray, Sir Henry Bessemer, John Ruskin, James Nasmyth, Charles Kingsley, Builders of the Forth Bridge, &c. With numerous Illustrations. **2/6**

> 'One of the most fitting presents for a thoughtful boy that we have come across.'—*Review of Reviews.*

GREAT HISTORIC EVENTS. The Conquest of India, Indian Mutiny, French Revolution, the Crusades, the Conquest of Mexico, Napoleon's Russian Campaign. Illustrated. **2/6**

RECENT TRAVEL AND ADVENTURE. Comprising Stanley and the Congo, Lieutenant Greely, Joseph Thomson, Livingstone, Lady Brassey, Vambéry, Burton, &c. Illustrated. Cloth. **2/6**

> 'It is wonderful how much that is of absorbing interest has been packed into this small volume.'—*Scotsman.*

LITERARY CELEBRITIES. **2/6**

> Being brief biographies of Wordsworth, Campbell, Moore, Jeffrey, and Macaulay. Illustrated.

W. & R. Chambers, Limited, London and Edinburgh.

SONGS OF SCOTLAND prior to Burns, with the Tunes, edited by Robert Chambers, LL.D. With Illustrations. 2/6

> This volume embodies the whole of the pre-Burnsian songs of Scotland that possess merit and are presentable, along with the music; each accompanied by its own history.

HISTORICAL CELEBRITIES. Comprising lives of Oliver Cromwell, Washington, Napoleon Bonaparte, Duke of Wellington. Illustrated. 2/6

> 'The story of their life-work is told in such a way as to teach important historical, as well as personal, lessons bearing upon the political history of this country.'—*Schoolmaster.*

STORIES OF REMARKABLE PERSONS. The Herschels, Mary Somerville, Sir Walter Scott, A. T. Stewart, &c. By William Chambers, LL.D. 2/6

> Embraces about two dozen lives, and the biographical sketches are freely interspersed with anecdotes, so as to make it popular and stimulating reading for both young and old.

YOUTH'S COMPANION AND COUNSELLOR. By William Chambers, LL.D. 2/6

> This is a new and enlarged edition of the first issue of 1857, which met with a gratifying degree of approval. The book offers friendly counsel to the young on everyday matters which concern their welfare; the hints, advices, and suggestions therein offered being the result of observation and experience drawn from the long and busy life of the writer.

TALES FOR TRAVELLERS. Selected from Chambers's *Papers for the People.* 2 volumes, each 2/6

> Containing twelve tales by the author of *John Halifax, Gentleman,* George Cupples, and other well-known writers.

STORIES OF OLD FAMILIES. By W. Chambers, LL.D. 2/6

> The Setons—Lady Jean Gordon—Countess of Nithsdale—Lady Grisell Baillie—Grisell Cochrane—the Keiths—Lady Grange—Lady Jane Douglas—Story of Wedderburn—Story of Erskine—Countess of Eglintoun—Lady Forbes—the Dalrymples—Montrose—Buccleuch Family—Argyll Family, &c.

W. & R. Chambers, Limited, London and Edinburgh.

Price 2s.

TWO GREAT AUTHORS. Lives of Scott and Carlyle. 2/

Concise biographies of two of the most notable authors of the century.

EMINENT ENGINEERS. Lives of Watt, Stephenson, Telford, and Brindley. 2/

'All young persons should read it, for it is in an excellent sense educational. It were devoutly to be wished that young people would take delight in such biographies.'—*Indian Engineer.*

TALES OF THE GREAT AND BRAVE. By MARGARET FRASER TYTLER. 2/

A collection of interesting biographies and anecdotes of great men and women of history, in the style of Scott's *Tales of a Grandfather*, written by a niece of the historian of Scotland.

GREAT WARRIORS: Nelson, Wellington, Napoleon. 2/

'As a prize for the upper classes of Board and National Schools, it can be recommended.'—*Standard.*

'Told concisely and yet with sufficient detail to make these heroes live in the imagination of the reader.'—*New Age.*

'One of the most instructive books published this season.'—*Liverpool Mercury.*

HEROIC LIVES: Livingstone, Stanley, General Gordon, Lord Dundonald. 2/

'Deserves a high place among the best of biographies for the use of children.'—*Schoolmaster.*

'It would be difficult to name four other lives in which we find more enterprise, adventure, achievement. . . . The book is sure to please.'—*Leeds Mercury.*

THROUGH STORM AND STRESS. By J. S. FLETCHER. With Frontispiece by W. S. Stacey. 2/

'Full of excitement and incident.'—*Dundee Advertiser.*

W. & R. Chambers, Limited, London and Edinburgh.

THE REMARKABLE ADVENTURES OF WALTER TRELAWNEY, Parish 'Prentice of Plymouth, in the year of the Great Armada. Re-told by J. S. FLETCHER, author of *Through Storm and Stress,* &c.   With Frontispiece by W. S. Stacey.   2/

> 'A wonderfully vivid story of the year of the Great Armada; far more effective than the unwholesome trash which so often does duty for boys' books nowadays.'—*Idler.*

FIVE VICTIMS: a School-room Story.   By M. BRAMSTON, author of *Boys and Girls, Uncle Ivan,* &c.   With Frontispiece by H. A. Bone.   2/

> 'A delightful book for children. Miss Bramston has told her simple story extremely well.'—*Associates' Journal.*

SOME BRAVE BOYS AND GIRLS.   By EDITH C. KENYON, author of *The Little Knight, Wilfrid Clifford,* &c.   2/

> 'A capital book : will be read with delight by both boys and girls.'—*Manchester Examiner.*

ELIZABETH, or Cloud and Sunshine.   By HENLEY I. ARDEN, author of *Leather Mill Farm, Aunt Bell,* &c.   With Frontispiece by Herbert A. Bone.   2/

> 'This is a charming story, and in every way suitable as a gift-book or prize for girls.'—*Schoolmaster.*

HEROES OF ROMANTIC ADVENTURE, being Biographical Sketches of Lord Clive, founder of British supremacy in India; Captain John Smith, founder of the colony of Virginia; the Good Knight Bayard; and Garibaldi, the Italian patriot.   Illustrated.   2/

OUR ANIMAL FRIENDS—the Dog, Cat, Horse, and Elephant. With numerous Illustrations.   2/

> A popular account, freely interspersed with anecdotes showing the personal attachment, fidelity, and sagacity of the dog ; the affection, courage, and memory of the cat ; the courage, revenge, and docility of the horse ; and the various characteristics of the elephant, including the famous Jumbo.

W. & R. Chambers, Limited, London and Edinburgh.

FAMOUS MEN.   Illustrated.   2/

Comprising Biographical Sketches of Lord Dundonald, George Stephenson, Lord Nelson, Louis Napoleon, Captain Cook, George Washington, Sir Walter Scott, Peter the Great, Christopher Columbus, John Howard, William Hutton, William Penn, James Watt, Alexander Selkirk, Sir William Jones, Dr Leyden, Dr Murray, Alexander Wilson, J. F. Oberlin.

LIFE OF BENJAMIN FRANKLIN.   Illustrated.   2/

'A fine example of attractive biographical writing. . . . A short address, "The Way to Wealth," should be read by every young man in the kingdom.'—*Teachers' Aid.*

EMINENT WOMEN, and Tales for Girls.   Illustrated.   2/

'The lives include those of Grace Darling, Joan of Arc, Flora Macdonald, Helen Gray, Madame Roland, and others; while the stories, which are mainly of a domestic character, embrace such favourites as Passion and Principle, Love is Power, Three Ways of Living, Annals of the Poor, Sister of Rembrandt, and others equally entertaining and good.'—*Teachers' Aid.*

TALES FROM CHAMBERS'S JOURNAL.   4 vols., each   2/

Comprise interesting short stories by James Payn, Hugh Conway, D. Christie Murray, Walter Thornbury, G. Manville Fenn, Dutton Cook, J. B. Harwood, and other popular writers.

BIOGRAPHY, EXEMPLARY AND INSTRUCTIVE.   Edited by W. CHAMBERS, LL.D.   2/

The Editor gives in this volume a selection of biographies of those who, while exemplary in their private lives, became the benefactors of their species by the still more exemplary efforts of their intellect.

AILIE GILROY.   By W. CHAMBERS, LL.D.   2/

'The life of a poor Scotch lassie . . . a book that will be highly esteemed for its goodness as well as for its attractiveness.'—*Teachers' Aid.*

ESSAYS, FAMILIAR AND HUMOROUS.   By ROBERT CHAMBERS, LL.D.   2 vols., each   2/

Contains some of the finest essays, tales, and social sketches of the author of *Traditions of Edinburgh,* reprinted from *Chambers's Journal.*

MARITIME DISCOVERY AND ADVENTURE.　Illustrated.　　2/

Columbus—Balboa—Richard Falconer—North-east Passage—South Sea Marauders—Alexander Selkirk—Crossing the Line—Genuine Crusoes—Castaway—Scene with a Pirate, &c.

SHIPWRECKS AND TALES OF THE SEA.　Illustrated.　　2/

'A collection of narratives of many famous shipwrecks, with other tales of the sea. . . . The tales of fortitude under difficulties, and in times of extreme peril, as well as the records of adherence to duty, contained in this volume, cannot but be of service.'—*Practical Teacher.*

SKETCHES, LIGHT AND DESCRIPTIVE.　By W. CHAMBERS, LL.D.
　　2/

A selection from contributions to *Chambers's Journal,* ranging over a period of thirty years.

MISCELLANY OF INSTRUCTIVE AND ENTERTAINING TRACTS.
Each　　2/

These Tracts comprise Tales, Poetry, Ballads, Remarkable Episodes in History, Papers on Social Economy, Domestic Management, Science, Travel, &c. The articles contain wholesome and attractive reading for Mechanics', Parish, School, and Cottage Libraries.

	s.	*d.*		*s.*	*d.*
20 Vols. cloth	20	0	10 Vols. half-calf	45	0
10 Vols. cloth	20	0	160 Nos. ....each	0	1
10 Vols. cloth, gilt edges	25	0	Which may be had separately.		

Price 1s. 6d.

With Illustrations.

SWISS FAMILY ROBINSON.　Their Life and Adventures on a
Desert Island.　　1/6

SKETCHES OF ANIMAL LIFE AND HABITS.　By ANDREW
WILSON, Ph.D., &c.　　1/6

A popular natural history text-book, and a guide to the use of the observing powers. Compiled with a view of affording the young and the general reader trustworthy ideas of the animal world.

W. & R. Chambers, Limited, London and Edinburgh.

RAILWAYS AND RAILWAY MEN. 1/6

'A readable and entertaining book.'—*Manchester Guardian.*

EXPERIENCES OF A BARRISTER. 1/6

Eleven tales embracing experiences of a barrister and attorney.

BEGUMBAGH, a Tale of the Indian Mutiny. 1/6

A thrilling tale by GEORGE MANVILLE FENN.

THE BUFFALO HUNTERS, and other Tales. 1/6

Fourteen short stories reprinted from *Chambers's Journal.*

TALES OF THE COASTGUARD, and other Stories. 1/6

Fifteen interesting stories from *Chambers's Journal.*

THE CONSCRIPT, and other Tales. 1/6

Twenty-two short stories specially adapted for perusal by the young.

THE DETECTIVE OFFICER, by 'WATERS;' and other Tales. 1/6

Nine entertaining detective stories, with three others.

FIRESIDE TALES AND SKETCHES. 1/6

Contains eighteen tales and sketches by R. Chambers, LL.D., and others by P. B. St John, A. M. Sargeant, &c.

THE GOLD-SEEKERS, and other Tales. 1/6

Seventeen interesting tales from *Chambers's Journal.*

THE HOPE OF LEASCOMBE, and other Stories. 1/6

The principal tale inculcates the lesson that we cannot have everything our own way, and that passion and impulse are not reliable counsellors.

THE ITALIAN'S CHILD, and other Tales. 1/6

Fifteen short stories from *Chambers's Journal.*

JURY-ROOM TALES. 1/6

Entertaining stories by James Payn, G. M. Fenn, and others.

KINDNESS TO ANIMALS. By W. CHAMBERS, LL.D. 1/6

'Illustrates, by means of a series of anecdotes, the intelligence, gentleness, and docility of the brute creation.'—*Sunday Times.*

W. & R. Chambers, Limited, London and Edinburgh.

THE MIDNIGHT JOURNEY. By Leitch Ritchie; and other Tales. 1/6
> Sixteen short stories from *Chambers's Journal.*

OLDEN STORIES. 1/6
> Sixteen short stories from *Chambers's Journal.*

THE RIVAL CLERKS, and other Tales. 1/6
> The first tale shows how dishonesty and roguery are punished, and virtue triumphs in the end.

ROBINSON CRUSOE. By Daniel Defoe. 1/6
> A handy edition, profusely illustrated.

PARLOUR TALES AND STORIES. 1/6
> Seventeen short tales from the old series of *Chambers's Journal,* by Anna Maria Sargeant, Mrs Crowe, Percy B. St John, Leitch Ritchie, &c.

THE SQUIRE'S DAUGHTER, and other Tales. 1/6
> Fifteen short stories from *Chambers's Journal.*

TALES FOR HOME READING. 1,6
> Sixteen short stories from the old series of *Chambers's Journal,* by A. M. Sargeant, Frances Brown, Percy B. St John, Mrs Crowe, and others.

TALES FOR YOUNG AND OLD. 1/6
> Fourteen short stories from *Chambers's Journal,* by Mrs Crowe, Miss Sargeant, Percy B. St John, &c.

TALES OF ADVENTURE. 1/6
> Twenty-one tales, comprising wonderful escapes from wolves and bears, American Indians, and pirates; life on a desert island; extraordinary swimming adventures, &c.

TALES OF THE SEA. 1/6
> Five thrilling sea tales, by G. Manville Fenn, J. B. Harwood, and others.

TALES AND STORIES TO SHORTEN THE WAY. 1/6
> Fifteen interesting tales from *Chambers's Journal.*

W. & R. Chambers, Limited, London and Edinburgh.

TALES FOR TOWN AND COUNTRY. 1/6

Twenty-two tales and sketches, by R. Chambers, LL.D., and other writers.

HOME-NURSING. By RACHEL A. NEUMAN. 1/6

A work intended to help the inexperienced and those who in a sudden emergency are called upon to do the work of home-nursing.

Price 1s.

COOKERY FOR YOUNG HOUSEWIVES. By ANNIE M. GRIGGS. 1/

A book of practical utility, showing how tasteful and nutritious dishes may be prepared at little expense.

NEW SERIES OF CHAMBERS'S LIBRARY FOR YOUNG PEOPLE.

Illustrated.

Price 1s.

'Excellent popular biographies.'—*British Weekly.*

POPULAR BIOGRAPHIES.

QUEEN VICTORIA: the Story of her Life and Reign. 1/

'A sympathetic and popular sketch of the life and rule of our Queen up to the present day.'—*Manchester Guardian.*

THOMAS CARLYLE: the Story of his Life and Writings. 1/

Gives in a concise form all that is known regarding the life and writings of the Sage of Chelsea, whose centenary falls in December next.

THOMAS ALVA EDISON: the Story of his Life and Inventions. 1/

A brightly written account of the wonderful career of the inventor of the phonograph, and perfecter of the electric light.

W. & R. Chambers, Limited, London and Edinburgh.

THE STORY OF WATT AND STEPHENSON.   1/

'As a gift-book for boys this is simply first-rate.'—*Schoolmaster*.

'A concise and well-written account of the labours of these inventors.'—*Glasgow Herald*.

'An excellent book to put into the hands of a boy.'—*Spectator*.

THE STORY OF NELSON AND WELLINGTON.   1/

'This book is cheap, artistic, and instructive. It should be in the library of every home and school.'—*Schoolmaster*.

THOMAS TELFORD AND JAMES BRINDLEY.   1/

Telford's autobiography is here largely reproduced, with an account of his labours and those of Brindley in connection with roads, bridges, and canals.

GENERAL GORDON AND LORD DUNDONALD: the Story of Two Heroic Lives.   1/

'Every boy's library ought to possess this little volume. It abounds in admirable teachings of duty and gallantry.'—*Academy*.

LIVINGSTONE AND STANLEY: the Story of the opening up of the Dark Continent.   1/

COLUMBUS AND COOK: the Story of their Lives, Voyages, and Discoveries.   1/

'Models of compact biography.'—*Christian World*.

'Is a fascinating and historical account of daring adventure.'—*Bristol Mercury*.

THE STORY OF THE LIFE OF SIR WALTER SCOTT. By ROBERT CHAMBERS, LL.D. Revised with additions, including the AUTO-BIOGRAPHY.   1/

Besides the AUTOBIOGRAPHY, many interesting and characteristic anecdotes of the boyhood of Scott, which challenge the attention of the young reader, have been added; while the whole has been revised and brought up to date.

W. & R. Chambers, Limited, London and Edinburgh.

THE STORY OF HOWARD AND OBERLIN.   1/

The book is equally divided between the lives of Howard the prison reformer, and Oberlin the pastor and philanthropist, who worked such a wonderful reformation amongst the dwellers in a valley of the Vosges Mountains.

THE STORY OF NAPOLEON BONAPARTE.   1/

A brief and graphic life of the first Napoleon, set in a history of his own times : the battle of Waterloo, as of special interest to English readers, being fully narrated.

'Present concisely and in a graphic manner the life-story of the celebrities mentioned. Much praise is due to the publishers for this very handy and useful series.'—*Bookseller.*

'Not less interesting than fiction.'—*School Board Chronicle.*

'Admirably written biographies.'—*Review of Reviews.*

STORIES FOR YOUNG PEOPLE.

MARK WESTCROFT, CORDWAINER: a Village Story. By F. SCARLETT POTTER.   1/

A HUMBLE HEROINE. By L. E. TIDDEMAN.   1/

BABY JOHN. By the author of *Laddie, Tip-Cat, Rose and Lavender,* &c. With Frontispiece by H. A. Bone.   1/

'Told with quite an unusual amount of pathos.'—*Spectator.*

'A beautifully pathetic and touching story, full of human nature and genuine feeling.'—*School Board Chronicle.*

THE GREEN CASKET; LEO'S POST-OFFICE; BRAVE LITTLE DENIS. By Mrs MOLESWORTH.   1/

Three charming stories by the author of the *Cuckoo Clock,* each teaching an important moral lesson.

JOHN'S ADVENTURES: a Tale of Old England. By THOMAS MILLER, author of *Boy's Country Book,* &c.   1/

W. & R. Chambers, Limited, London and Edinburgh.

THE BEWITCHED LAMP. By Mrs MOLESWORTH. With Frontispiece by Robert Barnes. **1/**

> 'Mrs Molesworth has written many charming stories for children, but nothing better, we think, than the above little volume.'—*Newcastle Chronicle.*

ERNEST'S GOLDEN THREAD. **1/**

> 'The story of a very little boy who tries to do right under trying circumstances. . . . The moral of the tale is excellent, and little boys and girls will follow Ernest's trials and struggles with interest.' —*School Guardian.*

LITTLE MARY, and other Stories. By L. T. MEADE. **1/**

THE LITTLE KNIGHT. By EDITH C. KENYON. **1/**

> 'Has an admirable moral. . . . Natural, amusing, pathetic.'— *Manchester Guardian.*

WILFRID CLIFFORD, or The Little Knight Again. By EDITH C. KENYON. With Frontispiece by W. S. Stacey. **1/**

> 'The author has certainly written nothing sprightlier or healthier. . . . Some of the incidents are exceptionally well told.'—*Spectator.*

ZOE. By the author of *Tip-Cat, Laddie,* &c. **1/**

> 'A charming and touching study of child life.'—*Scotsman.*

UNCLE SAM'S MONEY-BOX. By Mrs S. C. HALL. **1/**

THEIR HAPPIEST CHRISTMAS. By EDNA LYALL, author of *Donovan,* &c. **1/**

> 'A delightful story for children, simple, interesting, and conveying a useful lesson.'—*School Board Chronicle.*

FIRESIDE AMUSEMENTS: a Book of Indoor Games. **1/**

> 'A thoroughly useful work, which should be welcomed by all who have the organisation of children's parties.'—*Review of Reviews.*

THE STEADFAST GABRIEL: a Tale of Wichnor Wood. By MARY HOWITT. **1/**

W. & R. Chambers, Limited, London and Edinburgh.

GRANDMAMMA'S POCKETS. By Mrs S. C. HALL. 1/

THE SWAN'S EGG. By Mrs S. C. HALL. 1/

MUTINY OF THE BOUNTY, and **LIFE OF A SAILOR BOY.** 1/

PERSEVERANCE AND SUCCESS: the Life of William Hutton. 1/

DUTY AND AFFECTION, or the Drummer-boy. 1/
A thrilling narrative of the wars of the first Napoleon.

FAMOUS POETRY. Being a collection of the best English verse. Illustrated. 1/

STORY OF A LONG AND BUSY LIFE. By W. CHAMBERS, LL.D. 1/

Price 9d.

Cloth, Illustrated.

THE LITTLE CAPTIVE KING. **JOE FULWOOD'S TRUST.**

FOUND ON THE BATTLEFIELD. **PAUL ARNOLD.**

ALICE ERROL, and other Tales. **CLEVER BOYS.**

THE WHISPERER. By Mrs S. C. HALL. **THE LITTLE ROBINSON.**

TRUE HEROISM, and other Stories. **MIDSUMMER HOLIDAY.**

PICCIOLA, and other Tales. **MY BIRTHDAY BOOK.**

W. & R. Chambers, Limited, London and Edinburgh.

Price 6d.

Cloth, with Illustrations.

'For good literature at a cheap rate, commend us to a little series published by W. & R. Chambers, which consists of a number of readable stories by good writers.'—*Review of Reviews.*

'One contains three little stories from the pen of Mrs Molesworth, one of the most charming of writers for the little ones; and the name of L. T. Meade is a guarantee of good reading of a kind which children are sure to enjoy.'—*School Board Chronicle.*

CASSIE, and LITTLE MARY. By L. T. MEADE.

A LONELY PUPPY, and THE TAMBOURINE GIRL. By L. T. MEADE.

LEO'S POST-OFFICE, and BRAVE LITTLE DENIS. By Mrs MOLESWORTH.

GERALD AND DOT. By Mrs FAIRBAIRN.

KITTY AND HARRY. By EMMA GELLIBRAND, author of *J. Cole.*

DICKORY DOCK. By L. T. MEADE, author of *Scamp and I*, &c.

FRED STAMFORD'S START IN LIFE. By Mrs FAIRBAIRN.

NESTA: or Fragments of a Little Life. By Mrs MOLESWORTH.

NIGHT-HAWKS. By the Hon. EVA KNATCHBULL-HUGESSEN.

A FARTHINGFUL. By L. T. MEADE.

POOR MISS CAROLINA. By L. T. MEADE.

THE GOLDEN LADY. By L. T. MEADE.

MALCOLM AND DORIS: or, Learning to Help. By DAVINA WATERSON.

WILLIE NICHOLLS: or, False Shame and True Shame.

SELF-DENIAL. By Miss EDGEWORTH.

W. & R. Chambers, Limited, London and Edinburgh.

www.ingramcontent.com/pod-product-compliance
Lightning Source LLC
Chambersburg PA
CBHW030119030726
47498CB00007B/2455